A Promise Kept
The Legacy of Michael Malone
by
Statia Button Dougherty

A Promise Kept
The Legacy of Michael Malone

by
Statia Button Dougherty

Goose Flats Publishing ~ Tombstone, Arizona

A Promise Kept
The Legacy of Michael Malone
by Statia Button Dougherty

Copyright © 2018 by Statia Button Dougherty
ISBN# 978-1-939345-15-8
Library of Congress Control Number: 2018937760

Published in the U.S.A.

Print edition published in April 2018
First e-book edition published in 2013

Published by
Goose Flats Publishing
P.O. Box 813
Tombstone, Arizona 85638
(520) 457-3884
www.gooseflats.com

Book layout & cover design:
Keith Davis
Goose Flats Graphics
Tombstone, Arizona

Cover Image: Credit

Goose Flats Publishing ~ Tombstone, Arizona

Dedication

This book is dedicated to my wonderful husband Pat, for his undying support and constant faith in me.

I would like to thank my good friends Janice and Keith, for their help, encouragement and support.

I would also like to thank my daughter Brittney for helping with the first editing.

A Promise Kept

Chapter I
Michael

Michael stared at the buildings of New York as the ship slowly pulled into the harbor. It had been a long, and trying journey from Ireland by sea, and he was more than ready to test his land legs again. Although he was excited to finally reach his destination, he was also apprehensive. Some of his friends from Limerick had already completed the journey, but he had no idea how, or where to begin his search for them. He had almost no money in his pockets, and his possessions were meager. It seemed as though hours had passed before the passengers were called to disembark. The line of people leaving the ship, seemed to progress as slowly as the past few months had.

The year he set sail was 1863. The New Year had come and gone on the Escort without the least bit of circumstance, or celebration. Finally, it was Michael's turn to descend the gangplank. He turned and shook hands with the friends that he had made on the journey. They exchanged well wishes before Michael drew a deep breath, and said one final prayer of farewell to his motherland. He stepped out into the new world not knowing what his future held. He was greeted by noise, there were unfamiliar smells, and much commotion in the streets. So many people went bustling about, pushing and shoving their way through the crowds. Clutching his satchel a bit tighter, and drawing it a bit closer to his body, the young emigrant proceeded through the vociferous crowd of people. He had been warned of the pickpockets, and swindlers in New York. Now, he was to begin his new life, in a new country, with an emotional jumble of excitement, and cynical distrust.

"Here son! Over here! Come on over here for the chance of a lifetime! Today is your lucky day."

Michael glanced around, then back at the uniformed man. He put a finger to his own chest in a manner of a question.

"Yes lad, I'm talking to you! Come over here. You're from Ireland aren't you?"

"Aye, that I am," he replied, remembering his mother's last words to him. "Always remember where you come from, Michael. Never forget that you are Irish, and be proud of it!" she told him. "And never forget that you are a Malone"

The uniformed man spoke again. "Where are you going lad? Do you have family here? Do you have money? Are you hungry?"

The questions came so fast, that Michael hardly had a chance to consider the answers before another set of inquiries were hurled toward him. "How would you like forty dollars, and new pair of boots? How would you like to become an American citizen? It will only take you five minutes to sign these papers, and then you will be off to a nice dinner of bacon and beans. This is your lucky day son. You can become a citizen, and a soldier all at the same time. You are in America now; you should become an American right and legal. Join the army, and you can even be in the Irish brigade. Maybe you will find some of your friends from back home. Lord knows there are plenty of you Irish coming here. You people really know how to procreate, and populate the earth, don't you? You take the bible quite seriously, you Irish. Say, are you Catholic, or Protestant?"

It was too much to take in. Michael could feel the cold salt water from the deck seeping into his holey boots, right past the holes in his stockings, and down to his numb feet. His head was in a fog, and the feel of land beneath his feet was foreign to him. Yes, he was hungry, but he was used to being hungry. He was in America now. The words of the soldier played in his head, and then his mother's words again, "Never forget where you come from Michael." Finally he spoke up.

"But sir, I'm already a citizen of Ireland."

Well, that's OK son, you will always be a citizen of Ireland. But you can be a citizen of America, and a citizen of Ireland too!"

Michael looked over at another young man signing the papers on the table before him. He recognized his accent to be of Northern Ireland.

"Tis is a good opportunity, you should sign," the boy urged. "What Irishman is afraid to fight in a war? I've never known an Irishman afraid of a good fight, and they're goin' t' give us guns. The best guns money can buy. Nothin' like you can get your hands on in Ireland. Nothin' like you could ever afford. Sign mate! You're crazy if you don't."

The two recruitment soldiers looked at one another with a knowing glance, as they stood waiting for their target to swallow their sales pitch and sign the papers. Michael picked up the quill and signed his name.

Michael Joseph Malone
Age 18
Country of birth: Ireland
Next of kin: Mother, Molly Malone
28 Donegal Lane
Limerick, Ireland

And in that short space of time, Michael was off to fight a war that he knew nothing of, and cared nothing about. He learned quickly though. He learned the names of Generals, and battlefields. He became familiar with the politics, and causes of the statesmen, and likened their views, in some ways, to those of Ireland. North and South, always at odds about freedom, religion, and equal rights. Americans were not all that different than the countrymen back home.

In the following months, Michael spent many nights crying for his homeland, and his mother, amongst the wounded and the dead on the battlefields. He had never known the degradation of such hunger, cold, filth, and sickness. As quickly as he would befriend a comrade, he would lose that friend to the cause. He wondered, how could America be so grand, when all he had really seen was so much hatred, death, and depression?

The day was April 9th 1865, when General Lee surrendered to Grant at Appomattox, and the war was declared over. The Union had defeated the South at a devastating cost to both sides. It took three more weeks for the news to travel to Michael's regiment. His life had been spared, and once again, he picked up where he had left off on the docks of New York. He was still a wondering soul in a foreign land. Short pay from his service duties, boots holier than those he had worn that day on the docks, and hunger as he had never before known in Ireland, was all that Michael had to take away with him; but take with him where?

Michael had heard that soldiers of the civil war were being recruited to defend the forts, and citizens in the Southwest. The Natives in that region were becoming hostile, and emigration from East, to West was a dangerous journey. Young, unmarried men, were needed to escort pioneers across the country on the Santa Fe, Oregon, and Gila trails.

Santa Fe was a metropolitan city on the western frontier, and Michael was intrigued to see something new, and escape the oppressive environment in the South. Although he was tired of soldiering, he knew of nothing else, and soon found himself headed West, to New Mexico.

Chapter II

Magdalena

"Where are you going, Magdalena?" inquired Dona Maria Sandoval.

"I am going to the church to pray for my brother's return Mama. I will need two pennies for a candle."

"Very well, my daughter, but do not be gone for long."

She handed Magdalena the pennies, and watched from the stoop of the hacienda until her daughter had disappeared around the corner.

Dona Maria Sandoval was in a constant state of worry for her daughter. All of her attention could be concentrated on Magdalena, now that she was the last surviving child of Dona Maria's. Two infants had been lost in childbirth. One child was lost in a carriage accident at the age of five years. Her oldest, her son Guillermo, had left Santa Fe with a supply train to deliver goods to the Army at Fort Craig, three years earlier. Sadly, the wagons would never reach their destination. They had been reported to have been over-taken, and pillaged by Confederate soldiers, also on their way to the fort to take it over. No lives with the supply unit were spared. Magdalena refused to believe that her older brother was dead. She continued daily to await his return home. Guillermo was too strong, and too clever. There must have been a mistake. After all, no body was returned, and to Magdalena that meant that there was still hope that he might be alive. Dona Maria knew better however. She knew that her son was lying in a mass grave, somewhere along the Jornada del

Muerto trail. It worried Dona Maria Sandoval that her daughter refused to believe the truth, but even she, herself, refused in the beginning. Magdalena was more head strong than her mother, but her mother knew that she would come around in her own time. She knew that it was useless to try to change her mind, once it was made up.

~*~

Santa Fe was no place to raise a seventeen year old girl, in Dona Maria's mind. The city was full of pestilence in the form of beggars and thieves, orphans, and poverty. They were of another element. The Sandovals were aristocrats from Spain. Don Alfonso Sandoval, embellished his fortune in New Mexico with a mercantile. His store supplied the town with most of its needs. He possessed the means to invest in stock for the mercantile, and very few others had such means, in the days after the war. His real fortune came with a contract to supply the Cavalry. Through the entrepreneur, the Army could purchase guns, ammunition, dried fruit, hardtack, canvas tents, boots and uniforms, saddles and tack, and even horses. Almost anything the Army needed, could be procured through Don Alfonso Sandoval. It was a lucrative business for the gentleman, and he never missed the chance to display his fortune. He owned a fine, two story hacienda in the center of town. The walls were of double adobe. The hacienda boasted a large, well equipped kitchen, and there was a fire place in each of the bedrooms. The floors were paved with Mexican tile throughout. Wrought iron balconies opened up to the street from each of the upstairs bedrooms. Behind the grand house, was a long-house that served as living quarters for the servants.

Don Sandoval's women were adorned in the finest garments, made of the finest silks, linens, and wools that money could buy. The ladies wore gold combs in their hair, and each member of the family wore a gold ring, with rubies, and diamonds inset into the family coat of arms. This obscene display of fortune did not necessarily make Don Alfonso Sandoval a bad man, however. He was also very philanthropic by nature, and willing to contribute to the welfare of the good citizens of Santa Fe, if ever they were in need. But only the good citizens, by the standards of Don Sandoval. He often supplied medicines to the hospital, or paid the doctor for a visit to a friend who hadn't the fee. He was most generous to the Catholic church in town, and in his mind, that was his way of extending his generosity to the less deserving. He would give generously to the church, and the church could take care of the beggars and down trodden.

~*~

The water source for the town was the Santa Fe River, and the water was not always palatable, or healthy. The river was used for watering livestock, and washing laundry, as well as for irrigation and consumption. The more fortunate citizens of Santa Fe, drew pure, artesian, water from their own wells. Many of those who did not have this luxury, had succumbed to the bad water of the Santa Fe, and fell ill to malaria, and other diseases brought to town by the soldiers. There were too many people, living too close together, in squalid conditions. Naked children played in the dirty streets, their faces and bodies covered with so much dust from the earthen roads, that at times it was difficult to discern if the child was White, Indian, or Mexican. Many of these children were orphans, and depended on the charity of the town to feed, and cloth them.

Dona Maria Sandoval harbored an overwhelming desire to relocate to the outer limits of town. She wanted more space around her, and less people. She wanted to protect Magdalena from the sins, and sicknesses that were bred of such a town. The thought of losing another child, her last remaining child, was her greatest fear.

~*~

Magdalena entered the sanctuary, and approached a pew. She knelt to the floor, and crossed herself before taking her seat.

Bowing her head, she began to pray for her brother, and for his return. A tear rolled down her flushed cheek. Magdalena normally cried when she prayed for Guillermo. She felt that the angels would take pity upon her sorrow, and that her prayers would be more effective with this outward display of mourning. At times, the tears came without effort, but at times, the void inside of her would not allow them to come at all.

~*~

Michael was taken aback by the city. One thought kept playing in his head, over and over, "With all of the land, and space in the southwest, why do so many people live so tightly together, in this filthy area of a few square miles?" In some ways, it was like New York, only in the desert, and not on the seaboard. It smelled bad, there were too many people, and it was too noisy. The sooner he found the Cavalry and was on the trail out of town, the better he would be. He walked down San Francisco Street, aimlessly seeking something, or someone that resembled Cavalry. Pangs of hunger were gnawing at his insides. The noise of street vendors, carts and wagons, horses nickering, dogs barking all screamed inside his head like angry demons. The loud, clanging noise from the church bells, was almost too much to take. Michael felt as though he would faint at any moment. He sat on a bench to gather his senses.

"Church bells; how long has it been since I've been to church?" he thought to himself. It would make his mother proud and happy, if he paid a visit and said a prayer of thanks for his life. To Michael, his life seemed so pathetic at this moment. The bells kept clanging, louder and louder. Michael hadn't realized that he was sitting directly below them. Perhaps inside, he would find some peace and quiet. Perhaps if just for a while, he sat inside the church, he might be able to gather his thoughts. Michael rose, and walked into the sanctuary.

In comparison, it was nothing like the small, humble, churches that he was familiar with in Ireland. It was almost overwhelming.

He paused for a moment to consider the stained glass windows, the ornate chandeliers, and the gilded alter. "This is anything but humble," he thought. He approached a pew, and sat at the end. Crossing himself, he thought for a moment about what he should pray for. Again, he was distracted by the stimulus, and Gothic beauty that the sanctuary boldly displayed. While taking in his surroundings, he noticed the young woman at the opposite end of the pew, and wondered about the tear on her cheek. "She must be suffering from some personal tragedy," he thought. He could not divert his eyes from her. She was a lady. It had been a long while since he had seen anything so gentile, and civilized as she. He studied her profile, her dark skin, and shiny black hair, the flush in her cheek. Her taffeta dress was trimmed with fine lace. It was different from the lace that came from England, much more elaborate. She wore a collar of lace as well, that was adorned with tiny pearls sewn into the edges. He absorbed every bit of her femininity that he could.

While he had been off fighting the war for America, Michael had become a man. Many of his comrades carried daguerreotypes of their wives, or sweethearts from home. The images kept them going, gave them purpose and strength. Michael had longed for his family back home, and for Ireland, but he never missed a lover left behind. He'd never had a sweetheart. As he studied the young woman's profile, a voice in his head kept willing her to "turn your head this way, I want to see your face".

Magdalena pulled a crisp, white, linen handkerchief from where it had been tucked into her sleeve. She opened it enough to reveal an embroidered monogram. 'MS' on the linen. She dabbed her cheek, and her nose. Nearly an hour had passed since she'd been in the church. Suddenly, she remembered the promise that she had made to her mother. Not wanting to cause undue worry, she hastily rose and walked to the area where dozens of small candles burned. Each candle represented a different cause, a different prayer. Magdalena dropped her pennies in a jar and lit a candle. She folded her hands for one last prayer before she would leave. As she turned and headed toward the heavy, wooden doors, she paused as she spotted Michael staring in her direction. At last, he was finally allowed a glimpse of her face in full. She was the most stunning woman that he had ever seen. Her complexion was dark, and her lips were full. She had a dainty, chiseled nose, and high cheekbones. Magdalena's glance locked upon Michael's. When her eyes met his, neither moved for several moments, transfixed in the gaze. Each was waiting for the other to make their move, to say, or do something. Michael had never before seen eyes so black. They were so dark, that it was hard to discern a pupil. So piercing were they, that it made him feel uncomfortable, yet he could not look away. Magdalena, in turn, studied Michael's green eyes. How clear, and lovely they looked, framed by his long, black, curly locks of hair. After several lingering moments, Magdalena snapped herself into composure. She turned, and walked briskly down the aisle toward the exit. Michael could hear her stiff petticoats, rustling as she walked. He shamefully turned his head downward, even though he was not yet finished. He was not ready for her to take leave. He wanted to study her like a fine work of art. He wanted to absorb her essence, smell her perfume, examine her beauty with all of his senses.

A faint ray of light streamed in through the door, as it very slowly, closed behind Magdalena. The candles flickered as they caught a wisp of a breeze. She was gone.

Michael was startled by someone tapping his shoulder. He turned to find himself face to face with a weathered, old priest. The man had beady, deep set eyes, that startled Michael initially. His faced was lined and wrinkled with age, and nubby hairs protruded from the skin on his cheeks and chin. He was a shocking contrast to that which Michael had been gazing upon only moments prior.

"You must be hungry," said the priest in a gravely voice. "There is bread, and soup, in the garden outside. Supper is served until six o'clock, and then put away, so you must hurry if you are to have any."

Chapter III

A Change in Plans

Michael was grateful for the sustenance that the church had offered him. Sitting under the shade of an ash tree, he ate slowly, thinking about the magnificent woman in the sanctuary. Then, his thoughts turned inward toward himself. He was so thin, and frail, not the strapping young man who had left Ireland, so many moths ago. Even his muscles were smaller, from his own body consuming them, for lack of food. His clothes were filthy, loose, and tattered. He could not remember the last time he had bathed. No woman would give him a second glance, especially one of such refinement. Michael opened his satchel. He withdrew his Colt revolver and a small poke, containing the ammunition. He poured out the contents of the poke...fourteen bullets left. He removed another small poke from a hidden pocket inside of his shirt, and poured several coins into his hand. He counted out seventeen dollars, and sixty eight cents, plus a coin from Ireland that he carried for luck. Like his bullets, he was rationing his coins, trying not to spend either. Michael gathered up his scant belongings, and kissed his Irish coin before replacing in it the poke with the others. The sun was lowering in the sky, and it's rays streamed through the rustling leaves of the ash tree, reminding him that it would soon me dark. He started toward the river, and after some time found the perfect spot to camp for the night. Once again, he opened his satchel and looked at his gun. He thought for a moment about selling it, but quickly reconsidered. This was a foreign land to him, and he just might find an occasion to use it. From his satchel, he removed a bar of soap that had come all the way from Ireland with him. Rarely, had he found an opportunity to make use of it, but tonight he was going to bathe in the river, and wash his tattered clothing. Making himself look and smell the best that he could, he would go into town in the morning and spend some of his money. He needed a change of clothes, and stationary to write a letter to his mother. Soap in hand, he made his way slowly, into the chilly water of the swiftly flowing river. When his clothes had been scrubbed, he hung them on a mesquite branch to dry. He then rolled his cold and naked body up in his blanket. With belly full, and body clean, Michael slept well that night.

In the morning, he awoke with renewed hope and anticipation. He thought about his mother. She must be wondering about him. It had been so long since he'd written, and he had no way of knowing if she had ever received his letters. Now, he had no address, or way of receiving a letter in return.

Michael walked down San Francisco Street until he came to a sign that read:

Sandoval's Mercantile

He had second thoughts about parting with his money, but decided that it was for the best. He walked up the wooden steps of the store, across the porch, and through the swinging doors. Stepping inside, he stood for a moment, surveying the abundant inventory.

"Can I help you with something?"

Michael looked around to see a statuesque, dark, man behind the counter. The man had thick, wavy black hair, and a bushy moustache. Both were highlighted by a hint of silver. His eyes were narrow, and condemning, and turned downward in the corners, as did the corners of his mouth. Michael wanted to turn, and run through the swinging doors. "What if I don't have enough to pay for a new blouse, and trousers?" he thought to himself. He cleared his throat.

"Well, speak up won't you?" demanded the man.

Michael told the man behind the counter what he had come to purchase. The man led him to the area in the store where the dry goods, and ready made clothes were displayed.

"You could go to the tailor down the street. He's from Italy. He makes fine garments, but it'll cost you. I doubt that a street urchin like you has the money to pay for a tailor," said the looming storekeeper.

Michael was one of the downtrodden in the eyes of Don Sandoval. The sort that he despised. The lad could feel the merchant's contempt toward him. He felt diminished, by his sinister glare, but could hardly blame the man.

"I'll not be needin' a tailor sir, only a fresh change of clothes."

"Have you tried the church? They could outfit you with some clothes. They might not be new, but the price is right."

"I have money sir." Michael was becoming indignant. He had money, and wanted to spend it in this store. Why was this man giving him such a hard time? "I've just come from fighting the war in the East," Michael told Don Sandoval. "I'm in need of some fresh clothes, and have not had a chance to buy any. I'm goin' to join up with the Cavalry here in the southwest, and escort the wagon trains West." Michael was making nervous small-talk, but he was also trying to justify himself.

"If you're going to fight Indians, then I'd save your money. You won't need new clothes when you're six feet under. The Cavalry will outfit you with new clothes anyway, and they will come directly from this mercantile."

This was the last straw for Michael. The large man behind the counter was more than he cared to put up with.

"Where's th' owner of this establishment?" Michael demanded. "I would like a word with him!"

"And who are you?" Don Sandoval came back.

"I am a paying customer, that's who. And you are bad for business. I'd like to tell th' owner that you're chasin' away business."

Don Sandoval threw his head back, and began to laugh a hearty laugh.

"I am the owner," he announced with great pride. "I am Don Alfonso Sandoval, and I do not need your business, you Irish cuss." He laughed again, between his insults. "But since you have so much spunk, I will take your pocket change. Pick out what you need. The trousers are five dollars, and the blouse will be three, if you choose a plain one."

The old man picked up a newspaper and pretended to read, but never took an eyes off the downtrodden Michael. Michael was feeling somewhat elated at the fact that he didn't have to spend all of his money. He could buy what he needed, and still have something leftover. He selected what he came for, and added a pair of stockings. Taking the bundle to the counter, Michael remembered his earlier thoughts of his mother.

"I'll be needin' some stationary, and an envelope. And oh, the postage for a letter to Ireland".

The large man fumbled around behind the counter for a moment, and presented all that had been requested.

"Anything else?" he said.

"Yes, I'll take two penny candies," Michael said with pride, as though he had money to spare frivolously.

"Awh, a big spender. Since you're on such a big spending spree, why don't you buy yourself a decent pair of boots? What good is a new pair of stockings, when what's left of your boots is held together with twine?"

Michael lost his confidence again. The man was right. He desperately needed new boots, but that would have to wait.

"Never mind," said Michael, looking the man directly in the eye. "This is all for today, thank you. I wouldn't want me spending spree to carry me away now."

The merchant chuckled as he added up the bill. "That will be ten dollars and sixty six cents."

Michael paid the man, and started to walk toward the doors. He paused for a moment, then turned half way around.

"Yes?" said Don Sandoval. "Did you forget something, big spender? A new pair of boots perhaps?"

"I was just wonderin', what a big, important man like yourself is doin' behind the counter? Is your mistrust of mankind so great, that you cannot be hirin' a clerk to do the menial work for ya?"

Don Sandoval's eyes stared right through Michael.

"My son used to run the store for me. He was damn good at it too, I'll tell you. He would have been more than happy to take your last dollar. Ever since he died I cannot seem to keep good help in the store. There is nothing more that I'd like, than to be out fishing in the river, or at the gun club, enjoying a glass of brandy and a fine cigar. I don't care for tending the store, not one iota, but someone has got to do it. Someone who can be depended on to show up every day, and on time. My customers rely on the store to be open at regular hours."

"Oh, I see then," said Michael. "I'm sorry about your son."

He turned and continued toward the swinging doors.

"Perhaps you'd like to run the store," Don Michael called out.

"Me?" questioned Michael. "A poor Irish cuss like meself? But how could ya ever trust me then? How do you know that I can read, and do th' math? How do you know that I can count American money, being just a poor Irish cuss that I am?"

"Well, can you?" asked Don Sandoval. "Can you read, and do math?"

"Aye," replied Michael. "But I don't think that I'd care to work for the likes of an ogre such as yourself!"

"Have you had any better offers lad? You look like you could use some decent food... the kind that a good job, and good pay can afford you."

Michael thought about it for a moment. Maybe he could work for this man just long enough to save some money, and then head out west to Prescott to find a job there. It might be better than joining up with the Cavalry. He really did not come to America to fight their wars in the first place, and he certainly did not come to America to be hungry. That could be done well enough in Ireland.

"How much does it pay?" he asked confidently.

"I'll pay you a dollar a day, Sundays off. It's a good offer, better than you'll find anywhere in Santa Fe."

"Americans and their sales pitches," thought Michael. "There must be a catch."

"What's the catch?" he asked.

"There is no catch," said Don Sandoval. "I'm just sick of being in this store, day in, and day out. I want to go fishing. I need a break. The United States government pays me well, so I can pay you well."

"Well then," Michael said, "When shall I start?"

"Good!" said Don Sandoval. "You'll start tomorrow. The store opens at eight AM. Be here on time. And oh, you'd better buy yourself a new pair of boots. The ones you have will never do to represent me."

"Ha! I knew it!" said Michael. "I knew there was a catch! You just want to sell me a pair of boots!"

"It's no catch, but you can't work in those old scraps of leather. Those boots in the corner are twenty dollars. You take a pair, and pay me two dollars a week until we are even."

"But that will take ten weeks! I will pay you four dollars a week for five weeks, more if I can."

"Fine!" agreed Don Sandoval. "I'll take it from your pay. I hope you work well, and I won't have to let you go before those boots are paid for. And if you run off with them, I will call the Marshall on you, so I hope you have a fast horse."

Michael took the boots, and shook his head as he walked out the door. He only wished that he had a horse. "I'll be seeing ya in the mornin' then, eight AM sharp."

"I'm glad that you can do math!" Don Sandoval called to Michael as he walked through the doors.

At seven the next morning, true to his word and better, Michael was sitting on the steps of the mercantile, waiting for Don Alfonso Sandoval.

Chapter IV

A New Start

Don Alfonso Sandoval stepped out of his hacienda onto San Francisco Street, and strolled next door to his mercantile. He paused for a moment, at the sight of Michael sitting on the porch in front of the store, wearing his brand new clothes and boots. He was polished up, and looking his best. "Maybe this boy had some potential after all" he thought to himself. Walking up the steps to the mercantile, he held out a tin plate as an offering to Michael. It's contents were hidden by a linen napkin that covered the plate.

"My wife thought you might like some home cooking," he said. Michael accepted the plate, and removed the napkin, tucking it into his shirt. The biscuits and gravy were like manna from heaven. At first, he ate fast. Then he slowed his pace to relish the food, and make it last a bit longer.

"Where are you staying?" asked Don Alfonso Sandoval.

"I'm camping on the edge of town by the Santa Fe," replied Michael.

"I see," said Don Sandoval. "Well, you sure do clean up well for someone who is sleeping in the dirt. Have you a canvas?"

"No," said Michael. "I'm sleeping under the stars."

"Well, I can front you a canvas tent from the mercantile," said Don Sandoval.

"No, thank you anyway," said Michael. "I just may not want to be in debt to ya for th' rest of me life."

"Well then," replied Don Sandoval, "I will look for one in my own house that I can loan you. You can return it when you find yourself a permanent home.'"

"I'd be much obliged to ya sir. The nights are startin' t' get a wee bit cold now. Nothin' like I had to endure in the Northeast though."

"Well Michael, you will find that our pleasant weather here in Santa Fe can become rather cold in the winter, more than you might imagine. Let's get started now. I will show you how to open the store, and where everything is, and how to keep an inventory. Tonight I will show you how to close. Tomorrow I will open with you, and then I will go fishing."

The day progressed well, and after the past few months Michael considered his new job to be easy money. He was good with the customers, and was getting quickly acquainted with the townsfolk.

Michael was good with people much the same way that Guillermo had been, only better. He had a charismatic quality about him, and he was rapidly growing on Don Alfonso Sandoval.

At the end of the first day on the job, Michael and Don Sandoval locked up the store and each went their own way. The next morning Michael was waiting on the steps at seven AM. At seven forty-five Don Sandoval walked from his house and to the mercantile, again carrying a tin plate with a linen napkin covering it. Today's home cooked meal was fresh salt bread still warm from the oven, with melted butter and blackberry preserves. On the side was a generous serving of smoked ham.

"These are the best preserves I ever tasted!" declared Michael.

"My daughter and her mother put them up. My daughter is a natural in the kitchen, even better than her mother."

"You're a lucky man then, Don Sandoval," said Michael as he wiped the plate with the bread, soaking up every last bit of the savory preserves.

"Michael, I'm sorry that I forgot about the canvas yesterday. I hope that your night was not too uncomfortable. I have instructed my daughter to bring the tent over today, along with a few other supplies that I thought you might need."

"Thank you sir. That will be just fine."

"Now, I'm going fishing!" said Don Sandoval.

He started toward the door. "By the way Michael, help yourself to the apples in that barrel. I can't sell them fast enough and I'd rather have you eat a few than have them rot. I've instructed my daughter to take some home for pies, and if you're lucky enough you may get a taste of one." Then he was out the door.

Michael was beginning to think that he had made a good decision. Don Sandoval wasn't that bad after all. He had received at least one good home cooked meal each morning. He had his own space by the river, and now he was to acquire a canvas tent that could be called home for a while. With his new clothes, new home, and some decent food in his belly, Michael was starting to look and feel well again. There was hope for the future. He could work for a few months, maybe a year and save his money. Maybe he would buy himself a horse one day. Things were not so bad, and it was all just starting to get better.

Michael wasted no time in getting to work. He dusted, straightened and swept out the store. He would do everything that Don Sandoval told him to do, and more. Every customer was greeted with a smile the moment they walked through the door. At noontime there were no customers in the store, so Michael went out on the porch and sat in one of the willow chairs. He grabbed a green apple from the barrel on his way out, and rubbed it on his shirt before taking a bite. Next, he took out some jerked venison that had been wrapped in cheese cloth, and stowed in his satchel. Michael could not remove the thought from his mind, that he was the luckiest man alive. As he sat eating his lunch with the sun on his face, he began to daydream about what his future could possibly bring. He watched the people milling about the busy, dusty street, and sized up every horse that trotted past, trying to decide what sort of horse that he would ride one day. He was happy to be camped out by the river. He enjoyed the solitude, and didn't care too much for the noise, and smells of the city. Michael did liked the city people however, and enjoyed socializing with them, and learning things from them. At the end of the day he would go to his camp and light a fire, roll some tobacco and have a good smoke. Later, he would throw a line in the river, or snare a rabbit for dinner. Sometimes he would throw rocks at grouse, then skin his spoils so that he would not have to bother with removing the feathers. The birds were then skewered, and cooked over his camp fire. Grouse was his favorite. There were plenty of wild grapes growing along the river to complement the meat. Occasionally, people would pass by his camp, but nobody ever bothered him. They'd say their hellos and be on their way. As much as he enjoyed the people in town, Michael also enjoyed his solitude at then end of the day.

Michael's day dream was interrupted by the stage. "Mail!" called out the shotgun rider as he threw down a canvas sack that was heavily laden with letters and parcels. This would keep Michael busy for some time. He picked up the sack, and right away went to sorting the mail. It was enough work for someone to do as a completely separate job, but he was not about to complain. Michael was deep into his work, when he heard a woman's voice address him.

"My father told me to bring you a tent," she said.

Michael turned around and found himself, once again, face to face with the beautiful woman from the sanctuary.

Chapter V

The Canvas Tent

"You!" exclaimed Magdalena in a voice of surprise. "You are working for my father now? What is your name?"

"I am Michael," he answered. "Michael Malone."

The corners of her mouth drew up just slightly to reveal her amusement at his accent. "Well," she began, "you look a bit better than you did in the church the other day. And I might also mention that you smell better as well. Why, I could smell you clear on the other end of the pew."

Michael flushed with embarrassment.

"I came from the war in the east, and had not yet had a chance to do anything with me person. Me mother always taught us that cleanliness is next to Godliness."

"Good," replied Magdalena. "Your mother is right of course. It is a positive improvement. Your hair is a bit shaggy though. If you would like, I will bring my mother's shears tomorrow and give you a trim. Anyway, I do not know what my father was thinking by asking me to bring that tent to you. That tent must weigh more than one hundred pounds, I could never had carried it by myself. I have it outside on a cart. You can take the horse and cart tonight to your camp, and bring the rig back tomorrow. Do you know how to harness, and hobble a horse? You must not leave him all night harnessed to the cart. I have also brought a cot and a folding table. There are some other items as well, including a coffee pot. I did not know if you had one or not."

"No," said Michael, "I don't. But then I don't have any coffee either."

"Well take some from the store," said Magdalena.

"Oh no Miss, I already owe your father for the boots. I don't like being in debt to nobody, but your father insisted that if I were to work here, I would have to look the part. Me old boots were fairly fallin' apart."

"Yes, I remember." Magdalena went into the store room and took out a burlap sack. When she returned she started to fill it with food stores from the mercantile. First, a pound of coffee, then, a pound of sugar. Next five pounds of flour, a pound of lard, and three pounds of beans. She put a few green apples in the sack, and some jerked beef. On the very top, she placed six fresh eggs. Michael had assumed that she was gathering supplies to take home.

"I will just put this in the cart on my way out," said Magdalena. It should hold you for a day or two, especially with the meals that my mother insists on sending you each morning." She walked out of the store, but in another moment was rushing back in. "I must have left my head in here somewhere," she proclaimed. "I have almost forgotten, my father told me to bring home some apples. He is craving one of my apple pies," she said conceitedly. "Oh, and by the way, you can do the inventory for the supplies that I have given you, but you will not owe anything. Consider it a perk of the position. My father says that you need some decent food in you, and I think that I would agree." She put the apples in a sack, and rushed out the door before Michael could thank her.

Michael was locking up the store when Don Sandoval came strutting up from the river. He held up an ample stringer of trout.

"It was a good day fishing Michael! I see that Magdalena has brought you that tent, along with Blue. He's my best harness horse so you better take good care of him."

"Aye, that I will," said Michael.

Don Sandoval took two plump fish off his stringer, and threw them in the back of the cart. "Dinner!" he said with an accomplished smile.

At closing time Michael climbed up on the cart, and reined the horse around toward the river, and out of the city. He was still reveling in his good fortune. As he passed the sanctuary he crossed himself, as was his custom. How he loved that church! While he was at it, Michael said a quick prayer of thanks for his good fortune. He hummed an old Irish folk tune under his breath, to the steady rhythm of the horses clip clopping hooves. There were still a couple of good hours to be had before it would be dark, and he was anxious to get home, and set up his new canvas house.

Arriving at his campsite, Michael unharnessed Blue and hobbled him as promised. There was plenty of good grass close to the river, so he didn't worry about the horse wandering too far. He then pulled the tent from the cart and unfolded it. It was much larger than he expected it to be. He set up the frame and paced off the walls. It was twelve by fourteen feet! Michael had been expecting a small pup tent, but instead it was a tent much like the Union officers used. The tent had square walls with an "A" shaped ceiling, and it was tall enough to stand up in. There was a curtain door that could be tied up to stay open, or tied shut. On each of the other three walls were windows that could be tied up from inside the tent, or outside. Michael set the tent up on a flat piece of ground, not too close, or not too far from the river. He put rocks along the bottom edges of the canvas to keep out the wind, or running water in case it should rain. He then retrieved the rest of the supplies from the cart. First, he set up the cot in the corner of the tent. Rolled up inside of it was a clean, wool blanket. Next, he brought the folding table inside, and there was a chair as well. He set those in another corner. He began to go through the contents of a burlap sack that was in the cart. There were candles and matches, and two candle holders. The coffee pot that Magdalena had mentioned was there, as well as some other eating utensils, and a coffee grinder. He took a candle and placed it on the center of the table. The rest of the supplies were stowed underneath the table. The food stores that Magdalena had given him were placed on top of the table.

Looking around his new abode, Michael felt like a General. Stowing his satchel under the cot, he walked outside to check on Blue. The horse was content, and grazing a few rods from the tent. When Michael was satisfied with his work, he pulled some tobacco from his shirt pocket and rolled a cigarette. It was time to light the fire. Tonight he would cook the fish that Don Sandoval had given him, and have a green apple. Feeling too tired, too satisfied, and much too excited to bother making biscuits, he was pleased with the idea that if he wanted to, he had the makings for them. He sat on a rock and smoked, and stared at the fire. The fish were cooking, the sun was almost down. This was Michael's favorite time of day. He stayed outside and ate his dinner as the moon came up, and the stars came out. He then washed his tin plate in the river and went inside his new canvas house. Taking his place on the cot, he closed his eyes, and fell asleep listening to the bull frogs in the river bottom.

Chapter VI

A New Man

Michael awoke the next morning with much anticipation to greet the new day. The first thing he did, was check on Blue. Then, he washed up and prepared himself for work. For breakfast, he ate a piece of jerky, and then he combed his long, curly black hair. Michael thought about what Magdalena had said to him; it was getting very long. Today was Saturday, and the next day was his day off. Sunday, would be for taking care of his hair, and washing his clothes.

Michael was feeling anxious to get his work day started. Today he would take a small portion of his meager savings, and buy paper and postage for another letter to his mother in Ireland. There was so much that he wanted to share with her. After tying closed the flap door to his tent, he harnessed Blue and drove the cart the two miles into town. It was a nice change for him to drive. He normally didn't mind walking, but during the war, the troops had been marched nearly to death. It was the reason that his old boots were so worn out. Driving, would spare his new boots a day of walking, and help to keep them remaining new looking just a little while longer. Holding the reins loosely, and letting Blue take his own pace, Michael daydreamed again about owning his own horse. It was a favorite fantasy of his. Before he knew it, he was in front of the mercantile. San Francisco Street was already bustling, and alive with activity. There were people waiting on the porch for the store to open, even though it was only seven thirty. Michael tied Blue to the hitching post, and ran up the steps. He would oblige his customers, and open early for them. At seven forty-five, Don Sandoval walked into the mercantile to find it crowded with customers, and Michael busy at work. He smiled with satisfaction and waited for a free moment speak with him.

"Your first week went well," he told Michael. "I will come at closing tonight and give you your first weeks' pay."

"No need," said Michael. I only worked four days, so I won't be expecting anything this week. Put it down toward me boots please."

"Very well then, if you're quite sure," replied a satisfied Don Sandoval.

"Sir, I wanted to thank you for the loan of such a grand tent," Michael said, changing the subject. "I wasn't expecting such a large one. I will be forever in debt to ya I'm afraid," said Michael.

"Nonsense," replied Don Sandoval. "You're already starting to look healthier, and I can't have you getting sick. Winter will be here soon, and you'll be better off for the tent. I have some government business to take care of today. I shall see you at closing time."

Michael went about his business in the mercantile, and just before noon Magdalena walked through the door, accompanied by a dark woman who looked very much like herself.

"Good morning Michael," she said. "I would like to introduce you to my mother."

Trying not to stare, Michael studied the dark woman for a moment. She was a handsome woman, probably in her early forties. Her attire and demeanor were very proper. Michael felt a bit uncomfortable in her presence.

"It is nice to meet you, Michael. Magdalena tells me that you are from Ireland, and that you came here to help the Union win the war."

"Well Ma'am, that's partly true. I do come from Ireland, and I did fight in the war, but it was not my reason for comin'."

"Why did you come to America, Michael?"

"Well, me father got sick with the lung disease and died, and me mother has so many of me siblings to care for. Me older brother and I wanted to help her out, but we couldn't find any work in Ireland. Me brother joined the Royal Navy and went to England. I suppose I wanted a bigger adventure, so I came to America. Truth to tell, I never wanted to fight someone else's war, or any war for that matter. It just turned out that way."

"It certainly sounds like you found your adventure," said Dona Sandoval. "I suppose you must grow terribly homesick at times."

"Aye. I'm waitin' t' hear from me mum. I wrote her a few days ago, and plan on writing again tomorrow, on me day off. I suppose it might take a very long time to hear back from her."

"Yes Michael, don't hold your breath. The mail abroad takes a very long time. Michael, I have been hearing wonderful things about you from the town folk. People say that you do a fine job running the mercantile. Magdalena tells me that you are Catholic, and that you have already become acquainted with our sanctuary. Since you go to church Michael, and since you go to the same church that we do, I would like to invite you to join us for services tomorrow. Afterward you will take supper with us at the hacienda. I do hope that you will accept."

Michael looked at Magdalena, and back at Dona Sandoval. "I would be pleased to join you, Ma'am."

"Very good then, we will meet you in front to the hacienda at ten minutes before nine. Goodbye until then." She turned and started toward the door.

"Michael," said Magdalena, "I've brought you some lunch." Magdalena handed Michael a large basket that she was holding, and followed her mother through the swinging doors. Michael watched her until she was out of sight. He'd been so excited about his new job, his new boots, and his new tent, that he had hardly given Magdalena a recent thought. He knew that he still had a lot to do, before he could ever consider courting her. Even then, he knew that a lady of stature would probably never consider a poor boy, who worked for her father. It seemed hopeless. Michael turned his thoughts to his invitation. He hadn't planned on going to church, or anywhere else the next day. What he had planned for was cutting his hair, washing his one set of decent clothes, and penning a letter to his mother. This changed everything. He couldn't very well wear the same shirt to church that he'd been wearing to work all week. Setting the basket down on the counter, Michael walked briskly toward the racks of ready made garments. He found a nice, twill blouse, with buttons all the way down the front. It was dark green, and a much heavier weave than his other blouse. It would be appropriate to wear to church on Sundays, and it would also be a good winter shirt. The price on the tag was four dollars and fifty cents. This purchase would make a large dent in what was left of his money, but he had no choice. In another week he would have two more dollars in his pocket from his paycheck, and his boots would be almost half paid for.

Michael took the shirt to the counter, wrote it down in the inventory, and put the correct change in the cash register. He then took some paper and an envelope, and also wrote it down and paid for it, along with postage to Ireland. When a customer came into the mercantile, Michael greeted her in his normal congenial fashion. It was Mrs. Kit Carson.

Josepha Carson was heavy with child. It was a common state of being for her, even though her husband was often away from home for long periods of time. She was a regular customer in the mercantile, and was extended credit when needed. Her husband was sure to settle up in full, once he returned home.

"Good morning, Michael," she greeted. "I'm taking in another orphan," she told him. "I'll need some heavy muslin and thread. I can't tell you how it hurts my heart to see so many homeless children roaming the streets of Santa Fe. I don't know what Mr.

Carson will say when he comes home to find another child in the house. Perhaps two, if this baby comes before he returns."

Mrs. Kit Carson was one of the more favored citizens of the town. She came from good stock, and was very philanthropic by nature. Many of her friends were influential people in town, and the woman folk often relied on her for advice. Michael helped her with her shopping needs, and after she left he stood wondering what he was doing before she came in. His stomach reminded him of the basket that Magdalena had given him. Peeking inside, he thought again of his good fortune. The basket contained several pieces of friend chicken, two biscuits, and a whole apple pie. Michael was beginning to become cynical of his good fortune. What had he done to deserve it? What would he end up having to pay for it, in the long run? He was too hungry at the moment to dwell too deeply on it. Sitting down on the porch stoop, he began to devour the food. This morning, there had been no breakfast brought to him, but the lunch more than made up for it. Don Sandoval was right about the apple pie. It was the best Michael had ever tasted.

On Saturdays, the mercantile closed at four o'clock. Michael hurried to complete his chores before locking up. He grabbed the basket with the remaining food, so he might have it for dinner later. There was much to be done, since he would lose half a day on Sunday. Rushing to lock the doors, Michael scooped up his shirt and stationary, placing them on top of the basket. When he arrived at his campsite, everything was just as he'd left it. He went inside and placed the basket on the table, and hung his new shirt from a hook, in the ceiling of the tent. He rolled up the windows, to let the fresh evening breeze air out the tent. There would be no need to cook tonight, but Michael always enjoyed a fire in the evenings. When the fire was lit and burning, he rolled a cigarette, which had become his after work habit. There were still two and a half hours of good daylight. Michael relaxed on a tree stump that he had pulled close to the fire, and contemplated putting a line in the water. He made a list in his head of things that he wanted to do to improve his home. Wood and fuel needed to be gathered, and stored, so it would be readily available when needed. He also wanted to string a clothes line behind his tent. In the future, Michael would always have a clean change of clothes. It was his intention to add another pair of trousers to his wardrobe. Another line would be strung for the use of drying meat and fish, for the nights that he did not feel like cooking. Also, winter was coming and there may be days when he could not cook outside. Michael had a small piece of canvas in his satchel that he used at times as a lean-to. He was forming a plan in his head to use this canvas underneath the stand of trees that stood a few rods away from his tent. There, he would dig a fire pit for the nights that he could not cook out in the open. The wood could also be stored there to keep it dry. Michael was feeling very satisfied with his plan to make his home just a little more comfortable. A sudden turn of weather would not catch him off guard. Instead, he would be prepared.

As Michael sat contemplating the improvements to his campsite, his thoughts were interrupted by the sound of approaching hoof beats. He recognized the rider as Magdalena, when she appeared from around the bend.

"Hello Michael!" she called out.

"Hello yourself!" he replied. "How did ya find me?"

"I rode in the direction where you told me your camp was, and I followed the smoke from your fire."

"What might ya be doin' here anyway?"

"I am here to give you a good shave and a haircut, that is what I am doing here."

"If ya thought that I'd be disgracin' ya in church t'morrow, then why did ya ask me to go with ya in the first place?"

"If you will recall Michael, it was not I who asked you to church. It was my mother's idea."

"And was it your mother who sent ya here then?"

"No, coming here was my idea."

"And what might your parents think about ya ridin' out here all alone?"

"They thought it was a good idea. But I have to be back before dark, so let us get started, shall we? Go to the river and wet your hair; I will get your chair and bring it out."

Magdalena shaved Michael and cut his hair, being careful not to cut his curly, black, locks too short. She handed Michael a mirror that she had brought along. "There! You look so much nicer now! In fact, you are hardly the same man that I saw that day in the church."

Michael studied himself in the mirror. "It's so hard to shave with the tiny little mirror that I have. Thank you so much. I'm obliged to you too now I suppose."

"Not at all. You may keep the mirror with your other provisions. I will not be needing it. By the way, how is the tent working out? Is there anything else that you need?"

"Not a thing that I can think of. Can you sit by the fire with me for a while? How about a piece of apple pie? Today the prettiest girl in town, gave me the best apple pie that I've ever tasted.!"

"I'd love some, but just a small piece."

Michael went into the tent, and returned with two pieces of pie. He was embarrassed to serve Magdalena on his tin plate, but it was all that he had. They ate the pie and made small talk. Both laughed at the slightest things. Both were deeply content with the company of one another.

The sun was falling fast, and neither wanted the night to end. Michael still had a letter to write, and he still hadn't finished his fried chicken from earlier, but the pie seemed to satiate any hunger that he may have had earlier.

"You best be gettin' home before your parents start to worry. It's going t' be dark soon," said Michael.

"You are right, Michael. I will see you in the morning. Papa put a pig in the ground tonight. All of the hands are coming for supper tomorrow after church, and some of the town folk as well. Mama thought it would be a nice way for you to get acquainted; outside of the mercantile that is. If you are to be a part of this town, then you should have some friends here."

Magdalena mounted her horse, and started toward home. Michael watched as she disappeared around the bend. He stayed up for a while and watched the stars, being much too excited to sleep. If he washed his trousers now, they would never be dry in time to wear to church in the morning. It would have to wait. His mother's letter would have to wait as well. He just wanted to enjoy the evening air, and think about Magdalena. His previous thoughts about courting a lady like Magdalena, were replaced with the fantasy of her being his sweetheart. Surely she must have many suitors in town. Could he have a chance? Probably not, but he dreamed about it that night.

Chapter VII

Meeting the Town

Michael rose at the first light of day. It was Sunday. He picked up the mirror that Magdalena had left him, and considered his appearance. "Not so bad," he thought, although he wished that he had washed his trousers. Next pay day, he would buy a second pair. He really needed two entire changes of clothes. He still had the raggedy old clothes that he was wearing when he first came to town, but he'd save those for sleeping in when the weather turned cold, or working in, or wearing when his good clothes were drying on the line. There was plenty of time before he had to be in town. Michael opened the basket and ate a biscuit, with some blackberry preserves. He remembered that he had coffee, and quickly set out to start a fire in the pit outside of the tent. Returning inside he retrieved the coffee grinder and began to grind some beans. Putting the ground beans, and some water in the percolator, he placed the pot in the fire, and returned into the tent. He took out his stationary, quill, and ink, and sat down to write the letter which he had intended to do the previous night.

My Dearest Mother,

I miss you and the family so very much. I wish that you could see me now. The war is over and things are finally going well for me in America. I have secured a job as a clerk, in the mercantile in Santa Fe, New Mexico. I have you to thank for that. If you had not insisted on me going to school and getting book smart, I probably would not have been hired. Don Sandoval pays me a dollar a day. I had to buy some new boots and clothes, so as to be presentable at my new job. When I have settled my debt with Don Sandoval, I will send you some money. I am enclosing two dollars now. I know it is not much, but I hope that it will help. Today is Sunday, my day off. I know that you will be happy to hear that I am going to the Catholic Church with Don Alfonso Sandoval and his family this morning. Afterward, I am going to their hacienda (house) to have supper, and meet some of the town folk. Don Sandoval has put a pig in the ground for the occasion. I am anxious to try this, as it will be new to me. The Sandovals have been very good to me. Don Sandoval has loaned me a fine tent, much like the tents used by the Generals in the war. It is a very comfortable home indeed.

I must close this letter now, so as not to be late to church.

I love you very much,

Michael

P.S.

Don Sandoval has a lovely wife, and a beautiful daughter named Magdalena. I have high hopes that Magdalena will be my sweetheart some day.

Michael blew the ink on the paper, to hasten the drying process. Carefully, he folded it and placed it in the envelope. He addressed the envelope, and marked the return address as the mercantile. Then he affixed the stamp on the envelope and stowed it in his satchel. There was no use taking it to town with him today; he would take it with him the next day, when he reported to work. Michael dressed himself in his new green shirt, and combed down his curly hair. He pulled on his new boots, and started for town. At eight thirty, he was standing in front of Don Sandoval's hacienda. People were already heading toward the sanctuary for the nine o'clock service. It seemed to take forever before Don and Dona Sandoval appeared. Soon they were followed by Magdalena. Michael's eyes lit up when he saw her. She looked so beautiful, dressed in her fancy church clothes. They said their good mornings, and walked to church in relative silence.

Inside the church, Dona Sandoval entered the pew first, followed by her husband, and then Magdalena. Michael took his seat next to Magdalena. He was wondering if this latest stroke of fortune was intentional, or circumstantial. Michael looked at Magdalena, but she didn't return the glance. The service seemed to last hours, but Michael was content sitting next to Magdalena. In fact, he relished every moment. When the service was over, they mingled in the garden with the other parishioners. Michael was introduced properly to many of the townspeople. Some, he had met in the mercantile already. Others, he had met previously elsewhere. After socializing for some time, they headed for the Sandoval's hacienda. Michael was curious as to how it looked inside. When they entered the hacienda, the servants were busy with preparing the afternoon meal. Soon, many of the men who worked for Don Sandoval arrived. They would help with the preparations. The guests were shown to a large, shady courtyard. The hacienda had been built in a horseshoe shape around the garden. It was very magnificent, and soon, Michael was again changing his mind about courting Magdalena. There would never be any chance of him courting her. He could never support her in the custom to which she was used to. He hardly took his eyes off her as she approached her guests, and greeted them one by one. He studied every man who she addressed. He studied their faces, their body language. Surely they all must desire Magdalena, just as he did. He watched her face also, hoping that she would not catch him staring at her, but she never looked at him, not once.

Dona Sandoval took Michael by the arm.

"Come and meet my good friends, Mrs. Carson, and Mrs. Freemont. You will want to acquaint yourself with these ladies,

Michael. They are two of the best cooks in Santa Fe, and very charitable with their culinary productions. Mrs. Carson has brought fried sopes to our feast today, and Mrs. Freemont has brought peach and apple pies."

They chatted with the ladies for a while before Dona Sandoval took Michael around the grounds, and introduced him to so many people that he would never remember all of their names. Then, the dinner bell rang, and Dona Sandoval showed Michael to the front of the buffet line. There was so much food! Michael could hardly take it all in. He had been on the edge of starvation so many times in Ireland, and then during the war. Even in his times of hunger, he could never have imagined so much food. The diversified, and eclectic citizens of Santa Fe, were well represented by the dishes that they contributed to the feast. Dona Sandoval escorted Michael though the buffet line. First was the suckling pig. One of Don Sandoval's Mexican ranch hands was carving slices of juicy, tender pork, and Michael accepted a slice on his plate.

"Michael, be sure to try everything. Leave some room on your plate," said Dona Sandoval. Michael moved down the line a little. The Basque sheep herder had brought roasted lamb for those guests who were not inclined to consume pork. Another guest contributed a large platter of smoked sardines and oysters. There was a bucket of oysters "not from the sea" and Michael tried one. It had a mild flavor and tender texture. Michael put a few more on his plate. After the meat came the various breads. There were sopes and tortillas, corn fritters and buttermilk biscuits. Michael had always been intrigued by Mexican food, and wanted to try foods that he'd never had before. He took a fresh, warm, corn tortilla and moved on. Next on the table were roasted pecans, roasted pumpkin seeds, and boiled peanuts. Then the vegetables were presented. There were green chilies, roasted and stuffed with cheese, fried ochre, red cabbage shredded and soaked in red wine vinegar, corn and peas, squash fried with onions and garlic, fresh salsa, and potato pancakes. Michael was taking small portions of just about everything that he could. His plate was crowded with flavors from all over the world. He wondered how he would eat so much food, and there was still more on the table. Finally, there was plum pudding and baked apples. Another table displayed the many desserts that were donated to the feast, but Michael walked past that table. There were smaller plates on that table for the desserts, and if it were possible, Michael would try some later.

Magdalena was now watching her mother guide Michael through the buffet line. He didn't notice her watching him. She smiled at his innocent ignorance to the food on his plate. Michael sat at a long table and waited for Don and Dona Sandoval. Soon, the table was filled with revered guests, all company enjoying their meal. Magdalena approached the table and took a seat next to Michael. He was surprised by her presence; she'd seemed to be avoiding him all day.

"What's your favorite Michael?" she asked looking at the plate of food in front of him.

"I like the oysters 'not from the sea'." His answer was met with laughter. He set his fork down and looked at the faces of the guests at the table.

"Those are called mountain oysters, Michael," Magdalena explained him. "They come from sheep."

Michael needed no further explanation. In Ireland there was a similar delicacy from the same source, only prepared slightly differently. It was clear to him now what they were referring to. Magdalena leaned over and whispered into Michael's ear. "I like your new shirt, Michael. It brings out the color of your eyes."

After the feast, the men gathered at one end of the garden and the ladies at the other. The men talked politics and economics, and enjoyed cigars brought back from Virginia by one of Don Sandoval's esteemed guests. Kit Carson had recently returned home from a short business trip and enjoyed the relaxing conversation with his friends, away from a house filled with children and noise. For the most part, he was now retired. He tended his small ranch, and stayed home most of the time, which suited Josepha just fine. She was happy that the long stints, sometimes lasting two years or longer, were over.

Also among the guests were Josepha's sister, Mrs. Charles Bent, as well as John and Bessie Fremont. Michael had no idea what aristocratic company he was keeping, and it was most likely a good thing. Had he known, he may have been more reserved in his socializing. As it were, he made a wonderful impression of the guests at the party, and he was the talk of the town for the next few days. In fact, he didn't know it, and never would have dreamed it, but with the encouragement of Don Sandoval, Michael was to become a very popular citizen of Santa Fe.

Chapter VIII

Thieves in the Camp

It was past four o'clock when Michael offered his thanks and goodbyes to his hosts. The party was still in full swing, but Michael had chores that he wanted to finish before his day off was completely over. He still had not washed his one good pair of trousers, and now it would be too late for them to dry again. As he walked the two miles to his campsite, Michael was making a list in his head of things he needed to get done before the sun went down. Finally, he turned the bend in the river to where his camp came into view. Something did not seem right. He looked around the camp fire ring, but everything seemed fine there. As he approached his tent, he noticed a tear in the canvas near the bottom, below the last tie. Quickly he untied the door and entered his tent. Now he realized that the tent had been ransacked. The basket containing the last of the fried chicken was on the floor and the chicken had been devoured. So had the remains of his apple pie! That delicious pie, wasted on varmints! He studied the tracks in the dirt floor of his tent. Racoons! Now that they had discovered his tent, they would be back. Michael lost precious daylight with this unexpected interruption. He quickly tidied up his tent and took the pie pan to the river to wash it. The lean-to would have to wait until tomorrow. He would have to tie his food in an over-hanging branch, a very tall one, and hope that the coons would not be able to get to it. He knew that they were cleaver animals, and held out little hope. Michael gave up the rest of his daylight for lost, and lit a fire in his pit. He rolled his cigarette and turned away the thought of making any coffee, since the coons had gotten to that as well.

All of his food stores were gone; the flour, the sugar, the lard, everything. While Michael was out enjoying a feast, the raccoons had a feast of their own. He would have to do without until his next pay day. Tomorrow he would use most of his money for a second pair of trousers. One pair was just not enough. Now he would also have to buy a needle and thread to repair the tent, and possibly some shells for his Colt. He would have to take care of those coons, or they'd be a menace to him forever. He didn't want to think about the raccoons anymore this night. He had had such a wonderful day. Michael lay down on his cot with his arms folded behind his head, and replayed the day in his mind. He wondered about the mixed messages that Magdalena was sending him. He thought about the fine cigar he had smoked with the tobacco that came all the way from the plantations in Virginia. He wondered about the condition of the plantations in the south, and if the tobacco in his cigar had been harvested long before the Civil War, or more recently. Surely, it must have been a rare treat for the men to have these cigars at this point in time. He then thought about the brandy he was served. Who needed dessert when there was such sweet, smooth brandy to be had? Michael had tried many new things and met many new people on this day. He said a short prayer of thanks for his good friends and good fortune, and asked God to watch over his family back in Ireland. Feeling a tinge of guilt about living so well when he knew that his family was struggling back home, he could only hope that his older brother was able to send his mother more money than he himself had been able.

Michael fell asleep with much activity in his head that night.

Chapter IX
The Romance

Michael awoke early the next morning. He rolled up his blankets and tied them up with the tie that secured the window on one wall. The raccoons were not going to get a hold of his new blanket and shred that to pieces. He put all of his other possessions in a burlap sack and hung them from a hook on the ceiling of the tent. Grabbing his satchel he exited the door of his tent. He tied all but the bottom tie on the door. If the coons were going to get in, he'd make it easy so they wouldn't do any more damage. He arrived a half hour early to work. A customer followed him in the store, happy that Michael opened early so he could buy his provisions and get his day started. Michael then put the letter that he had written to his mother in the pile of out-going mail. He walked over to the dry goods and picked out a pair of trousers. This pair was a bit darker in color that his others. Finding a large curved needle and some sinew to repair the tent with, he took his provisions to the counter to pay. There would be a whole week until he was to be paid again, and even then he would only receive two dollars. The rest would go toward his boots. Michael knew exactly how much money was in his pocket, but he took it out and counted it just the same, which was his habit. There would be precious little left, and his food was all gone. He'd have to go back to snaring rabbits, and fishing, and eating the wild grapes and blackberries by the river, at least for a while.

"Too bad raccoons aren't good eating," he thought. Walking to the place behind the counter where the guns and ammunition were stored, he took ten shells out for his Colt. As he stood near the guns, he studied the shotguns in the glass case. How he longed for a shotgun and a rifle so that he could do some real hunting. If he had a rifle he could shoot a deer or an elk, and have meat all winter. He stared at the guns until his daydream was interrupted.

"Good morning, Michael! You're here early this morning!" It was Don Alfonso Sandoval. He was anxious to see Michael and recall the details of the party the day before. "You made quite an impression on our guests yesterday, Michael. What is it about you that makes people like you so easily?"

"I don't know," replied Michael. "You tell me. You didn't like me much when you first met me, sir."

"Of course I did, I was just testing you, Michael. Did you have a good time at the party last night?"

"Aye, that I did. Thank you, and Dona Sandoval for throwing such a fine feast and invitin' me. I won't be forgettin' it for a long time."

"Were you thinking about buying a rifle?"

"Yes sir, well, no sir. Not now. There are things I might be needin' more at the moment, but perhaps some day. Today I am just goin' to buy some shells for me Colt. I've something to tell ya, sir. Some raccoons got into the tent yesterday and ransacked it. They ate all my food stores, and they tore the canvas gettin' in. I feel real bad about it sir, but I'm goin' to sew it up and make it good as new, or almost good as new that is."

"So that's what the shells are for?"

"Yes sir," Michael replied as he walked over toward the inventory sheet. He wrote down his purchases in the inventory and added up the cost. Don Sandoval watched as he put his money in the register, and the goods in his satchel.

"Michael, don't worry too much about the tent. It's something I rarely use. In fact I never use it. I used it only once. My son

Guillermo used it a few times. I'm happy that you can make good use of it. Really, it is of little concern to me."

"I washed the pie tin and brought it back with me sir. The damn coons made off with a good portion. I only hope that they enjoyed it half as much as I did."

Michael went to reach for it, but Don Sandoval stopped him.

"Never mind about that now Michael. Magdalena will be over later, you can give it to her. I'm going to visit with the Carsons this morning. I need to talk to Kit about making a trip into Mexico for me to procure some coffee beans and vanilla, and some of their good cactus whiskey. When he returns, we shall share a bottle Michael. I shall see you later." Don Sandoval walked out the door, but he didn't walk toward the Carson house. Instead he walked to his own hacienda.

"He must have forgotten something," Michael thought to himself.

The mercantile was very busy that Monday. Michael never had a chance to sort out the mail when the stage brought the sack. It would have to wait until the next day. At noontime his stomach was feeling more empty than usual. It must have been from the large meal the day before. He had no breakfast, and nobody brought him biscuits this morning. That must have been only his first week at work; he would be on his own for meals from now on.

Don Sandoval went into his home and found the ladies of the house sitting down to a late breakfast. He helped himself to a corn tortilla and smothered it with fresh butter. Missy, one of his house servants, poured him some coffee and placed the cup in front of him.

"Michael has your pie tin Magdalena," he said. "He even washed it. Maria, have you given the servants all the leftover food from the party?"

"Goodness no Alfonso! There are twenty or thirty pounds of pork still. I have given the servants food, but there is still plenty for us to eat for days."

"Michael's not eaten today. The raccoons ransacked his tent yesterday and ate all of his stores. Magdalena, take him a box of groceries."

"Papa, the raccoons will just eat them. I will take him lunch in a while. There is no use in feeding the raccoons too."

"Have Diego harness up Blue to the buckboard and get that old foot locker out of the cellar. He can store his food in that. The coons will never be able to open it. Make sure that the lock and key are still with it. That will keep human varmints out as well. And I want you to go through Guillermo's clothes and pull out anything that is still in good condition. That boy is still wearing the same trousers that he was a week ago." Don Sandoval got up from the table and started walking toward the door to leave.

"Mama, I know that Michael is sweet on me, but he tries to hide it. He acts so indifferent. What is the matter with him?"

"He knows his place!" called Don Sandoval as he left the house.

"What does he mean by that, Mama?"

"Never mind Magdalena. The poor boy must be famished. It is already after two o'clock. Take him some of those mountain oysters that he favors so well, and some tortillas. Oh, and take him a big piece of Mrs. Fremont's peach pie. Make him a lunch big enough to be dinner too. I will have Diego get the trunk and the clothes ready."

Magdalena jumped up from the table and happily followed her mother's instructions. Michael still had her basket so she looked for another. She found a very large basket that she normally used when she was picking apples or peaches, and crammed it with food left over from the feast the day before. Rushing from one end of the kitchen to the other she put together a care basket ample enough for a family of six. She placed some linen napkins on the top. The regular stores like coffee, flour, sugar, and salt, would have to be replaced as well. The mercantile would supply those things. Magdalena could hardly pick up the basket. It was crammed with biscuits and preserves, pork and lamb, tortillas and corn fritters, and Michaels favorite, mountain oysters. She struggled to carry the heavy basket the short distance to the mercantile. Outside on the street a young rancher saw her and ran to her rescue.

"Good morning, Miss Magdalena. Can I help you with that basket?"

"Why yes, Mr. Sanderson. I am taking it to the mercantile; if you don't mind that is."

"It would be my pleasure, Miss Magdalena."

She entered the mercantile followed by the rancher. This was the day that Michael had long anticipated; the day that he would meet Magdalena's suitor.

"Just set it there on the counter please, Mr. Sanderson. That will do nicely. Thank you very kindly."

"Is there anything else that I can help you with, Miss Magdalena?"

"No, thank you. That will be all."

"Well, if that's all then." The rancher slowly backed away, obvious that he didn't quite want to leave.

"Thank you again, Mr. Sanderson," Magdalena repeated herself and waved. She turned toward Michael, but he was looking down, adding up the day's sales and trying to appear indifferent.

"Has the store been busy today, Michael?"

"Yes, quite," he replied without looking up.

"Have you had time to take your lunch?"

"I forgot it," he said, still looking down.

"My father told me that raccoons got it. He said that they ransacked your tent."

"Aye, they did. And it is your father's tent, not mine."

"That's horrible!"

"They even ate the tallow candle that was on the table."

"You must get rid of them!"

"I intend on doing just that."

"My father told me that you have my pie tin."

"Aye, and your basket and linens too."

Michael took the basket out from under the counter. The pie tin and the linen napkins were inside.

"What do you intend to have for lunch Michael?"

Michael's stomach was gnawing at him, and Magdalena was starting to unnerve him with her interrogation.

"I'm too busy to eat. I'll go fishin' when I get home tonight."

"Michael, I made you a basket of food from the leftovers of the party. It was my father's idea. He told me that the coons stole all your stores. He said that you should replace them from the mercantile. Just write it down in the inventory."

"I already owe your father too much. I hate bein' beholdin'."

"You are not beholding Michael. I told you before. It is a benefit of the position. I think your hunger is making you cranky."

"YOU are making me cranky!" he snapped back.

"Fine then! I will just leave the basket on the counter. Perhaps you will feel better after you eat something." Magdalena picked up the smaller basket and hastened through the door.

"Awh, why did I do that?" Michael asked himself. He lifted the linens and peeked into the basket. "Why did I do that?" he repeated.

Chapter X

The Apology

Magdalena slammed the door behind her. "That stubborn Irishman!" she ranted.

"What is this all about?" her mother asked.

"That Michael Malone, he is so ungrateful! He did not even so much as look inside the basket, or say thank you when I took the food to him this afternoon! Nothing!"

"That is not at all like him," said Dona Sandoval. "Something must be wrong. Help me with these clothes of Guillermo's. Diego has the buckboard ready. I will take it over to the mercantile and have a talk with him, see if I can get anything out of him."

Dona Sandoval noticed the time. "Oh no! The mercantile closed half an hour ago! I am afraid that I may have missed him."

"Wonderful," said Magdalena. "The raccoons eat again tomorrow! I cannot bear the thought of feeding raccoons all that wonderful food."

"I will have Diego take the buckboard out to his campsite. Here, take this box of clothes down to the cart. I will be finished up here in just a moment. I want to get Guillermo's winter coat and his slicker. I am sure that Michael can use them. Winter will be here before we know it."

Michael had worked late that day. He never did get around to eating, but was looking forward to digging into the basket that Magdalena have brought to him. He felt badly about the way he treated Magdalena. After all, she was not promised to him, so what if she was talking to another man? And after all, she was doing something nice for him. As he walked he contemplated his apology.

"There! That is the last of it," said Dona Sandoval. "There is still a fine pair of boots, hardly worn. They were always a bit too tight for Guillermo. I do not know if they will fit Michael, but we can address that later."

"I will drive out to the camp myself Mama. I know where it is, and Diego will never find it. You know how he conveniently gets lost every time you send him on an errand, and then comes home drunk."

"Very well then, but come right back. The days are getting shorter and I do not like you out after dark alone."

"Yes, Mama."

Magdalena climbed up onto the seat of the buckboard and commanded Blue to go. She wasn't quite to the edge of town when she saw Michael walking.

"I thought you would be at camp by now," she called down to him from her perch.

Michael felt uneasy. "I worked a wee bit late. The mercantile was busy today, and I still had work to do after I locked up."

"Well, you must be tired, and I know that basket is heavy. I had to enlist help just carrying it over to the mercantile today. It was much too heavy for me to manage."

Michael felt even worse now. He put the basket on the back of the buckboard along with his satchel and climbed up into the seat along side Magdalena. Taking the reins from her, they rode for a while without saying anything. Finally, Michael swallowed his pride.

"I wanted to tell ya that I'm truly sorry for the way that I acted today at the mercantile. I don't know what got into me. I think maybe I was just mad at those coons for eating the best pie I ever tasted."

Magdalena wanted to be stubborn, but instead she laughed out loud. "It is alright Michael. I forgive you. I could never be mad at you for long."

Magdalena knew that the sun would be down soon. She clicked her tongue at the horse to hurry him along, so that she could sit for a while with Michael at his camp. It was inviting there, and she felt comfortable. They went around the bend in the river, and to the clearing where Michael's camp was. At first appearance, everything looked normal. Michael jumped down from the cart and went inside. Everything was just as he had left it. He put the satchel under his cot, and the basket on the table. Magdalena was still sitting on the bench in the buckboard.

"Can you stay a while?" asked Michael.

"I was wondering if you would ask."

Michael helped Magdalena down. "Would you like to stay for dinner? I have plenty!" They both laughed.

"I'd love to Michael, but I promised to be home before dark."

Michael made a fire in the pit. Once again there was a change in his plans. At least tomorrow he'd have clean trousers to wear to work.

"I bought me self some new trousers in the mercantile today."

"Oh! I almost forgot! I have brought you a trunk to store your food and provisions in. It has a lock on it so the varmints will never be able to get in it. Papa says that it will keep the human varmints out too, so you can stop dragging that satchel everywhere you go."

"That will be fine!" said Michael. He and Magdalena looked at each other for a long pause. He wanted to grab her into his arms, and draw her near to him, but he didn't dare. That could ruin everything. What if he offended her? He would lose his friend, and most likely his job too.

"Why is your family so good to me?" he asked.

"Because we love you, Michael. In a way, I think you sort of fill a void that was left when Guillermo did not come home. You are nothing like him, but Mama and Papa think the world of you, and so do I."

Michael was satisfied with the answer. That was probably as close to "I love you" that he would ever hear from Magdalena.

"Let's sit in front of the fire Michael; it is starting to get chilly."

He sat down on his log in front of the fire, and she sat next to him. She moved in closer.

"It is getting colder in the evenings now, winter is coming. Put your arm around me, Michael. Keep me warm."

"Shall I get you my blanket to cover yourself with?"

"No Michael! I do not want your blanket! I want your arm!"

She took Michael's arm and put it around her shoulders and snuggled in close to him. She looked into his eyes, and he into hers, and then, without thinking about the consequences, Michael kissed her very gently on the lips. She didn't resist, so he kissed her again, and this time with passion.

"I love you, Michael Malone."

"I love you too, Magdalena Sandoval. I have from the first moment I saw you."

Chapter XI

The Bounty

"Oh no!" Magdalena exclaimed. "It has gotten dark without me realizing, and I promised my mother I that I would be home before dark! She will be so worried."

Michael and Magdalena hadn't noticed the sun going down. They hadn't noticed that the cicadas had stopped singing, and the bullfrogs had picked up where they had left off. Michael jumped up and struggled to get the heavy trunk off the buckboard. Magdalena ran to his aide.

"Those two crates are also for you Michael. They are Guillermo's clothes. Mama thought there might be some things that you could use."

Quickly, they took everything into the tent. Michael took a corn fritter, and locked up the rest of his food and valuables in the foot locker. He stowed his Colt in the waist of his trousers and helped Magdalena up on the seat of the buckboard. Taking the reins, he prompted the horse toward home. They had not gone very far when Don Sandoval, mounted on his horse, met up with them on the road.

"You're mother is worried sick about you Magdalena. You promised to come right home. What sort of nonsense have the two of you been up to?" His voice was stern.

"Sir," started Michael. "'Tis entirely me own fault. We were just talkin', and sittin' by the fire, and I didn't realize how fast the sun was goin' down. I promise you sir; I was going to see Magdalena all the way home. I would never let anything happen to her."

"I see. Well you better be off in haste. I don't appreciate having to saddle up and come out here to fetch my daughter home. I think maybe she should not be allowed to come to your camp in the future."

"But, Papa!"

"Just get home, Magdalena! I can see her from here, Michael."

They said their goodnights and Michael turned the reins over to Magdalena. He walked back to his camp with his head down in deep contemplation. When he walked around the bend, a movement caught his eye from in the direction of his tent. "Those damn coons are back," he thought to himself. He took his Colt from his waist and slowly approached. He would take them by surprise and be done with them once and for all. But it wasn't the coons. From the back of the tent came a very large gray wolf. He was looking at Michael, but trotting in the opposite direction. Michael took the wolf down with a single shot. The smells of the food coming from his tent must be attracting every critter in the area, he thought. But this time it was Michael's good fortune. The wolf was in healthy condition. It had a very nice thick coat, and measured neatly six feet in length. Michael quickly skinned the rogue, and then dragged his carcass a long way from the tent where he left it for the varmints. He rolled up the hide and stashed it in a tree limb. Then he put a pot of water on to boil so he could wash up. Hungry and exhausted, he still had things to do before he could get some sleep. After washing up he went inside his tent, lit a candle, and took out a piece of salt bread and some sliced pork. His hunger had finally caught up to him. After he ate, he decided to survey the contents of the boxes. On top of the first box were the wool coat and the slicker. These things pleased Michael very much. They would get much use, he was sure. There were several nice blouses and shirts, nicer than anything Michael had ever worn before. There were also four pair of trousers and several pair of long underwear and stockings. Everything looked so new and unspoiled. He'd never had so many clothes before. Michael could tell that the blouses would fit, but he'd have to try the trousers later. The buckle in the back would allow him to adjust up to a couple of inches, so he felt fairly sure that they would do. He pulled on a pair of the long underwear. With the nights getting colder, he could sleep in these and spare his street clothes undue wear. He lay back on his cot and was asleep in an instant.

The next morning, Michael woke up with the first light of day. Quickly, he washed and shaved and picked out a clean blouse and pants to wear. He combed his curls and packed some food in a linen napkin. He was not going to miss lunch again today. He put five shells in his Colt, and resigned himself to carrying it and having it handy at all times. Taking the wolf hide from the tree limb, he started off to work. Michael opened early again, and went straight away about his business. Customers started arriving to the store early, and it looked as though it was going to be another busy day. Don Sandoval came in and waited patiently for Michael to finish up with his customer.

"I'm sorry again about last night," Michael told Don Sandoval. "I promise it will never happen again."

"And what makes you think that you will have the opportunity for it to happen again? Magdalena's mother was not at all happy about the incident. I was not that happy about it myself, but I was confident that she was in good hands with you. Unfortunately, the two of you used poor judgment. Magdalena is the only child we have left. Her mother tends to be a bit over protective of her. The real question here is what are your intentions toward my daughter? She thinks that you are in love with her, and I know that she is quite smitten with you."

"Well sir, the truth of the matter is that I am in love with your daughter. I think that you should know that I would lay down me own life before I would ever let anything happen to her. I truly am very sorry for making Dona Sandoval worry last night. You are right, we... I used bad judgment. We were having a heart to heart, and well, I'm just not used to keeping track of time when I'm in me camp. There has never been a need to, but I will from now on, and that is a promise."

"I'm afraid that my wife will not permit Magdalena to go back to your camp, Michael, especially in light of these new facts."

"Sir, I would never, never dishonor Magdalena."

"Let me talk to Maria and give her some time to get used to things. Now I should let you get back to work."

"Don Sandoval, I have something I want to ask you. Do you know where I can sell this wolf hide?" Michael brought the hide out from behind the counter. Don Sandoval walked back and unfurled the hide.

"This is a very nice hide Michael. Where did you get it?"

"When I got back to me camp last night after I left you and Magdalena on the road, I caught him peeping about me tent. I dropped him with one shot, and I skinned him."

"Mr. Carson has done some trapping. He can probably tell you where to sell it. You do know that wolves have a bounty in these parts don't you? If you want cash right now, just take him to the Marshall's office. It might not be as much as you would make selling the hide, but you'd get your money right away. The Marshall will probably sell it himself and make a profit. If you want, I'll watch the store for a while and you can go see to it right now."

"Thank you sir! I'll be back directly." Michael took the wolf hide and bolted toward the door. "And tell Dona Sandoval thank you for all the fine garments she sent me. I've never had such fine things before in me life!"

As he ran in the direction of the Marshal's office, Michael thought the conversation with Don Sandoval had gone well; much better than he expected. He really had thought that the idea of courting Magdalena would be met with much resistance. Now he felt that it might not be as impossible as he first imagined. As he ran through the streets, the sight of the wolf hide drew much attention. People stopped to look and wonder where the wolf had come from. Wolves were not at all welcome in these parts. There were too many sheep and cattle ranchers, and they posed a threat to the children in town as well. There were so many orphans living on the streets. Michael ran into the Marshall's office. "Good morning, sir! Don Sandoval told me that there is a bounty on wolves. I've come to collect. I shot this wolf last night near me camp."

"This is a fine hide, Michael. He was a big one! You could probably get twelve or thirteen dollars for it, but I can pay you ten dollars right now. That is what the bounty is on wolves."

"Ten dollars! I'll take it, please."

The Marshall paid Michael with ten silver coins, and Michael quickly ran back to the mercantile to relieve Don Sandoval.

"Don Sandoval! The bounty on wolves is ten dollars! That was the easiest ten dollars that I've ever made. I'll be keeping me eyes open for wolves from now on."

Michael handed the coins over to Don Sandoval. "Now I only owe you six dollars. After payday I'll only owe you two and be done. Then I can start sending me mum some money."

Don Sandoval smiled as he left the mercantile, coins jingling in his pocket. This young man certainly was not what he'd envisioned for a son-in-law, but if it came to be, it would be alright with him. Michael was a good man. He was happy and animated, and had good morals and integrity. He loved his family, and the whole town loved him. What more could a father want for his daughter? Dona Sandoval might be a harder sell though.

~*~

"Mail!"

Michael ran outside and caught the mail sack as the stage driver threw it down to him.

"How goes it, Michael?"

"Good! I shot a wolf last night and collected a ten dollar bounty!"

"That is good news all around!" said the teamster. "Don't spend it all in one place now!"

Michael went about his chores in the mercantile. It had been especially busy the past couple of days. People were getting ready for cold weather. Kit Carson had agreed to go to Mexico to procure some provisions that would do well in the mercantile. There was talk about Michael going along with him. In one way Michael wanted to go. He thought it would make a good adventure, but in another he didn't want to leave Magdalena or his comfortable routine, not even for just one week. The morning came and went in a rush. Michael finally found time to have some lunch. He went outside on the porch and sat in the willow chair, as he always preferred to be outside when he could. Just as he had finished the last bite of his lunch, Magdalena came walking up with a brisk pace in her step.

"Michael!" she sat down in the chair beside him. "I had hell to pay last night."

"Now what sort of talk is that for a fine lady to be usin?"

They both laughed. Magdalena could say or do nothing wrong in Michael's eyes. She was perfect in every way.

"What did your mum do? I felt so bad, and after she went to all the trouble to send me all those beautiful garments."

"Do you like them?"

"Aye. I've never had anything like them before. I never had much clothes of any sort really. Please tell your mum thank you, and I appreciate it much. I'll tell her me self when I see her next.

What did she say to you when you got home last night?"

"Oh, she was crying and carrying on like I'd committed the worst mortal sin. She was very angry with me and not so happy with you either. It was a good thing that Papa took sides with me, or I would still be hearing about it. At breakfast this morning Mama hardly spoke to me. Then to make it worse, Papa came home from the mercantile and told her that we were in love. You told him so, and he told Mama. She'd have to find out sooner or later, so I guess sooner is better. It will give her time to get used to the idea. Papa told us that you shot a wolf in your camp last night! I wonder if that wolf was watching us the whole time." Magdalena shivered at the thought. "It just made Mama feel worse about me being out after dark. Papa said it was huge. He said you got a bounty on it, and you're almost finished paying off those boots you're wearing. Oh, I almost forgot, Mama found a pair of boots that Guillermo hardly wore. They're real fine boots, made from iguana skin. Guillermo only wore them once or twice. He had them made down in Mexico. They were too tight on him though. I'll bring them later today. It will be an excuse to come back and see you. Oh Michael, I can't stand to be apart from you. I think of you constantly."

Magdalena was running on and on, barely stopping to take a breath. She spoke rapidly and without giving Michael a chance to speak back. He didn't mind, though. He loved listening to her, and he loved watching eyes dance as she spoke. He was just happy to be near her. Finally, he took his chance to get a word in.

"Magdalena, your mother has already given me so many fine things, and so has your father. I feel like I'm taking advantage. I already have a pair of boots, and I'm still paying on them."

"But they're just in the closet gathering dust, Michael. Why shouldn't you have them? Besides, like I said, it gives me a chance to come back."

"Well, I must be gettin' back to me job now. I don't want to get fired. I need to start saving for a ring."

Magdalena smiled. Michael was insinuating marriage.

Chapter XII

Time Moves On

The next few weeks went by quickly, but Michael knew that the coming weeks would pass more slowly. The trees were bare, and the nights were cold. It was dark when Michael walked to the mercantile in the morning, and dark by the time he arrived home. He was saving as much money as he could, offering a little with each letter he sent to his mother back in Ireland. He still didn't know if she was receiving his letters, as he had not yet received a letter in return. Don Sandoval was overseeing the project of a small house being built behind the hacienda. Michael hadn't assumed anything, and had never even given a thought that the house was for Magdalena and himself when they were married. He did not want to ever buy anything on credit again, so he was saving to buy her a ring with cash.

Michael had fallen into a routine of spending Sundays with Magdalena's family. He would go to church with them in the morning, and take an afternoon meal with them afterward. Some Sundays Michael had to decline in order to get his wash done, and letters written, and any other chores that had been piling up. He felt comfortable in his campsite, although the nights were bitter cold. He would put on his long underwear and woolen stockings and cap, and pile the blankets on top of himself.

~*~

Several weeks passed, and one morning Michael woke up and knew that winter would soon be over. He could feel spring in the air and was happy for it. He felt an unexplained happiness as he made his way to work that morning. He crossed himself as he passed the sanctuary, as was his habit. Although the air was brisk, the sun was peeping out and casting a glint upon the river. The trees were starting to grow their leaves again, and tender shoots of succulent grass were springing up along the banks of the Santa Fe. The air smelled clean, with a hint of wood smoke from the hearths and stoves of the homes along San Francisco Street. The smell of fresh bread was wafting out from the bakery. Life was good, very good.

Michael unlocked the mercantile and went in. He went straight to work sorting the mail that had been piling up. Magdalena was going to begin working in the store taking care of the mail duties, and Michael was very happy about that. Sorting the mail took up so much of his time, and he was always behind in that chore. Now Magdalena would be keeping up with it, and he would be spending more time with her while they worked together. By the time Magdalena arrived at the mercantile, Michael was half finished sorting the mail. He kissed her hello, and looked into her black eyes. "Magdalena, I want you to have dinner with me tomorrow night at Hanna's restaurant. Will you?"

"Yes Michael, I'd love to!"

Magdalena had no idea that Michael had saved enough money to buy her a ring. Today he would pay for it, and tomorrow he would present it to her at dinner. Then they could set a date to be married, and in the meantime Michael would save all the money he could to start buying materials to build a house. He was still unaware that the house Don Sandoval was building on his property was for Magdalena and him. Magdalena did not know either. As far as she knew, it was just another of her father's projects. Michael could not wait to put the ring on Magdalena's finger. Then a new thought occurred to him. He hadn't asked Don Sandoval for Magdalena's hand yet. Everyone knew that they were sweethearts. Should it be assumed that they would marry, or should Michael go through the traditional process? His thoughts were distracted by the swinging doors. He tended to his customer while Magdalena kept busy sorting mail.

When the sanctuary bells announced the noontime hour, Michael and Magdalena assumed their usual spot on the willow chairs on the porch to have their lunch together. This was a new routine for them. They sat together eating, both in a dreamy mood. Each wondered what the other could be thinking so deeply upon.

After Magdalena finished her job at the post office she kissed Michael goodbye. It was close to four o'clock in the afternoon. As she was leaving, her father came through the swinging doors.

"Hi Papa! Bye Papa!" she kissed him on the cheek as she hurried past him on her way home.

"She's in a hurry, I guess," said Don Sandoval.

"Sir, I would like to ask your permission to marry your daughter," blurted out Michael.

Don Sandoval just stood, staring.

"Sir?"

Michael's heart sank. What if Don Sandoval would not grant him permission to marry his daughter?

"Sir?"

"Michael, I have only one question for you. What took you so long? Everybody in town has been waiting for you to ask Magdalena to marry her. Magdalena drives her mother half crazy. It's all she talks about, and has for weeks."

"I needed to save money for a ring. If you will give me permission, I am going to ask her tomorrow. I have asked her to have dinner with me at Hanna's."

"So you have already bought a ring?"

"No sir, but I have picked one out and I have the money to pay for it in me pocket. Would you like to see the ring I've chosen?"

"Of course I would."

Michael went to the shelves behind the counter that were always kept under lock and key. He pulled out the case of rings and opened the glass cover. "It's this one here" he said pointing out a gold band with a diamond solitaire.

"That's very nice, Michael. You do well with your money if you've already saved enough for that ring. What about your mother back home? I thought you were sending her money."

"I was sir, but I haven't in a month or two. I haven't heard a word from her and it's been almost a year since me first letter, so I don't know if she's getting my letters or not. I don't want to keep sending money if some thief is getting it, so I decided to save until I hear from her."

Well, Michael, tomorrow when you and Magdalena are having dinner, I shall tell her mother that the two of you are going to set a date...Finally! She will be so happy for something to do. I think she has been planning this wedding in her head for the past two months now. I have to admit that I've given a fair share of my own time thinking about it, myself."

Michael smiled. He took the ring from the case and walked over to the register and placed the money in. He wrote down the transaction in the inventory. Don Sandoval waited for Michael to lock up and they walked together as far as the hacienda.

"Why don't you come in for dinner, Michael?"

"Thank you, but no, sir. I have things to do in the camp tonight. I have to get ready for tomorrow."

"Alright then Michael, I'll come by the mercantile tomorrow. I have some things I need to talk with you about. I'll be going away for a few days to buy some mules and wagons. I have to take some provisions to Fort Craig soon. We'll talk more about it tomorrow."

Chapter XIII
The Promise

Michael and Magdalena were seated in the corner close to the hearth. They sat close to one and other and held hands under the table. After ordering their dinner, still holding Magdalena's hand, he brought it up to the table. With his free hand he produced the solitaire and placed it on her finger.

"Oh Michael, I was beginning to think that you'd never ask. It is just beautiful!" Tears began to well up in her eyes.

"I probably never would have been able to, if it weren't for your father giving me a job and all. I will be in debt to him for the rest of me life. I have him to owe for all that makes me happy today. But we must have a long engagement so that I can save money to buy us a place to live. I can't very well take you down to me campsite, now can I then?"

"Michael, I wouldn't mind! I'd be happy living anywhere with you, I really would."

"Well, a tent is no place for a fine lady to be livin'." Michael looked deep into Magdalena's eyes and knew that what he was telling her was true. She was much too fine of a lady to keep her modestly. But he knew that she was also telling him the truth. He knew that she would live anywhere with him. He thought about the times that she came to visit him at his campsite. They would sit for hours in front of the fire, or by the river. The time always passed too quickly, as they were always so content just to be in each other's company. He realized all of the things that he really loved about Magdalena. Although she was raised a lady, and with all the privileges that come with that, she was totally unspoiled by her background. She could go to tea with the finest ladies in town, or walk the streets with the downtrodden, and see nothing but the good in people. She could ride a horse, and shoot a gun, and harness a team, and still, always be a lady. And although they had servants and kitchen help, Magdalena was a very fine cook.

"Magdalena, promise me that you'll always be by me side and never ever leave me. I can not imagine life without you."

"I do, Michael. I promise. I could never be away from you, either."

Chapter XIV

The Letter

The following day, Michael was already busy at work when Magdalena showed up at the mercantile to sort the mail. She chatted almost non-stop, as she would do when she became excited.

"Michael, Mama and Papa want you to come for dinner tonight after work. They have things they want to discuss with us. Mama was so excited when I showed her the ring last night. She's taking me to Miss Ursula's today to be fitted. We are going to look at patterns for my wedding dress. We have invitations to send also, and we have address them in a hurry. We've picked a date and it's only six weeks away."

"Hold on now, Magdalena. I told you that we needed a long engagement so that I can save some money."

"And I told you that I could live anywhere with you. We can save together, Michael. I have a job now, and with both of our paychecks it should not take us too long. Anyway, Papa wants to talk to you tonight. You've been running the mercantile for over a year now, and he is very pleased with what you are doing. I think he may offer you a promotion in wages. Well, I better hurry and sort the mail. I want to leave early today. Mama and I have much to do, and we need to get started. She is so excited to plan the wedding!"

Michael was left to wonder about their future as Magdalena went about her task of sorting mail.

"Michael!" she called. "Michael!"

Michael dropped what he was doing and ran to the mail room.

"What is it? I thought something was wrong and there you stand with a smile on your face!"

"It is for you! A letter from Ireland!"

Michael took the envelope from her and stared at it for a long moment. "T'is from me mum."

"Well, are you going to open it?"

"Aye, but I've waited this long, what's another moment? I just want to take me time and make it last." Slowly, Michael opened the yellowed envelope that he had waited so long for. Now he knew that his mother had received at least one of his many letters. Carefully, he unfolded the letter.

My dearest Son,

I was meaning to write you sooner, but I was sick for more than a month. I am feeling much better these days. I have received three letters from you now. I want to thank you for the money you send. It helps so much, and the American silver dollar goes far in Ireland. I am happy to hear that you are serving with the American Army and making your home there. Your brother Matthew is doing well in the Royal Navy. He also sends money when he can. I am earning some money with my sewing and taking in laundry, now that I am stronger and have resumed my work. Your brother Liam has been working in the coal mines, and saving all his money. He will soon have fare for passage to New York. I hate to see another of my babes leave me, but what must be must be. He should be in America by summer of next year. Your sister Kathleen will be married by the time you receive this letter. She seems too young to be married. Where does the time go? She is to be married to David Mayo; I think you should remember the family. David is doing very well now and can take better care of Kathleen than I can. The house will seem so empty with just the twins and me. Your little sisters are not so little anymore. It seems they grow a wee bit taller every night. It is the hardest thing keeping them with clothes on their backs and shoes on their feet. I so wish that they'd stop growing, but I thank the Lord every day that we have food on the table and my children are healthy. The weather has been so cold and damp lately, and so many are sick in the borough. Mrs. O'Connor's youngest died last month of consumption.

It seems that time doesn't heal my heartaches at all. I miss your father more and more with each passing day, especially now that all my children are leaving the house to start their own lives. Your father would be so proud of you my son.

Thank you again for your letters. I look forward to receiving them and news from you.

I hope that this letter has found you well.

All my love,

Mother

"Michael! Your brother is coming! It will be so nice to meet him. I wish that he could be here for the wedding. This is so exciting!" Magdalena finished sorting the mail shortly after the sanctuary bells chimed their noontime announcement. She and Michael took their lunch together on the porch. The days were growing longer and warmer. The cicadas were especially vociferous this time of year, and Michael didn't care for it much. His pleasant mood had been suddenly altered with Magdalena's proclamation of an early wedding date. He had so much to do still. His mother's letter, although welcomed, weighed heavy on his mind. There was a sad undertone about it. His brother Liam would be coming to live in America. Now that Michael needed to concentrate on his new family, he would be burdened with helping his brother find work and a home as well. It would be expected of him. Michael was not ready to bring his brother into his home with his new bride. He decided to put it out of his mind and cross that bridge when he came to it. At the moment he had a wedding to prepare for, and a house to build, and land to acquire to build it on. There was much to do and much to plan for, and little time to do it in. As happy as he was, Michael was feeling the strain of the whole situation.

He finished up at the store and walked slowly over to Don Sandoval's hacienda. Why was he feeling so daunted? He should be excited, the way that Magdalena was excited. Of course, she didn't have the burden of figuring everything out. Perhaps he would go to Prescott and see what kind of work he could get there. He needed to make more money and he didn't want to be forever obligated to Don Sandoval. He and Magdalena could start a new life there, if only he could find a decent position. He walked through the wrought iron gates and knocked on the heavy wooden door. One of the servants opened it and showed Michael to the parlor where his soon-to-be family was waiting for him.

Don Sandoval poured Michael a glass of brandy and sat down in his leather chair. "Michael, Dona Sandoval and I would like to tell you how happy we are that you are marrying our daughter. We are both very pleased that you are to be our son in law. When the two of you are married, I would like to make you a partner in my business. You won't be an equal partner, but a partner just the same. I'm sure that you've been worried about how you are going to take care of a family on your income. You don't need to worry any longer. I still would like you to run the mercantile, but I want you to start going with me on buying trips and learning that end of the business. I also want you to learn how to negotiate contracts. I will be teaching you all the ropes, so that when I'm no longer here, you and my daughter will be set for life. I always planned on Guillermo being a partner in the business, but you and Magdalena are my only children now, and it will all be left to you. How do you feel about this Michael?"

Michael was in no way prepared for such a proposal. Coming to America was the best decision he'd ever made. Everything just seemed to fall into his lap. Back in Ireland he never would have been able to marry out of his station, and here he was being elevated into high society with the marriage of his one true love.

"Sir, I don't know what to say. You've treated me so well. I...I...I... intend on doing me very best to be a good husband to your daughter, and a good business partner to you."

Michael was having a hard time containing his emotions. He quickly wiped a tear away from his face with the sleeve of his shirt.

"You've already proved yourself a good business partner, Michael. Your word as a gentleman is as good as any written contract. You showed me what you were made of when we first met and we made a deal on a pair of boots. Now, there is more. I have an early wedding present for you and Magdalena. I hope you are in for a good stroll before we eat, because I have it stored on the far end of my second acre. Mama, are you coming with?"

"Of course, I wouldn't miss this for anything," she replied.

The four walked together along a newly constructed path of gravel, lined with river rocks on each side. Don and Dona Sandoval took the lead walking arm and arm. Michael and Magdalena walked hand and hand behind them. They walked past the long house that was home to their servants. They walked past the massive barn which sheltered the livestock when they were rounded up for work. They passed a small garden with a fountain and wooden benches set up in a circle around it. In between the benches were shrubs of flowering plants and cacti. Behind the benches were Peppertrees and Palo Verdes for shade. They followed the path around a corner and there sat Don Sandoval's latest project. The reason for his clandestine absents in the past few months. It was a small addition to his grand Hacienda. A little guest house, perhaps.

"Here is your new home," announced Don Sandoval with great satisfaction. "Here is where you and Magdalena will live. This is your house, and you can move in any time you like, Michael. It is ready for you now."

Michael stood gazing in disbelief. This was just too good to be true. He was afraid that he would awake and find that it was all a dream.

"Let's go in," said Don Sandoval. He opened the heavy wooden door and the four of them entered directly into a large room. There was terracotta Mexican tile on the floor and beautiful woven Navajo rugs placed strategically on top of the tiles. On one wall was a fireplace with a magnificent hearth of river rock. There were chairs and sofas upholstered with cow hide, with the hair still on. Oil paintings of New Mexico sunsets hung on the walls. An arched opening on one side of the room lead into another section of the small hacienda. There, was the kitchen and dining room area. The kitchen was well equipped with copper pots and pans, a wood burning stove, and a work area in the center of the room with a butcher block counter. An opening on the other side of the great room lead to the bedroom. The bedroom had a grand four poster bed with buffalo skin blanket spread over it. There was a vanity against one wall with a large mirror and three small drawers. A chifforobe for their clothes stood in the corner. In this room there was yet another fireplace with a river rock hearth. In front of it sat a porcelain tub with brass feet. Although all of the rooms in the small hacienda were inviting and comfortable, the great room was the bulk of the house area. Michael went back to survey it closer. On one wall was a gun rack. Michael walked over to it to take a closer look. Most of the racks were barren, but on the top two racks were a rifle and a shotgun. Michael looked at the guns, and looked at Don Sandoval, and back at the guns. On the top rack was a

Rigby rifle. Michael had never seen one like this before. It was the newest rifle on the market, and there it was, never been fired. He took the gun down from its perch on the rack and balanced it on the flat palm of his hand. He then drew it to his shoulder and looked through the aperture sights, and then brought the gun down to hip level. Again he looked at Don Sandoval in total disbelief. Retuning the gun to its place on the rack, he began to examine the gun on the second rack. He picked up the Westley Charles pin fire, and examined the engraving and the beautiful natural pattern of the ebony wood.

Don Sandoval watched smiling, as he was very pleased with himself. "I figured if I was going to recommend you for acceptance to my gun club, that you should at least have a couple of nice guns. And anyway, I'm going to be sending you out with some supply wagons soon. You'll need a fire arm besides that Colt of yours."

This news did not settle well with Magdalena.

"Papa! You must not send Michael out with a supply train! You sent Guillermo out and he never came home. We do not even know where he is buried so we can go visit him!"

"That will be enough, Magdalena," said Dona Sandoval. "Do not spoil the evening. We have a nice dinner waiting for us in the hacienda, and it is getting late. Let us go have dinner, shall we?"

Chapter XV
The Wedding

With the preparations for the wedding in full swing, the next few weeks passed by quickly. Magdalena worked at the mercantile as often as her hectic schedule would allow, but left Michael with much of the work to do himself as she and her mother secured all of the wedding preparations. Michael was still living in his camp by the river. The weather was warm, and he'd grown comfortable in his own space. As he went through his normal routine at the store, his mind was consumed with fleeting thoughts about his wedding and his future. Everyone had big plans for him. What if he could not live up to Don Sandoval's expectations? Was he really ready for married life? He did not really know what was required to be a husband. He would have to learn as he went along.

The wedding was to be on Saturday evening at five o'clock. A reception would follow at the Sandoval's hacienda. Friday, Michael would close the store at noon and move into the casita behind Don Sandoval's hacienda. Saturday the store would be closed all day. Michael posted a sign in front of the store so give the town advanced notice. That particular day he would need to treat himself to bath and shave, and get a haircut so as to look his best for the wedding. He took a folded piece of newsprint from his pocket and carefully unfolded it. It was a wedding announcement that he'd been meaning to send to his mother in Ireland. The announcement included a photo of himself and Magdalena.

"Well, there's no time like the present," he said to himself as he went for the stationary to pen a quick note to his mother.

At that moment, Magdalena hurried through the front doors.

"Michael, this heat is so oppressive," she announced as she fanned herself. "I hope that it will not be like this for the wedding. How will our guests sit through the wedding and a full mass in this heat? I am sorry that I have left so much of my work in the mailroom to you these past couple of weeks. I intend to be all caught up by the end of the day. You will have me for the whole day today, and when I am finished with the mail, I will help you with the mercantile. What is it Michael? You seem so far away."

"It's just, well, the day is almost here. I was jest wonderin' what me life is goin' t' be like. I hope that you don't get tired of havin' me around all of the time."

"Michael, I promised you that we would be together forever, and I meant it. I cannot wait to have you around all the time! Oh Michael, if you are not happy and excited about this wedding it would break my heart."

Michael looked at Magdalena with his piercing green eyes and gave her a sheepish smile.

"Of course I'm happy Maggie, I've never been happier in me life."

"What did you just call me? Michael! You called me Maggie. Nobody has ever called me that before."

"Well, it jest seems fittin'," he said. "Magdalena is too formal for me to be callin' you that anymore. I need a pet name for you, and Maggie is a good Irish name."

"Yes, well, I am not Irish, but if it suits you then it suits me as well."

"You might not be Irish but you're goin' t' have lots of Irish children."

"Half Irish, Michael."

They both laughed at the thought, then went about their tasks. Michael penned a quick note to his mother and included the wedding announcement He wished that he had the time to write more, but it was all the time that he could afford to spare at the moment. Magdalena sorted the mail. They both kept busy the whole day to get accomplish everything that they needed to, since the store would be closed for two and a half days. The towns people knew that if they needed something desperately, they could go to Don Sandoval and ask him for it.

"Michael, you have another letter from Ireland. This one is post marked six months ago. It must have been mailed right after the first one."

Michael took the letter from Magdalena. The instant his fingers touched the envelope, he was struck by a daunting feeling.

"Michael, what's the matter with you? You have been acting oddly all day."

"Oh, 'tis nothin'. I suppose that I'm just tired."

"Well, are you going to open that letter?"

"Aye." He opened the envelope and slowly removed the letter. It was from his mother.

Dear Michael,

It is with great sorrow that I write to inform you of another tragedy in the family. The twins took sick with the cholera right after Christmas, and our dear Christina was not strong enough to endure it. We lost her on the first day of January. It took most of my money to give her a modest funeral. Most of the town was there, even though it was a cold and rainy day. The good lord spared Caitlin, but she's not been the same since the passing of her sister.

Your brother Liam is filled with anger toward Ireland, and toward England also, for creating the problems here. He was much encouraged by your letter and took passage to America on the Village Belle. He has almost no money with him, and I pray that he makes it safely, and in good health. I've heard that one in five passengers will die before they reach the shores near Philadelphia. I hope that he finds the means to New Mexico when he arrives, and that he can find you without delay. I know then that he'll be fine.

Hoping with all my heart that this letter finds you well,

Your loving mother.

"Michael, what is it? What is the matter?"

"Oh, 'tis nothin'. Me brother has left Ireland for Philadelphia. He left the first of January ."

"That was almost eight months ago. He must be in Philadelphia by now. How exciting Michael! I wish he were here in Santa Fe. I wish that he could come to the wedding."

Michael didn't mention the death of his sister. He did not want the news to over-shadow Magdalena's big day. He would save that news for later.

They finished up their work and closed the mercantile for the day. Michael walked slowly to camp that night. There was so much on his mind. He wanted to be happy, but he didn't know just what he felt. He supposed that it was a mixture of emotions all battling for precedence inside of him. One moment he was elated by the impending wedding. Another moment he was as frightened as a lost child. And then there was the news of his sister Christina. He remembered her as she was the day he left Ireland. She and Caitlin were waving to him from the shore as he boarded the ship to America. He wondered if he'd ever see his mother and sister and brothers again. He was holding out hope of seeing Liam one day soon, although he really didn't want the responsibility of taking care of his brother. He was going to have enough to do in the coming months.

When Michael arrived at his camp, he took a long, and thoughtful moment to look around. This had been his home for over a year, and tomorrow he would be packing it all up and moving to the casita. Michael loved living outdoors. He had everything he needed, and life was simple. But now it was time to move forward. Things were going to be even better, but he couldn't hold back the melancholy feeling that had taken over. He lit the fire and rolled a cigarette, and took out a bottle of the Mexican spirits that Kit Carson had brought back from his buying trip. There, he sat in front of his fire with his bottle, watching the sun go down and the stars come out. It was a warm summer night. He was finally enjoying some relief from the hot temperatures of the day, as he took in all the comforts of his home for the very last time. He remembered sitting on that log with Magdalena the very first time he kissed her. As he listened to the bullfrogs singing their familiar songs, a smile came across his face. In two days he would be the husband of the prettiest girl in New Mexico. Michael remained up late that night, and morning arrived much too early. He jumped up and stoked the still burning coals and threw on some small branches to boil water and make coffee. He cleaned himself up and dressed, and hastened to open the store much earlier that day since he'd be closing at noon. The heat of the day was already stifling. A mosquito landed on his arm and he swatted it. "This is one thing I'm not going to miss about me camp," he told himself.

Magdalena showed up at the mercantile with Blue and Rhoney harnessed to a stock wagon.

"Why didn't ya bring th' buckboard?" Michael asked her.

"This way we can get everything in one trip. I am going with you to your camp after we close the store and help you load everything up."

Again Michael felt that oppressed feeling of leaving his camp behind. "That's goin' t' be too much weight for Blue and Rhoney to pull," he said.

"Nonsense, Blue is plenty strong, and so is Rhoney. Now let us get the work done so we can get to your camp and move you."

At noon, they locked up the mercantile, and drove the wagon out to the camp. Michael's camp, his home, was dismantled and packed on the wagon by three o'clock. They drove back to the hacienda and unloaded the wagon, stowing the tent and provisions in the big barn. Don Sandoval came out to greet them just as they were finishing up.

"Keep those supplies handy, Michael. You may need them when I send you with the supply train. Kit Carson won't be going on too many more trips, but I am hoping that he will go on the first one with you. He can teach you a lot, but right now he just wants to stay home with Josepha and grow vegetables, and raise chickens, and children.

Magdalena gave her father a scolding look. "Must we talk about supply trains the day before my wedding, Papa?"

"No, we mustn't," he replied. "Supper will be at six sharp."

Magdalena went to the hacienda, and Michael to the casita to rest and clean up before supper.

The next morning, Michael woke up and walked to the hacienda.

"You are just in time for breakfast, how did you sleep?" asked Dona Sandoval.

"Very well, thank you ma'am. The casita is very comfortable, and there are no mosquitoes there."

"Very good! I am very glad that you are comfortable. After breakfast a barber will be coming to the house to groom you for the wedding, Michael. Are you ready?"

"Yes ma'am."

Dona Sandoval laughed. She could hear the reluctance in Michael's voice and knew that it was normal.

"You will find your clothes in the chifforobe. The tailor just brought them by yesterday afternoon. I was really beginning to panic. I can not stand last minute arrangements, but you should try them on after you bath in case there are still any alterations to be made. He assured me that he would make himself available in just such a case."

"Yes ma'am."

"You will not be seeing Magdalena today Michael. You will not see her until the wedding. Don Sandoval and I will be here for you all day today if you should need anything. You will go to the sanctuary with him this afternoon at four o'clock. Magdalena and I will follow and she will ready herself for the wedding there. Be sure that you take time to rest today. You will want to be fresh for the wedding. There will be much standing, and a full mass."

"Yes ma'am."

"Alright then, eat your breakfast. I will have Juana bring you some refreshments to the casita around two o'clock. We do not want you fainting at the alter now. Make sure that you eat!"

"Yes ma'am."

Dona Sandoval left the room chuckling to herself. "Poor boy," she thought. "He is just as Don Sandoval was when we were married twenty two years ago."

Michael finished his breakfast and went back to the casita. He tried on his wedding attire, and everything was perfect. "Perfect," he thought. "Just like everything. Everything is too perfect." Michael quickly put away his clothes, as the heat of the day was already upon him, and he was beginning to sweat and did not want to spoil them. The Mexican tile and adobe walls did their best to hold in the coolness of the night, but the windows were all closed, and it was making Michael feel boxed in. He paced around the casita for a time, and then walked outside to where the benches were placed around the fountain underneath the Peppertrees. Taking a place on a bench, he looked around and let his mind wonder. Don Sandoval approached and sat next to him.

"Don't worry, Michael. We all feel this way before the wedding. But you will soon see that life is so much better and more complete when you have someone to share it with. It gives life more purpose."

"So, you were nervous the day you got married?" inquired Michael.

"Yes, both times!" Don Sandoval laughed.

"Both times?"

"I was married once before I married Magdalena's mother. I was very young. The marriage didn't last a year; she died of cholera and took our unborn child with her."

"Oh, I'm so sorry. I wonder sometimes why God lets that happen. It seems to happen a lot." Again Michael's thoughts turned to his sister.

"Well Michael, there are no answers for tragedies. Perhaps God gives them to us so we might appreciate life. But, don't worry; I assure you that you will be happy. You are marrying the best woman in the county; the best available woman I suppose I should say. I don't think anyone can hold a candle to my Maria, but Magdalena comes from good stock. I can assure you that."

"Aye," replied Michael. He looked up at the sky and saw the reason for the dampness of his body. The monsoons were building thunder heads in the mountains and soon it would be raining.

"I hope that we'll not be walking through mud puddles to the sanctuary this afternoon."

"Well, that's not a big concern, Michael. Why don't you and I walk down to the gun club and have a cigar and a brandy. We can be back before the barber comes to clean us up, and nobody will ever miss us."

The two rose to their feet and walked the five blocks to the gun club. There they passed some time together with friends, taking

Michael's mind off of the wedding momentarily.

"We better get going, Michael. The barber will be at the house, and Dona Sandoval will be looking for us. Let's not give her provocation to start and argument with me. I always lose."

They exited the gun club into the pouring rain and ran down the street, splashing through puddles of mud and muck. The summer storms could come out of nowhere in a great fury, and leave just as suddenly as they appeared. Afterward, the sun would shine down on the newly washed earth, leaving everything fresh and restored. The rainbows would come, birds would warble and frolic in the puddles, and spider webs would glisten in the dampness. Horses standing in front of their carts and wagons held their heads down, unconcerned at the welcomed refreshment. Clouds would break up and open their portals for the rays to shine through, and everything seemed renewed.

Michael went straight to the casita, being warned of Dona Sandoval's scorn. He left Don Sandoval to face the wrath on his own. After all, it was his idea to go to the gun club in the first place, even if it were for Michael's benefit. The barber was waiting to take care of the men in the hacienda. After their shaves and cuts, they cleaned up and dressed, and headed out to the church. Already, the towns people were gathering in the church gardens. Some entered the sanctuary early to offer a small prayer in advance. Three hours later, the ceremony was finished. The bells were ringing a joyous refrain, as if they were trying to outdo one another. Then, the large crowd streamed in procession to the hacienda of Don Sandoval for a great feast and reception. There was much festivity as the guests ate, drank and danced to their heart's content. The first dance was for Magdalena and her father. Afterward, Michael took Magdalena across the courtyard tiles in a close embrace. He didn't know that would be his one and only dance with his bride that night. One by one, all of the male guests at the reception approached Magdalena and offered her gold and silver coins to dance with them. Dona Sandoval stood close by to make sure that nobody was out of hand, and to guard the silk reticule as it became engorged with coins.

"Do not worry, Michael. It is a custom of the Mexican people in these parts. It is a good custom, and after tonight, Magdalena will be all of your own."

As they were speaking, Mrs. Carson approached.

"Do you think that I could steal Michael away from you for the price of a dollar Maria? I would very much like a dance with him."

Dona Sandoval smiled. This was very unusual for a woman to offer coins for a dance with the groom, but soon it caught on, and Michael was just as busy dancing with the lady guests at the wedding as Magdalena was with the gentlemen. Soon, his pockets also were bulging with coins.

When midnight came around, the guests were still in full celebration, but Magdalena and Michael were ready to retire to the casita. It had been a very long and exhausting day for both of them. They said their goodnights to the guests and thanked them all for coming before they departed hand and hand to their casita. The guests all whistled and yelped and made much commotion until the newlyweds disappeared around the bend in the path leading to their new home together.

Chapter XVI

After the Wedding

When Michael and Magdalena entered their casita, there were fresh cut flowers adorning every room. The flowers had been brought from the sanctuary and placed in their dwelling after the wedding. In the kitchen on the butcher block table, there was a small feast spread out for the two of them. There were smoked sardines and oysters, grapes from the local vintners, roasted pecans from the local orchards, freshly baked breads and goat cheese from the Basque family who had brought the 'oysters not from the ocean' to Michael's introduction party. In the center of the butcher block was a bottle of champagne and two silver goblets; one identified as "bride" and the other as "groom".

"Oh Michael, I am so happy!" declared Magdalena. "I do not want tonight to ever end."

"But it must Maggie, if we are to have a long and happy life together. But for now, let's just not think upon it. Let's enjoy the moment, Maggie."

Michael looked into Magdalena's deep black eyes.

"I love your black Spanish eyes Maggie."

"Michael, I have something to tell you that I have never told you before. I have never told anyone. I have been sworn to secrecy, but I need to tell you now. You are my husband, but you must promise me never, never, to repeat what I tell you now."

"Maggie, you can trust me with your confidence; I promise."

"I am not Spanish Michael, not completely. My mother is not Spanish, as everyone believes her to be. Her father was Mexican and her mother was Mescalero Apache. I am sorry that I did not tell you before Michael; please do not hold it against me."

"I don't understand, Maggie. Why are you sorry? Why is it a secret?"

"It would compromise my father's position in this community and his relationship with the government. He could lose his contract if we were to be found out. I have never told another person. My parents made me promise when they finally told me. I have been sworn not to tell a soul."

"Maggie, I will not forsake you, but I still don't understand. Kit Carson's wife is Mexican, and before her he had two Indian wives, and nobody seems to care."

"It is different Michael, and people do talk. They talk behind his back. It is just best if we leave it alone."

"I will leave it alone Maggie, for you. But when we have children it might be different. I was taught to be proud of who I am and where I come from. Me mum always taught me to stand up and be proud. The Irish are persecuted in th' old country by the English, but 'tis nothin' like it is here in the new world. People hate us here even more than back home. But me, I'll always be proud t' be Irish. And when you and I have a brood of our own, I want them t' be proud to be Irish, and Spanish, and Mexican, and Mescalero."

"Michael, I love you for that, but it is not that easy. My father worked hard to get where he is today, and I will not ruin it for him. My mother used to speak to me when I was little in her native Apache tongue, but my father made her stop when I was about seven. He was afraid that I would repeat the native language in public and my mother would be discovered. Michael, my father accepted you, because you are honorable. My mother accepted you, because she holds no prejudice against anyone.

I was raised to be that way; but unfortunately society does not feel the same."

"Then, I suppose we should stop the talking, and take the secrets for gibberish. We'll worry about it when the time comes t' worry about it. Tonight is our weddin' night Mrs. Malone. Mrs. Maggie Malone, I love you."

"I love you too, Michael."

Magdalena and Michael spent the whole next day in their casita without ever emerging to greet the family. Nobody bothered them. When the church bells rang for the Sunday service, the happy couple closed their eyes and smiled as they held each other tightly in their grand four posted bed.

Chapter XVII
The Trail Ride

The holidays arrived quickly, and the women of the hacienda busied themselves with preparations. They canned and jarred and secretly knitted stockings and scarves for their men folk in their spare time. Magdalena still worked side by side with Michael at the mercantile every day. She assumed more authority over the store, as were her father's orders. Don Sandoval had other plans for Michael. Thanksgiving Day was approaching and Magdalena was helping her mother put up cranberries when she suddenly became overwhelmed by the smells generated from the stove in the kitchen. She sat down quickly, holding her hand to her mouth.

"Magdalena, what is it?" her mother asked. "You are as white as a ghost. I hope you're not coming down with the influenza. There is so much of it going around at the moment. I am going to speak to your father about you working in the mercantile. I do not like you around so many people. You never know what they are going to give you."

Dona Sandoval put down what she was doing and called Missy to finish up for her. She removed her apron and took Magdalena by the hand. "Come now. We are going to see Dr Finny."

It was Sunday afternoon, but the doctor worked from his house and readily accepted patients at any time of day or night. He normally did not like to work on Sundays, but would make exceptions. The ladies were warmly greeted when they walked through the door.

~*~

Michael and Don Sandoval had been out fishing. When they returned to the hacienda, the women were sitting in the parlor, Magdalena with a shawl over her lap drinking tea. Immediately the men sensed something unusual. Magdalena looked at the stringer of fish that Michael was carrying.

"I hope you do not expect me to cook those smelly things! I do not even want the smell of them in the casita. If you are planning on eating them, you cook them yourself. And do it outside!"

"What's the matter with you Maggie? You love fresh trout. I'll just go put them in the smoke house." He took Don Sandoval's stringer from him. "How about your fish, shall I smoke them too?"

"That sounds like a good idea," Don Sandoval answered.

Michael left the hacienda through the kitchen. The servants stared at him as he walked passed, and Michael stared back. "What is going on here?" he thought to himself. After putting the fish in the smoker, he went into his casita to wash up. Afterward, he lay down on the bed to take a siesta before dinner.

"What was that all about?" demanded Don Sandoval to his daughter.

"Watch your tone husband. Your daughter is not feeling well."

"That seems apparent, but does she have to take it out on her husband? Are you mad that Michael went fishing with me? Because if you are, then you best get over it quickly."

"I am not mad father. In fact, I just could not be happier!" she said with an air of sarcasm. "In fact, I am going to go tell him now!"

Magdalena discovered Michael asleep in the casita. "Well, this is just fine. I am home canning and jarring and getting everything ready for Thanksgiving dinner, and you go fishing with my father. I suppose that it wore you out so that now you have to take a nap!"

Michael starred sleepily at Magdalena in disbelief. "Well, what 'tis it that you'd like me to do? I'd be happy to help, but I don't know a thing about cannin' or jarrin'."

"Maybe you could just be here when I need you Michael. I had to go see Dr Finny today."

Michael sat up quickly. "Why? What's the matter with ya, Maggie?"

"There is nothing the matter with me, Michael. I am going to have a baby, that is all."

"A baby?" Michael beamed.

"Yes, a baby." They embraced each other for a long moment in silence.

"Michael, do you not have anything to say? Why are you so quiet?"

"I'm scared Maggie. I'm happy, but I'm scared. What if something goes wrong?"

"I know that mama is scared too, but she did not say so. She lost all of her babies but me. I am the only survivor. I think she is afraid that I might die in child birth, or that the baby will die and we will be adding a head- stone to the family plot."

"Me own mother lost a lot of babies too. I never told you Maggie, but the last letter I received from my mother was news of me sister Christina. She died of the cholera."

"Oh, Michael, I am so sorry. You know I still pray every day for Guillermo to come home. I know how hard and how sad it is to lose a sibling."

"You know, I'm lucky me self to be alive. I was born during the great famine; so many died of starvation. Me mother converted to Protestant in order to save her babies. She was an outcast in the burrow for a long time because of it. You see, the Catholic Church was more interested in making money. They were selling their crops and produce to England, shipping it off to the mainland. There was plenty of food in Ireland, just none for the poor, or the Irish. The Protestants would feed the hungry. Every day they opened a soup kitchen, and if you were Catholic, all you needed to do was convert and they'd feed ya. Me family practically lived on boiled onions, cabbage, carrots, and beef suet for three or four years. They'd put it all in a big pot, and boil it, and that's what they called soup. Some days they'd put some barley in it, and that was a special treat. Of course, I don't remember much of it, only the stories me mum tells. It's like she has to tell them over and over; like she never wants to forget. She wants us to be grateful for our lives and whatever we have. When we got older, she went back to the Catholic Church and begged for forgiveness. I don't know why, but they took her back."

"Michael, I am a little afraid also, but I am strong. Our baby will be strong. You shall see. With all the good blood between us, how could our baby be anything else? We are survivors, Michael, and our baby will be too. So let us be happy about this, shall we?"

"Yes, we shall. Tomorrow I will write to me mum and tell her. I wish she were here, Maggie. I wish she could see me now, and meet you. She would love you, and you would love her. Some day, I will save enough money to send for her and Caitlin."

"That will be nice, and I look forward to meeting them. Now let us go over to the hacienda and have dinner Michael. I am perfectly famished! I only hope that I can keep it down. I have felt queasy all day."

Michael took Magdalena in his arms and held her for a long moment. He thought of his mother in Ireland and all that she had to endure, raising and losing children. He thought of his sister Christina. She was always so warm and happy, and pleasant to be around. He thought of his sister Caitlin and wondered how she would ever get along and be happy without her twin. She always seemed to be the weaker of the two. How she must be suffering now. A tinge of guilt came over Michael for having such a good life in America.

The couple strolled hand and hand along the path leading to the hacienda. It was their custom to have Sunday dinner with Don and Dona Sandoval. Tonight they sat down to a dinner of chicken and dumplings, and roasted green chilies stuffed with warm goat cheese. As usual, warm corn tortillas freshly made by their Mexican servants were also served. A prayer was offered by Don Sandoval sitting in his place at the head of the table. The four ate in silence for some time before Don Sandoval finally spoke up.

"So, we are expecting a baby! It's time that you expanded your interest in the business, Michael. My ranch foreman, Cotton and his top wrangler, Charlie are getting some cowboys together to go to Chama to buy some livestock. I want to put you in charge. You will learn how to drive livestock, but most importantly, you will be in charge of the purchase. I need some good strong oxen and mules for the wagons. There are several forts that need supplies, and I don't have enough livestock to pull all the wagons. I also want you to buy some beeves. I'll give you more details later. And you'll need to buy some good saddle horses. While you're at it, pick yourself a good sturdy and sound horse. Don't waste money on something that's ready for the glue pot in order to spare a few dollars. That would only be a waste. Spend what you need, but buy something good. A good working quarter horse that can stand a long trail. You'll be needing it in the future."

Magdalena gave her father a scornful look of disapproval, but she knew not to argue with him, especially at the dinner table.

"Will Mr. Carson be going along Papa?" Magdalena knew that Michael would be much safer in the capable hands of Kit Carson. He was the best trail guild alive, and he was familiar with the Indians of the country.

"No, Mr. Carson won't be going this time. Ever since that horse reared over with him he's had a pain in his chest where the saddle horn went into it. He's going to Chimayo to try to find a miracle at the santuario, since there's nothing the doctor here can seem to do for him."

"Who will watch the mercantile, papa?"

"You will, of course. You've been working with Michael long enough to know all the ins and outs of it by now."

"No!" interrupted Dona Sandoval. "She will not! She is expecting a child. She needs to be out of the public and save all her strength. There is so much sickness in this town, and I do not want her around it."

"Very well then, I'll do it myself until I find a capable person to take over. I swear, it's so much easier to find a cowboy in these parts than it is to find a storekeeper."

"I will thank you not to swear at the dinner table," said Dona Sandoval.

"When will I be leaving?" asked Michael.

"At the first sign of springtime," said Don Sandoval. "Perhaps in three, four months. You should reach Chama in seven or eight days. It's a little over one hundred miles, but an easy trail, and there are plenty of water sources. The way back will take much longer. I don't want to lose any livestock, and I don't want the livestock to lose a lot of weight and be all straggly when they arrive. I will give them little rest before they will be put to work, so they need to arrive in good shape. I'd plan on being away almost two months if I were you Michael."

"Aye sir, but".... Michael hesitated. "I know nothing of purchasing livestock."

"Don't worry Michael. I will coach you, and you have Cotton's expertise to call on as well. Everything will be fine. I am well known in these parts, and nobody would dare to cheat me.

They'd lose all my business in the future. Well now, Mama, what's for dessert?"

Chapter XVIII

Liam

The holidays came, and went, and the following months passed quickly. As springtime approached, Michael would open the mercantile an hour early each morning, and after his noon meal Don Sandoval took over, or the store would be closed in order that Michael spend as much time with Cotton as possible before they were to leave for Chama. It was important for Michael to learn as much as he could from Cotton, and it was important for Cotton to realize that Michael was ultimately in charge on this trip, even though he himself was the trail boss. They needed to have an understanding, and a close bond. Michael had no problem with this. He and Cotton took an instant liking to one another. They had much in common, even though they were both very different. They spoke together about their time served in the war, something neither man ever talked about with other people. They spoke of the hardships growing up, and family members lost prematurely to war and illness. Cotton was born and raised in Virginia. He saw his life turn from one of privilege, into one of desperation and hunger. Michael enjoyed hearing his stories of growing up on a tobacco plantation. Cotton had grown up around horses of fine thoroughbred quality, but he took to working horses as though he'd been around them his whole life. He wasn't much older than Michael, but he was taller and more muscular. He had lines in his face from hours in the sun, and his hands were like leather. He acquired his name from his blond hair, which was bleached from the sun, and quite a contrast with his sun darkened skin. Nobody knew what his real first name was, or even his last name, he was just Cotton. There had been a time when Cotton had designs for Magdalena himself, but those ambitions faded quickly. He somewhat envied Michael, but held no grudge against him. What he envied wasn't that Michael had won over Magdalena, or was living in good position in the community, it was more that he had someone to love, and someone to love him back. Cotton wanted that more than anything, and worked hard to save his money so that some day he could court a proper woman in the accustomed way.

Cotton always welcomed a cattle drive. There would be a good bonus for him in the end if the animals were delivered in good condition. No financial agreement about the trip had been discussed between Michael and Don Sandoval, but Michael was more than excited to have a horse of his own. That would have been plenty payment for him; however, he had no idea how hard those few weeks would be. He'd be sleeping on the trail in all kinds of weather, living on salt pork and beans, and not bathing for days, maybe weeks on end. The worst part would be being apart from Magdalena for so long. Don Sandoval was a fair man, and knew the value of a loyal and trusted employee, and both Michael and Cotton were more than willing to do a hard day's labor for him.

When the day finally arrived for them to leave, Michael's apprehensions about the trail ride were somewhat put to rest with Cotton's confidence and friendship. It was just as Don Sandoval had planned, and Michael was more than happy to have a friend that he could hunt and fish and share a story with at the end of the day. He kissed Magdalena goodbye, and she stood and waved to him with tears in her eyes until he became a speck in the distance. Even then, she stared into the horizon hoping that something might drive him back. Her mother came to her side and took her hand.

"Come in and rest now, my daughter."

"No mama. First I want to go to the church and light a candle, and pray that my husband returns home safely to me. What will I do without him all this time?"

"The time will pass quickly, my daughter, and you will take care of yourself and your unborn child. That is what you will do. Come along, I will go with you and also light a candle for my son-in-law."

~*~

Every day, Magdalena arose and crossed a day off the calendar. Michael had been gone a month. She was seven months with child now, and the baby inside her was growing. She had stopped wearing her corsets, and was showing under all of her petticoats that almost drove her crazy. By the time her husband would return, she figured that she would be eight months along, or more. It made her nervous to think that he might not be there for her when their child was born. She paced around the casita, worked in the garden, and busied herself in the kitchen of the hacienda. Her nervous energy was almost more than she could take. One day, she decided to make some pies. She could not find the pie tins, and was banging and slamming things around the kitchen in an unorganized frenzy. Finally, her mother came into the kitchen to see what all the commotion was about.

"What is all this about, Magdalena?"

"I cannot find the pie tins. I need something to do! How did you ever stand all these petticoats around your waist, mama? I cannot stand all of these clothes!"

"Why do you not walk over to the store and see if you can help your father, just this one time? He still has not found permanent help, so maybe you can help him out a bit, but do not get too close to anyone. Let your father handle the public."

"That is a great idea mama. I need something to keep my mind busy."

Magdalena strolled over to the mercantile and found her father unpacking and stocking bolts of yard goods.

"Just look at me, Magdalena! A store keeper! Why can't I find decent help in this town?"

Magdalena began to admire the new fabrics, when a man walked through the swinging doors. They both looked up. Neither said a word. Magdalena's mouth dropped open. A man looking almost exactly like Michael did the first day she saw him had just walked through the doors. At first glance she thought it was her husband, but upon further inspection realized that it wasn't.

The man finally broke the silence. "I was wonderin' if ya might be helping me out a bit. Ya' see, I'm lookin' for me brother."

The Irish accent, the voice, all just like Michael's, was too much for Magdalena to comprehend, and she fainted dead away. Quickly, her father and the stranger picked her up off the floor, and placed her in a chair. She could hear her father's voice calling to her. Slowly, she opened her eyes. Staring at her was her father and the dark haired stranger. She studied his face for a moment. His green eyes studied her back.

"Magdalena, you shouldn't have come here. Are you feeling well enough to take yourself home? You need to lie down and rest." Magdalena's father was speaking to her, but she didn't hear a word. She and the stranger continued to stare at one another.

"I'm sorry if I frightened you somehow, Miss," he said.

"Who are you?" Magdalena asked. "Where did you come from?"

"Well," started the stranger. Me name is Liam Malone. I came from Ire..."

"Liam!" Magdalena interrupted. You are Michael's brother! We were expecting you months ago!"

"Well, I was hopin' to be here sooner, but I had to gather up some money. I took a job working in the coal mines in Pennsylvania for a few months so I could buy me self a horse and come out west. So, here I am. And where might me brother be? 'Tis been years since I've seen him."

"I am afraid that he is not here. He went on a cattle drive and he will not be back for another month or so. I am Magdalena, his wife, and this is my father Don Sandoval."

"As pleased as I am t' meet ya both, I'm as disappointed not to see me brother. I've come all this way. I can't believe it. Me own brother, a cowboy." Liam chuckled at the thought.

"Magdalena, take Liam to the hacienda to wash up and rest. You will stay with us tonight, Liam. Dinner is at six o'clock sharp. You're family now."

"What a wonderful surprise for Michael when he returns!" Magdalena was very much revitalized now. She led Liam to the hacienda and introduced him to her mother. Then she showed him where to wash up, and the room where he would spend the night.

"We have so much to talk about over dinner. Oh, Liam, I am so happy that you are here! Michael has told me so much about you and your family. I have been hoping for so long to meet you." She could not stop smiling. In an instant, everything seemed better.

"You rest a bit, dinner is not for three more hours. Just come to the dining room at six o'clock. If you want something to read, papa has a wonderful library in the parlor. Please make yourself at home."

"When is your baby due, Magdalena?"

Magdalena placed her hand on her swollen belly, realizing that it was now very obvious that she was with child. "In about two more months. I cannot wait for the day. Liam, will you be staying in town? Will you wait for Michael to return?"

"I'm not really sure what I'm going t' do with me self. I don't really have much of a plan in fact."

"Oh, I see. Well, we can talk more at dinner. Do not be late; it is a peeve of my father's."

Magdalena turned and walked away, closing the guestroom door behind her. She hurried to her mother, and in a much excited voice began to talk about Liam.

"Can you believe how much he looks like Michael? I just cannot wait to hear what he has been doing in the past year since we received word that he was coming. Can you just imagine the look on Michael's face when he comes home and sees his brother? You should have seen me when I first saw him, Mama! I was in so much shock from the resemblance to Michael, that I fainted! Papa and Liam had to pick up off the floor!"

"Magdalena, you are much too excited. Go to your casita and rest until dinner."

"Oh, I couldn't possibly rest mama. I am going to make some pies like I started to do earlier. Did you find those tins for me?"

~*~

At six o'clock sharp and after a very comfortable rest, Liam made his appearance at the dinner table. Everyone was already seated and waiting in much anticipation. Liam took a seat at the table, and one of the servants poured him a glass of brandy. The food was served, and the conversation commenced. Don Sandoval spoke first.

"So, what are your plans, Liam? Where do you go from here?"

"Your daughter asked me the same thing. To tell you the truth sir, I haven't got a real plan. I came out t' see me brother, but me brother's not here. So I supposed I may go to Texas for a while. I don't really know."

"Texas! What will you do in Texas? You should stay put for a while Liam. Stay here in Santa Fe and see what it has to offer.

Wait for your brother; it won't be much longer."

"Are there mines here in Santa Fe? Coal mines? That's about the only work I've ever done."

"Well, Liam, I have a proposition for you. Why don't you come to work for me? I'm looking for someone to take Michael's place running the mercantile. It pays a dollar a day, and Sunday's off, if you can read and write that is, and change money."

"Really? I can do those things. That sounds like a deal, and much nicer than workin' in the mines! When would I start?"

"The sooner the better. Why don't you take tomorrow to look around town, and then start the day after?"

"I'll do that. Thank you sir. I appreciate it so much. I'll check into Fanny Sullivan's boardin' house tomorrow. I stopped by there t'day to check out th' rooms, and I was quite pleased with what I saw, if you know what I mean."

Everyone around the table laughed. They knew exactly what he meant. Fanny Sullivan was quite the looker, and Irish too. She ran a lovely boarding house just a few blocks away. She was also known for her good cooking.

"I think that you should like it there Liam. It's a nice, clean place," said Don Sandoval. "But don't be getting too fresh with Fanny. She won't take any nonsense from you."

The Sandoval home almost seemed complete again. Everyone enjoyed the food and conversation, and Magdalena's famous apple pie.

Chapter XIX

Fanny Sullivan

The next morning, Liam woke up early and refreshed. He found himself in a warm, comfortable house, and in a warm comfortable bed. These comforts he'd seldom experienced in his lifetime. As he lay in bed and looked around at the lavish furnishings about the room, he felt as though he may be dreaming it all. For a long while he just laid there taking it in, and envying his brother for having such a fine wife and family in America. After some time, he arose and washed his face, dressed, and went to the kitchen to see what the good aromas were that wafted down the hall and into his room. His new family was sitting at the table having their breakfast. They greeted him with good mornings, and invited him to join them. Liam was in no way used to being waited on by servants. Again, he pondered his brother's good fortune. Magdalena had come to the table with her black hair loose and flowing, and her night clothes and lacy robe. Mornings were still difficult for her in her condition, and it took her much longer to pull herself together. Liam studied her face and hair, and could hardly believe her exotic beauty.

Liam was lavished with fresh milk, coffee, peaches, eggs, ham, and corn bread. He gorged himself as though it were his last meal, appreciating every bite as though it may all disappear at any moment. Magdalena watched him in an amused way. She had never seen anyone eat with such gusto. After breakfast Magdalena walked down the path back to her casita. She knew that Michael would return any time now, and anticipated the day.

After packing up his meager belongings, Liam walked down San Francisco Street to Fanny Sullivan's boarding house. When he arrived, she was sweeping the front porch.

"So, you're back. I thought ya might be. This is the finest rooming house in all of Santa Fe."

Liam walked up the steps to the porch and greeted her. Fanny noticed at once that Liam was cleaned and shaven. She leaned in a bit closer and sniffed the air.

"Where did ya sleep last night that you were able to get a bath and shave? I have to admit that you smell a wee bit nicer today than ya did yesterday."

"Aye, well, I didn't want to enter your fine establishment in the condition that I was in." Liam spoke with a tone of sarcasm. "I stayed with me brother's in-laws, the Sandovals."

"Ah yes, I should have known that you were Michael's brother. You're th' spittin' image of him yourself."

~*~

Fanny Sullivan had boarded a ship with her father to come to America when she was just seventeen. The rest of her family had all succumbed to an epidemic. Fanny's father had been a successful horse breeder and trader in Ireland. When they came to America he sold everything that he owned and brought his fortune with him in gold. On the ship to America, he fell sick and died half way through the journey. Fanny was so afraid that she'd be robbed or taken advantage of that she sat with her dead father for two days before she told a steward on the ship that he'd died. By that time, she'd stashed her father's fortune in various places, in the hems of her skirts, her pockets, and in her luggage. Her father was buried at sea, and seventeen years old, Fanny disembarked alone when the ship reached New York. After the long journey and death of her father, Fanny was exhausted and wished only for a place to rest and to clear her head, but she knew the moment she arrived in New York that she did not want to stay there. She found her way to the train station and inquired as to other metropolitan cities. Something inside had told her to go west, so when Santa Fe was mentioned, she purchased passage. It would be a long and complicated journey by train and by stage. When Fanny boarded the train, the rhythmic sound of the wheels on the tracks, and the gentle swaying of the car put her right to sleep. The other passengers on the train seemed to be of respectable stature. There were families, ladies with fine garments, and businessmen. All seemed very refined, and Fanny felt safe enough at last to close her eyes. When finally she reached Santa Fe she hired a buggy to show her the town. As they made their way down San Francisco Street, a large and beautiful, Victorian gabled home caught her eye. It was painted blue with white shutters. There were white steps leading to a white porch that was the length of the house.

"Stop, driver!" she commanded. "Who lives in that grand house?"

"Nobody lives there ma'am. That house has been empty for almost two years. The old man that use to live there died of a broken heart when his young wife ran off with another man, and most of his fortune as well. He had some very fine thoroughbreds. There is a barn in the back of the house that's nicer than most of the homes around here. I tried to buy it once, but the bank won't sell the barn without the house."

"Driver, take me to the bank that owns that house please."

The driver clicked to urge his team on for several blocks, then stopped in front of the bank.

"Where is the closest hotel?" Fanny inquired.

"There's one across the street, but I wouldn't recommend it to you."

Fanny knew what he was trying to tell her.

"There's a nicer one about three blocks down the street."

"Very well then, driver. Please take me there so I can settle in. I'll walk back to the bank from there."

The driver stopped in front of the El Dorado Hotel. He helped Fanny from the buggy, and took her luggage to the lobby. Fanny paid the driver and tipped him generously.

"You've been very helpful," she told him.

After she checked into the hotel, she walked to the bank to inquire about the house.

"It's a very fine property for the money," the banker told her. "However, it doesn't come cheap."

"Well, may I see it just the same?"

"Have you any assets Miss? I wouldn't want to waste your time showing you something that you can't afford. We do have some other properties that I would be happy to show you."

"Why don't ya just tell me what th' cost of the house is, and I will decide for me self whether or not I can afford it."

The banker told Fanny the cost of the property, four thousand dollars, and she paused for a moment. Her father had left her a good fortune. She had the money to pay for the property outright and still have a good nest egg, as well as money for improvements.

"Well, that would be rather difficult for me," she told the banker "but I'd still like t' see it jest th' same."

He sighed out loud and rolled his eyes. "Let me just get my hat."

Together they walked to the house. The banker fumbled with the keys. "Nobody has been here in several months. We stopped having it cleaned or maintained when interest in the property died down. It still has all the original furnishings. Mr. Silverman's wife never returned for them, and he had no other heirs."

It was all Fanny could do to contain her amazement and keep composed. The house was beautifully furnished with fine furniture, Persian rugs, and oil paintings on the walls. They walked from room to room. The kitchen was fully furnished, and large enough for many servants to work at one time. There was a large sitting room and two bedrooms downstairs. Upstairs, there were six more rooms, each decorated for a person of grand stature. Fanny knew that she had to have this house. It would take almost half of her father's fortune, but she already had ideas for it.

"May I see th' barn?" she inquired.

"Look Miss, ah, it is Miss, correct? Is there a Mr. somewhere? Perhaps you'd like to come back later with your husband and I can show you the property at the same time. I'm a very busy man you know and I..."

"I'd like t' see th' barn please. I'd like t' see it now if ya don't mind."

The banker huffed. "Right this way, and let's hurry shall we?"

The driver had been right. This was the most magnificent barn that Fanny had ever seen. There was a large saddle room with racks on the wall. The saddles and bridles were all still there. There were English saddles, Western saddles, and side saddles. With each saddle was a bridle, and above the saddle an engraved wooden placard with a name for the horse it belonged to. There was also a large section in the barn for storing hay and grain. Fanny looked around the spacious barn and noticed a staircase leading to the loft.

"What's upstairs?" Fanny inquired.

"It's an efficiency for the groom and his family," answered the banker. "Now if you're quite finished, I really need to get back."

"I'd like t' see it," insisted Fanny. She started up the stairs, as the banker became more and more agitated. Upstairs she found a completely furnished apartment. There was a kitchen, two bedrooms, and a large parlor. The furnishings were of the greatest comfort and quality, and Fanny felt that she herself would be quite comfortable living in this apartment. "Is the price firm on the property?" she asked the banker.

"The bank needs to recover all of the losses that it incurred through Mr. Silverman. There is very little room for negotiation here."

"Well, th' property isn't generatin' any revenue jest sittin' here, and th' longer it sits, th' more work it will be goin' to need, and the less it will be worth."

"Young lady, you have tried my patience until I have no more. Now I must be getting back to the bank."

Fanny followed the banker almost running to keep pace with his brisk step. They walked down San Francisco Street. Fanny was so excited inside, but she knew that she must remain calm on the outside. She asked the banker many questions on the way back to the bank, but he mostly just ignored her.

"Are you the top person in charge?" she asked. "At the bank, are you in charge? Do you have a manager? Who owns the bank?"

By this time, the banker felt that he'd been duped by a young woman who wasn't quite right in the head. He was sure that he had wasted his time, and would be chastised for it when he returned to work. He stormed through the front doors of the bank. A tall well dressed man was standing at a teller's window closest to the door.

"Mr. Barton!" the banker exclaimed, surprised to see his manager.

"Where have you been Smith?" the man asked the banker.

"Well, I was showing this young lady here the Silverman property. She'd like to make an offer."

"Really? The man gave Fanny an amused look. He was taken by her red hair, milky white completion, and crystal blue eyes.

Most of all he was taken by her young age. Like the banker, Mr. Smith, he also found it difficult to take her seriously, but Fanny so amused him that he offered her his time. "I'm Charles Barton, owner of this bank. Shall we step into my office?"

"Aye sir, and thank you. It seems your man Smith doesn't want t' sell that property. Perhaps he wants it for himself. I asked him if the price was negotiable, and his answer was not satisfactory to me. In fact, he really did not answer me at all. As I was telling him, the longer th' house sits, the less it will be worth."

"Hmmm." Mr. Barton looked at Fanny as though he hung on every word. He knew that this conversation would lead nowhere, but he smiled and listened and watched her as she poured out all of the reasons why he should lower the price on the property. "You have some very good points Miss, I'm sorry I didn't catch your name."

"Sullivan, Fanny Sullivan."

"I can see that you have a good head for business Miss Sullivan. Perhaps I should hire you to work at my bank. Have you ever worked at a bank before Miss Sullivan?"

"No sir. I've never worked for anyone before, except for me father tha' tis. Me plan is to buy th' property and make it a rooming house."

"You mean a boarding house?"

"Call it what ya will, those are me intentions. That house will make me money."

"So, would you like to make a down payment on the house and put it up as collateral then?"

"No sir. I do not wish to carry a debt. I would like to buy it outright."

Barton laughed out loud now. "Your girls must bring you a good profit, Miss Sullivan. You look so young to be so enterprising."

A Promise Kept

"Well Mr. Barton, I thought your banker, Smith was insulting, but now you've jest outdone him. When you're ready t' sell that house you can find me at the El Dorado Hotel." She rose and started for the door.

"Wait a moment, Miss Sullivan. I didn't mean to insult you. Please come back and sit down. Now, if you are serious about purchasing one of the most distinguished properties in Santa Fe, I will need to know how you intend to pay for it."

"I intend to pay for it in gold."

"In gold?" Mr. Barton smiled.

"Yes, in gold. That is if we can come to an agreement."

"Alright then, I will sell you that property for thirty-five hundred dollars."

Fanny took a moment to reply. This was five hundred less than the banker told her, and she was more than prepared to accept the offer.

"It's a deal then," she said. "I will bring you th' gold tomorrow at noon. That will give you time to draw up the papers. I will expect the deed at that time."

"Miss Sullivan, it's customary to make a deposit, to show good faith."

"Oh, yes, of course." She reached into her reticule and produced a smaller poke. "How much of a deposit?"

"How does, say, a thousand dollars sound?"

"Very well then."

When she emptied the contents of gold coins on the table, Mr. Barton's eyes widened. For the first time he took her entirely seriously. He counted out a thousand dollars, and Fanny put the remainder of the money back into the poke. Even if she could not come up with the balance, this would make a sufficient deposit with the house being collateral.

"Do you always walk around with so much money on you, Miss Sullivan?"

"No, not always, just when I want t' buy something," she replied.

"If you can wait just one moment I'll have a receipt made up for you."

Mr. Barton walked out of his office and over to his banker. "Good job, Smith. Can you make me a receipt for a thousand dollars? Make it out to Fanny Sullivan."

"Will you please make it out to Francis Sullivan?"

Mr. Barton spun around. "Oh, I didn't know that you were right behind me, Miss Sullivan."

"Francis is me given name, I go by Fanny though."

"Oh, of course, Francis Sullivan." Mr. Barton handed the receipt to Fanny. She looked it over.

"Everything seems to appear in order. I'll be seein' ya tomorrow at noon then. And you'll have the deed?"

"Yes of course. It will be ready and waiting. Oh, and Miss Sullivan, may I take you to lunch at La Fonda tomorrow in celebration of your new home?"

"Yes sir, ya may, and I thank ya very kindly."

That had been five years prior, and Fanny had since made a success of her proper boarding house, which she preferred to call rooming house.

~*~

"Well, Mr. Malone, how do ya intend t' pay me for a room? Have you a job?"

"I start work tomorrow for Don Sandoval in his mercantile."

"I see then. Well, let me show ya around." She took him to his room on the second floor. "Here's your room. I serve breakfast at seven sharp and dinner at six sharp. If you're not here in time t' eat then it's your own problem. I change the sheets on your bed every Monday. There is t' be no whiskey or women brought into your room. If you want hanky panky, you take your women to the hotel. Is that clear? I run a clean establishment here, and there will be no mistake about it. I am well respected in this community, and I intend to remain that way."

Liam watched her crystal eyes dancing as she spoke, and he knew that she meant every word. Fanny had long, wavy red hair, but it was never seen. She always kept in a tight bun on the back of her neck. She wore crisp, linen, high collared blouses buttoned to her chin, and tailored walking skirts. She was plain and simple, and proper, but still, she couldn't help but be beautiful.

"Are you listenin' t' me sir?"

"Aye, I've heard every word."

"Good then, it will be two dollars in advance."

Liam paid her the money, and she turned to leave.

"Oh, and one more thing," she turned around. "If you have a horse I have a fine barn in the back. It cost two dollars a week to board your horse. That includes feed and grooming."

After Fanny had bought the Silverman house, she found the teamster who showed her the town, and offered him a job. He worked for room and board running the livery and taking care of her private horses, and he still kept his buggy business and shod horses. The money he made doing that was his own. But the money made from the livery was hers. It was a good arrangement for both of them. The driver, Mr. Blackwell, occupied the efficiency in the loft of the barn.

Chapter XX

The Baby

Magdalena sat crocheting a blanket for her baby in her casita, when she heard a commotion in the back pasture. She stopped to listen. There were men hollering and hooping it up, dogs barking, cows mooing and horses nickering. She dropped what she was doing, and ran outside to see what all the commotion was. The sun was just beginning to go down, and there was a slight chill in the air. As she looked over the landscape she could make out the sight of several men driving in mules, horses, beeves, and oxen. It was Michael. He was home!

Magdalena grabbed her shawl and wrapped it around her as she ran out the door. She ran toward the pasture where the livestock was being brought in. From a distance, Michael saw her, and loped his exhausted mount toward her. He jumped from his horse before it had fully stopped and embraced his wife. "Oh, Maggie, I've missed ya so much!"

"I have missed you so much too, Michael! I am so happy that you are home! I do not think I could have managed another day without you."

Michael laughed and put his hands on Magdalena's swollen abdomen. "I think this child of ours has decided to come between us, Maggie." They both laughed.

"We do not need a child to come between us Michael. The smell of you is almost enough in itself. I will go put some water on to boil for your bath while you finish up here. I think Papa will want to speak with you, but please try not to take too long."

Magdalena looked at Michael's horse. It was beautiful. A stocky grulla colored gelding.

"What a beautiful horse, Michael! Is this to be your horse?"

"Aye! He's a good one too, has a lot of heart. I call him Blaze, because he's a good trail blazer."

"Well, I hope that all of the equines that you have purchased are as fine as Blaze. That will please Papa." Magdalena turned to walk back to the casita. "I will put that water on now, Michael."

Michael, along with the trail hands, left the livestock out to graze. They would be left to rest and fatten up for a several days before the horses would be brought in and tried out, then stabled. Their own mounts were put in the barn right away, and given a generous helping of grain along with their hay. Don Sandoval walked out to the barn to speak with Michael.

"How did it go, Michael?"

"Very well sir. I think I could be a cowboy if it weren't for being away from Maggie for so long. I loved being on the trail."

"Well, I see that you've bought yourself a fine horse. I will ride out with you tomorrow to see the rest of the stock. I'm very anxious to see what you've purchased for the money that I gave you."

"Oh, you've reminded me sir." Michael pulled a poke from his trouser pocket and handed it to Don Sandoval. "There was money left over. I bought the best mules and oxen that I could, but some weren't worth the trouble. They wouldn't have made the trip back so I didn't bother with them. I found some good horses too, and beeves. If you need more than I brought back, I'll be happy to make another trip, but I think that I bought the best that is t' be had at the moment."

"We'll see tomorrow, Michael. You must be very tired, and I know that you are in need of a bath. Go get cleaned up and rest a bit. We'll expect you and Magdalena for dinner at seven thirty tonight."

Michael finished up with Cotton and Charlie in the barn, and Don Sandoval walked back to the Hacienda. As he passed the casita, Magdalena ran out.

"Papa!" she called out to him. She ran to meet him as he turned toward her. "Papa, please do not mention anything about Liam to Michael. Let us tell him tomorrow, shall we? I want Michael to myself tonight, and we can surprise him with Liam later. Please promise me, Papa?"

"Very well, then. I don't see why a few more hours should make any difference. I'm only glad that I didn't already mention it."

Michael hurried to the casita, where Magdalena had a warm bath waiting for him. As she scrubbed his back his eyes began to close, and in another moment he was asleep in the tub. Magdalena looked at him with contentment and smiled. She let him rest a while so he would be fresh at dinnertime.

There was much conversation at the dinner table. Although Michael was still tired from his long journey, he was happy and excited to be home. A good home-cooked meal was always welcomed. While on the trail, he had reverted back to his days of roughing it in the outdoors, and as much as he enjoyed it, the luxuries of home appealed greatly to his senses. A warm bath and shave, a comfortable down bed, good food to eat, a warm fire, and the company of womenfolk were all very welcomed.

"Tomorrow we'll ride out and look at the livestock, and then we will gather all the trail hands and we will pay them together, Michael." announced Don Sandoval. "Then, perhaps a drink and a fine cigar at the gun club."

"Of course, sir, but what about the mercantile? Don't you think that I should get back to my duties there as soon as possible?"

"No, Michael. I've found a very capable person to run the store. You will still oversee it, but I assure you that it is in very good hands. I was as lucky finding the new clerk as I was to find you. I tell you, the two of you have very much in common. The customers love him just as much as they love you."

Michael looked perplexed, and slightly disgruntled. "As good as me, huh?"

"Yes indeed. I'll take you by tomorrow to meet him on our way to the gun club. I feel positive that you will like him as we all do. Having him here will give you more time to help me with more important business matters. Now let us enjoy this special meal that has been prepared especially for you!"

When the meal was finished, Magdalena and Michael were invited into the parlor for brandy, but graciously refused and returned to their casita. They spoke about the coming of the baby and snuggled in the comfort of each other's embrace. The next morning, after sleeping in late, Magdalena made breakfast in their own home and they had a quiet meal together.

"Papa will understand you sleeping in Michael, but he will be very anxious to see the livestock you bought. You better get dressed and ready to ride out with him."

"As much as I love me new horse, I'd sure like a few days out of th' saddle. Perhaps he'd like to rest as well. I'll take a fresh mount t'day.

I guess I'd best get ready now."

Michael dressed, and he and Don Sandoval rode out to the pasture. Michael's father-in-law was very pleased with the selection of fine animals, and there were more animals than he had expected, given the amount of money that Michael brought back.

"You did very well, son. I am relieved to know that you will be able to carry on the business. I'm getting old and tired. I would much rather go bird hunting or fishing than worry about beeves and wagons and money and such. From now on, you shall make the money, and I shall spend it. There will be a nice bonus for you and the boys. Now, let's go pay them and then see about the new man at the mercantile, shall we?"

Michael was none too excited about meeting his replacement. How could anyone be as good as he was? And where did Don Sandoval find him anyway? He had much on his mind, and was determined to know the answers to all of his questions. After putting the horses up, Michael went for Magdalena while Don Sandoval fetched his wife. Together they made the short walk to the mercantile. By this time it was already past Liam's noontime meal, and he was occupied inside the store. With every step closer, Michael grew more apprehensive. He was already determined to dislike this new person who was so capable. He followed Don Sandoval into the mercantile with the ladies close behind.

"Good morning, Liam," said Don Sandoval.

"And top o' the mornin't' ya, sir."

Michael just stood with his mouth gaping for a long moment.

"Have ya nothin' t'say t'yer brother after all this time?"

"Liam!" Michael ran to him and embraced his brother. "Liam! When did you arrive? Nobody told me." He turned and looked at Magdalena and then Don Sandoval, who both stood smiling. "I'm so happy t' see ya! You must tell me everything of home, and what you've been up to these past couple o' years. I want t' hear everything!" His eyes began to well up, and the tears spilled over his flushed cheeks.

"Aye, but there will be time for that. I see me customers are gettin' angry. I must tend t' them now, and I'm sure that yer family has things in mind for ya t'do today. Your father in-law has invited me t' dinner t'night. He says they are serving elk; somethin' I'm excited to try. I'll be seein' ya t'night then brother."

The four exited the mercantile, and as they made their way down the steps Michael remarked, "I haven't seen me brother in over two years. You'd think he'd want to spend a little more time with me. He practically pushed me out th' door. Did ya see that? His customers are waiting. His customers could wait just a wee bit longer, I'd say."

"You see what I mean Michael? He's very capable."

The ladies laughed as the men turned one way toward the gun club, and they turned back toward home.

Later that evening Michael enjoyed his favorite dish of "oysters not from the sea". A lamb was slaughtered and tamales with cheese and green chilies were served, and of course elk. Liam enjoyed his first American cook out, and brought Miss Fanny as his guest. Everything was perfect. Michael offered up his thanks for his family, new and old. He and Liam talked about bringing their mother and sister to New Mexico. Together, they would save money for their passage. They would have to find a place for them to live as well. The goals they set added purpose and joy to their lives. Fanny was vicariously excited as well. She wanted to be included in the plans, as she had no family of her own. It would be wonderful to have a family from Ireland, and in her mind she was trying to figure a way to add onto the home that the Ferrier was now occupying, and offer the efficiency to the Malone family. She kept her ideas to herself, though. She did not want to barge in on their family and their plans; she would ease in gently.

The next few weeks passed, and summer would soon arrive. Along with summer, new fabrics and patterns arrived at the mercantile. The ladies would be fashioning new summer wardrobes before the weather became too warm for their winter attire. They were exited to see the new patterns and styles from back east.

The new livestock had to be branded and inoculated. The young steers were castrated, and there was a big barbeque at the Sandoval's with all of the usual people. Magdalena was growing more anxious for the baby to arrive, with each passing day and the constant swelling of her belly. The weather was turning warmer, and she was constantly in a state of discomfort. Sunday morning arrived, and the family walked together to church. Magdalena felt quite satisfied with her growing family.

Liam joined them regularly for church, and Miss Fanny normally accompanied Liam. The two seemed to be an item these days, and people were starting to talk, but in a good way. Don Sandoval was very pleased to call them friends, and family. As they sat in church that Sunday late in June, Magdalena was growing increasingly fidgety. The baby was kicking, and she was feeling all sorts of new and unusual pangs. Before dismissing his Parrish, the Father made an announcement of the Fourth of July picnic in the church garden. Of course, everyone in town had already made their plans for it, as it was a long standing tradition. Upon their returned home, Magdalena informed her parents that she did not want to take dinner with them that night. It would be the first Sunday night that they did not have a family dinner together at the hacienda. She was not feeling well, and wanted to rest. Dona Sandoval had her servant Missy take the young couple a light meal at five o'clock, but Magdalena just picked at her food, barely eating a thing.

The next few days seemed to drag on very slowly for Magdalena. On Thursday morning, when everyone was preparing for the picnic, she did not seem as enthused as she should have been.

"Magdalena, are you all right?" asked Dona Sandoval as they were preparing their baskets in the kitchen.

"I've been askin' her that for the past two days," Michael said. "She's just been moping about like she is now; can barely pull a word from her mouth."

"I am fine!" she replied sternly. "I am just so sick of lugging around all this weight! It makes me tired."

"Well," her mother said, "If you do not feel like going to the picnic, you do not have to."

"Mama, I really do not feel like going, but maybe it will be a good diversion. I will be ready in an hour."

Liam and Fanny stopped by the hacienda to join the family for the short walk to church. Magdalena was lagging. Her thighs ached from the weight of the baby, and she wondered how much more could she take. At the church, a large group of citizens were already gathered. People had their blankets spread out on the ground, and some were already sampling the contents of their baskets. There were relays and sack races, as well as horse races and pie, and preserve contests. Liam and Michael were enjoying each other's company, and most of all the celebration of an American holiday. They spoke to one another about how wonderful their new country was, and how glad that they were to be in America. Fanny agreed. They were deep in conversation when Michael happened to notice Magdalena across the garden speaking with her mother. The look on her face told him that something was wrong. He jumped up to run to her. Liam was asking what was wrong, but Michael didn't answer. As he approached the women, Dona Sandoval told him to take Magdalena straight home. She was going to fetch the doctor and be along directly. When they saw Michael walking Magdalena home, Fanny and Liam caught up and walked with them.

"She thinks it may be time for the baby to come," Michael told his brother.

"Oh 'tis a glorious moment!" exclaimed Fanny.

"Dona Sandoval has gone for the doctor. Perhaps you can help Fannie," said Michael.

"I'll be happy t' do whatever I can."

Michael escorted Magdalena to the casita. He waited with her until the doctor arrived.

"Michael, I think it best that you wait in the hacienda with the others," said Dona Sandoval. "I will call for you if I need you."

"Aye," Michael replied, and left the casita with some reluctance.

In the hacienda the small group was gathered in the parlor. Don Sandoval poured Michael a glass of brandy.

"Here you are son; this will steady your nerves. You might as well relax, these things can take time." He handed Michael the brandy and went to his humidor to begin the selection of the finest cigars in his collection. "People will be coming to visit. I will offer them cigars and brandy, but I think it would be best if you kept the public away from the baby and Magdalena until they are strong enough to receive visitors. They will both be delicate for a while. We must do everything in our power to keep that baby healthy."

"Aye, sir." Michael was in a daze, and at the moment more frightened than ever. A new life was coming into the world. He was excited, and happy as well. For a moment his thoughts drifted away, and to his own mother. How sad it must have been for her to bury so many children, and in pauper's graves to boot. He quickly dismissed the malevolent thoughts and returned to the present moment. Hours passed and the conversation was sparse. Michael and Don Sandoval took turns pacing the floor.

At last, the doctor came to the hacienda and announced, "There is a fine, healthy new girl in the Sandoval family!"

"Can I go t' her now?" inquired Michael.

"Yes, Michael, you and the family may go and meet your new daughter. Congratulations! Now I suppose I'll go to the picnic and see if I can rustle up some leftovers from somebody's basket."

"I'll have Missy prepare you a meal Dine here tonight!" invited Don Sandoval.

"No, thank you. I'd like to join the celebration now. But I will always remember this day, July fourth, eighteen sixty seven, as the day that Magdalena brought her baby girl into the world; very patriotic planning of you, Michael."

In the casita, Dona Sandoval was just finishing up with bathing and swaddling the baby. She handed the infant to her daughter.

"What do you think of that, Grandpa?" said the new Grandmother.

"I think she's the prettiest baby girl that I've ever seen, next to Magdalena, that is. What is her name?" Don Sandoval looked at Magdalena, Magdalena looked back at him, and they both looked at Michael.

"We haven't talked about a name," he said. "I just assumed that it would be a boy, and we'd name him after me."

Everyone laughed.

"Well, we better let the mother rest now." Don Sandoval could see that Magdalena's eyes were heavy. They left the two alone with their infant.

"What are we going to name her Michael?"

"Well, I was just thinking that I'd like to name her after me mum. Molly's her name."

"Molly." Magdalena repeated it. "I like it. It sounds very friendly. Molly Malone. Yes, indeed. That is a fine name. Perhaps her middle name can be Maria after my mother. Molly Maria Malone."

Both smiled. "Then we have it!" said Michael.

"Molly Maria Malone.

Chapter XXI

The Plans

The days were filled with happy activities after baby Molly was born. Her parents loved to put her in the perambulator and parade her around town. She was a beautiful baby, and people always remarked. She had a mop of thick black curly hair. A lot for a baby. It framed her perfect rosy face, and bright, green eyes.

Michael was becoming more involved in the family business, and Liam was managing the mercantile mostly on his own. He and Fanny were officially courting and planning a marriage, but Liam was putting it off until he could save some money and bring his mother to America. Michael was earning very good money, and with almost no expenses, he was putting much of it away and giving generously to his brother for their cause. The Sandovals were very happy with their extended family. Now, at the Sunday table were six adults and one baby. The family was growing, and Don Sandoval was quite pleased with the quality of souls that he had inducted into his clan.

One Sunday in early January, Liam and Fanny had an announcement to make. Everyone at the dinner table listened intently while Liam told the family that passage had been secured to bring their mother and sister, Caitlin to America. They were to live in the apartment over the barn. A small apartment was being built next to the barn for Fanny's business partner, who was in total agreement with the situation, since the stairs were starting to bother his knees. He was getting up in age, and shoeing horses was hard on the body. The second part of the announcement was that as soon as the family arrived in New Mexico, he and Fanny were to be married. There was no date yet, but they were starting to make the plans. They would be married in the Catholic Church, and have a reception at the boarding house. It would be as grand of an affair as Magdalena and Michael had. Everyone at the table was pleased with the announcement, and after dinner Don Sandoval called for brandy and cigars in the parlor. There was much to talk about, and Magdalena was especially pleased that she was finally going to meet Michael's mother. The celebration continued until the clock announced the midnight hour, and Liam suddenly remember that he needed to be up early in the morning to open the store. Baby Molly was fast asleep in her perambulator in front of the fire. Michael and Magdalena wheeled her back to the casita, and everyone retired for the evening.

That night, Michael tossed and turned in his bed. He was too excited with anticipation of his family's arrival to shut his eyes. How wonderful that their mother's dream would come true; to see her family in America. There would be a warm home waiting for her, with a good stove to cook on, and always food on her table. She would never have to see her family hungry or sick again. She would never be cold again, or worry about where the money would come from to buy coal. Michael knew how proud she would be when she saw him, and Liam, and what nice homes and families they had. She would love Fanny, and Magdalena, and dote over little Molly. Finally, as Michael's eyes began to grow tired and close, the rooster started crowing his announcement of daybreak. Magdalena rose out of bed and decided not to wait for one of the servants to milk the cow. She would do it herself and have fresh cream for Michael when he got up. She lit her stove and started for the barn. She finished the task of milking, and on her way back to the casita she collected a half dozen eggs from the henhouse. Carefully, she placed them in the pockets of her apron. She turned toward the rooster they called Jake and told him that he could stop his noise, that surely the whole town must be awake by now. Inside the casita, Michael and baby Molly were still fast asleep. It was unusual for either of them to sleep so late, but then, they were up late the night before. Magdalena checked on Molly as she had the habit of doing frequently when the child was sleeping. Then she went to Michael and gently spoke to him.

"Michael, you'd better get up. Papa said last night that the two of you had a meeting to attend with the Army this morning. He said it was important. I am making you a good breakfast now; it will be ready soon."

When Michael came to the table, Magdalena had a hearty breakfast of ham and eggs, fresh cream, coffee, sliced oranges, and corn bread waiting for him. Michael ate and cleaned himself up before dressing. By the time he left the casita to walk up to the hacienda, Don Sandoval was already walking toward the casita. Together, they walked to the town square to the office building where they would meet up with the Army purveyors. At the meeting, a proposal was presented to Don Sandoval. He needed time to think it over before presenting it to his family. When the meeting was over, Michael and Don Sandoval walked the short distance to the gun club. There they sat with a drink, and discussed the proposal, and how it would affect their futures.

Don Sandoval began the conversation. "If we accept this proposal, I would expect you to take charge, Michael. It would be a huge move for you, but a good move for you and the family. I just don't know how the women will react. Most likely not in good favor I expect. What do you think about moving, Michael? You would be a long way from your family. Your mother is coming soon. This is a great opportunity for the business, though, and if you didn't like it out west, perhaps we could send Liam eventually. But then, he will be tied to Fanny, and she has a good business going here in town. There is a lot to be considered here, but ultimately it will be up to you, Michael. I would not ask you to do anything that you and Magdalena do not want to do.

Why don't you discuss it with her tonight, and let me have an answer in the next day or two?"

"I want t' do it," said Michael. I'm all for it. Let's present it t' the wives next Sunday at dinner. Do we have that much time t' consider the proposition? I was thinking that if we wait a week t' give our answer, perhaps it will give us more time to really consider all of the aspects of the proposal.

"Yes, that's a good point. We can take the week to think about it, discuss it, and weigh the pros and cons. You are a wise businessman, Michael. I like the way you think, and I am in total agreement."

They spent the rest of the afternoon at the gun club, enjoying the company of Don Sandoval's friends. On their way back home, they ran into Liam locking up the store.

"You're working late again, Liam," Don Sandoval called out. "You'll be in trouble at home if you keep this up. Dinner at six, don't forget." The men enjoyed funning at the domestic life that Liam had so easily fallen into, but none of the lot would trade it for the single life.

Sunday morning, the six adults and one baby made their way to the sanctuary together. After sitting through a lengthy sermon, they strolled back to the hacienda, which had become their Sunday custom. Being a beautiful January afternoon, the women took their tea in the garden, and the men took their drinks in the parlor. They discussed business, and let Liam in on the proposition.

"We are going to present it to the ladies toward the end of dinner," said Don Sandoval. "I don't want to mention it too early in the evening, in case of a bad reception. Liam, it might mean that you will be making trips out west occasionally. I want to know if you are good with that. I'm sorry that I did not mention this sooner, so you would have time to think about it. I just wanted to keep it from the women until Michael and I had time to think, and discuss it."

"Sir," started Liam, "I am ferever in debt t' you. I will be happy t' serve you in whatever way that I can. If I am away from me family for a while, it will only mean I will be all the happier t' see them when I return. I'm just so pleased that you have offered us this opportunity in America. Without you, my family would not have been able to make the trip to America. I'm sure that I can speak for me brother as well as me self when I tell you that bringing the family here to a new and better life is worth anything that you might ask of us."

"Aye!" chimed in Michael. "I agree! To a better life!" He lifted his glass, and they toasted... "To a better life!"

At that moment, the women were just coming in for dinner. "What is all this about?" asked Dona Sandoval.

"You shall find out soon enough," answered Don Sandoval. "Now let's eat, shall we? I'm starving!"

As the dinner plates were being bussed, and the dessert being served, Don Sandoval felt the time was right to make the announcement.

"A proposal has been presented to me by the Army. It will involve all of you, so we would like your vote, even though we've pretty much made up our minds." He looked at the men, and then men returned his glance and then turned their eyes toward the women. The room was filled with nervous energy, but Don Sandoval retained his stalwart composure. He was, after all, the head of the family, and was not about to allow the women to undermine his authority. He only wanted them to think that their opinion was important.

After noticing the anxious glare from the table, he began his speech.

"The Army has made me a proposal. They want to open a supply post out west, and have offered this great opportunity to me first. I have decided, uh, we have decided, to accept their offer to open a post in San Diego."

He spoke quickly so as to get in everything before the protests began. "Michael has agreed to run the post. This is a wonderful opportunity for us to expand our business and secure the futures of everyone at this table."

"San Diego?" questioned Dona Sandoval. "California?" You are going to send Michael all the way to California while he has a wife and child here in Santa Fe?"

"Oh, well," began Don Sandoval. "Michael will be taking his family with him."

"What?" Dona Sandoval was about to protest.

"San Diego!" said Magdalena. "We are going to California!" Magdalena's sense of adventure and her lifelong desire to leave Santa Fe was about to be fulfilled. She was elated, but her mother was not so enthusiastic.

"How can you send away your only child and grandchild? Have you lost all of your senses, husband? There are many dangers out there. They will have to cross hundreds of miles in the desert, in Indian territory. We will miss the pleasures of seeing our granddaughter grow up, and more grandchildren born. What are you thinking, Alfonso?"

"Sir," interrupted Fanny. "You mentioned that this would affect everyone at the table. How would this affect Liam and me self?"

Dona Sandoval watched and listened, still slightly in shock from the news. Her dinner was suddenly not agreeing with her. She wanted to run from the table for air, but she did not dare. She did not want to miss a word.

"Well, Liam will have more responsibilities here, for one. He will be promoted in the business, make more money, and have more of a say in what goes on in the business. He will be a partner, just like Michael."

Fanny smiled. The way she saw it, there was nothing about the proposition that was distasteful to her, other than her sister-in-law being so far away. She would still have Liam's little sister and mother as family. She would still have Liam right there in Santa Fe, and he was to become an important person in the town. Fanny was more than satisfied with the proposal.

"Also," continued Don Sandoval, "Liam may have to make some trips from time to time to California to deliver provisions. He will have plenty of wagons and the Army along with him. It will be as safe as can be. I may also ask him to make buying trips to Chama, and Mexico."

Fanny did not care for the addendum, but she could see that Liam was happy about it, and so she reframed from further comment.

"Oh, Michael! California! San Diego! I have never seen the Pacific Ocean before. I have never seen any ocean before. When do we leave?" inquired Magdalena.

Dona Sandoval could see Magdalena's excitement. She wanted to be happy for her, but all of her thoughts were of dread. She would speak more to her husband in private later. There was nothing more to be said at the moment.

"You won't leave until summer," answered Don Sandoval. "We need time to gather provisions and get ready. Michael might need to make another trip to Chama in spring for more oxen and mules. There are things that you can buy when you get to San Diego, but I want to send you prepared to settle and make a home. Prices are much higher out west. Much, much higher."

"Out west? Out west?! We are out west! We are in New Mexico!" Dona Sandoval's opposition was obvious.

"Oh, Mama, I have always dreamed about this moment! Please do not argue it. I want to go. Michael wants to go. We can visit you, you can visit us! I shall write at least once a week, I promise."

Dona Sandoval knew that she was outnumbered. She wanted Magdalena to be worldly and see things; she was just filled with apprehension. But there was no use fighting it; everyone else seemed to be happy about the plans.

The next few weeks were spent making preparations for the wagon train West. Kit Carson agreed to see the train as far as Fort Craig. He was not feeling all too well these days, but he had a history at Fort Craig and was very fond of the post. Furthermore, it was not all too far from Santa Fe. He could see the train to the post, and be back in no time. Liam and Fanny were making plans for their wedding. The new house was being built next to the livery for the Ferrier, and everyone was making plans for the rest of the family to arrive from Ireland. The next several weeks were filled with plans, preparations, and anticipation. It was an exciting time in the lives of the younger and more adventurous generation.

One afternoon, there was a knock on the door of the hacienda. It was a young neighbor named Olivia Sanderson. She was only nineteen years old, like Magdalena, and the two of them had attended the Catholic school together. Dona Sandoval answered the door when her house servants neglected to do so.

"Good afternoon, Olivia. Have you come to visit with Magdalena?"

"No," she replied. "I am here to speak with your husband regarding a business proposition."

"I see," said Dona Sandoval. "Well, come in then and wait in the parlor. I will fetch him directly."

She escorted the young woman into the parlor and showed her a seat. "Would you like some lemonade?" she asked.

"No thank you, ma'am. I won't be staying very long." Dona Sandoval could see that the young lady was nervous. She wondered what such a young woman could be so troubled over. Olivia was from a prominent family in town. She had been afforded the best of everything growing up. Dona Sandoval wondered what sort of business proposition she could possibly have with her husband, but she knew and practiced patience. She knew well that her husband would disclose everything to her at an appropriate moment, as he always had.

Don Sandoval entered the room and sat in a chair beside Olivia. His demeanor was approachable, and he was always very receptive to the younger generation, as he always expected the same from them. Olivia felt a bit more at ease as Don Sandoval made small talk about the weather, which was his intention.

"So, why don't you tell me what brings you to me today, Olivia. I am just a little bit more than curious."

"Well sir, I understand that you are forming a wagon train out to California. You see, I have been offered a teaching position at the Mission in San Gabriel near Los Angeles, and I was wondering if I might join your train."

"Is that all?" asked Don Sandoval. "I'm sure that can be arranged. However, my wagon train will only be going to San Diego. Los Angeles is several days north of there by stage. Do you have arrangements for that travel?"

"Why, yes sir, it is as you say. I will be taking the Butterfield. The problem is, Don Sandoval, I do not have a wagon for the trip to San Diego. I was wondering if I could hire one from you, but I do not have much money. I was wondering if I could work something out with you. I am a very good cook, and I know that you will have family and employees on that train to feed. I thought that perhaps I could drive the chuck wagon and do the cooking for your folks, and that way I could sleep in the chuck wagon in exchange."

"Why, I think that's a splendid idea, Miss Olivia. I would have to hire a cook anyway, and the wagon would be part of the deal. I have not even begun to look for a camp cook. You have crossed one thing off my list of things to do. But you will also be paid according to how many people you will be cooking for, and how long it takes to get to San Diego. I'm sure that Magdalena will be happy to have a woman, a companion, along on the trip as well. She can help you with the cooking some. She also is an excellent cook you know, but she will be too busy tending to her child to take on the task of camp cook. It will be good for her to have a friend along. As the time gets closer, I will speak with you again about wages. I still don't know how many wagons I will be sending, or how many hands I will be sending. I am certainly happy that you came to me today, Miss Olivia. Yes, this is one less thing that I have to worry about now. And congratulations and good luck to you with your teaching position."

Don Sandoval showed Olivia to the door, and she smiled as she bid him goodbye. Olivia was much relieved that she had gathered the courage to approach Don Sandoval with the proposition, as it had turned out much better than she had hoped or expected. Don Sandoval seemed genuinely happy to accept her proposition.

~*~

March came around, and Michael was off to Chama once again to buy horses, mules, and oxen. He said his goodbyes to Magdalena and baby Molly one chilly, March morning. There was still snow on the ground in Chama, as it had been a particularly cold winter that year, and the wind blew hard. Don Sandoval knew that the trip would take close to two months, and he wanted to get the wagon train started in early summer, if possible. Timing would be somewhat up to the army as well, as they would be escorting the emigrants traveling to San Diego. In addition, nobody knew quite when Michael's mother was to arrive from Ireland, and he wanted Michael and Magdalena to be here to greet her and attend Liam's wedding.

In the weeks while Michael was away, Magdalena was rekindling her acquaintance with Olivia, and becoming ever closer to Fanny. The three women would talk over tea about how their lives had evolved, and what was to come. Most excited was Olivia. She was about to embark on a grand adventure out on her own. One day toward the end of May, the ladies were gathered at Fanny's house.

"I am so pleased that you will be traveling with us, Olivia," announced Magdalena. It will keep us from getting too homesick, and we shall have each other for companionship. I have heard that there are nine men to every woman in California, Olivia. You will have to watch yourself, because the men will all be watching you!"

The ladies had a good laugh. Life was so perfect as of late, except for the absence of Michael. This time it was much easier for Magdalena though. She had more confidence in her husbands safe return, and the baby kept her busy. Her friends with common interests also occupied much of her time.

Baby Molly started to fuss in the middle of their conversation.

"I best take her home and put her down now. She needs her nap, and she is especially fussy since she is cutting another tooth.

Magdalena started toward home after saying goodbye to the other ladies. When she arrived, she was happily surprised to find Michael home and in the tub, cleaning up.

"Where've ya been, wife? I expected you'd have a hot bath waitin' fer me when I got home."

"Michael!" She ran to her husband threw her arms around his neck, giving him a loving kiss. "Look, Molly, Papa has come home!" Molly reached for her father and started to chuckle. "That is the happiest I have seen the baby since you've left. She has been just horrid!"

"Well, of course she was. She missed her Papa. Can't say as much for you though."

"Oh, Michael, stop teasing. You know I miss you every second that you are away. A lot has happened since you've been gone."

"Do tell me, beautiful wife."

"Well," she started in easy; "Molly cut two teeth and is cutting another now!"

"Is that right? Well, that is grand news."

"And," she continued, "your mother's ship has landed and she is on her way to Santa Fe!"

"More grand news indeed! I'm so happy t' hear this. I was worried that we'd have t' go to California without seein' her."

"Oh, Papa would never have that, Michael. You know that."

"Aye, you're right, me beautiful wife."

"There's other news, Michael, not so nice. Kit Carson died two days ago. His funeral is tomorrow."

Michael sat up.

"Oh tha'tis bad news. I'm so sorry t' hear it. I know that he and your father were very close friends. I me self was very fond of the gentleman. What happened?"

"The doctor said that he had an aneurism in the area of his heart. He knew he was dying Michael. He died laying on the floor on his buffalo robe. He will be wrapped it in when he is buried somewhere near Taos."

"I'm so sorry for his young wife, and all those wee ones he left behind. How will they get along now? They aren't wealthy by any means."

"The town will take care of them, Michael, and my parents will help of course. Now get out of that tub! I am putting Molly down for a nap, and we should probably rest up, too, before dinner. Papa will have you very busy the next few weeks and I want you to myself before he gets a hold of you. I am so excited, Michael. Olivia and Fanny and I have done nothing but talk about your mother coming, and the trip to California. There is much to look forward to. But first, we must get through this funeral tomorrow."

"Do you know what I was thinkin' Maggie? I was thinkin' that when we get to California, I want to have some sheep."

"Sheep! Michael there are a lot of cowboys out west, and you know how they feel about sheep."

"But they haven't tasted one, I bet. The whole trip, all I could think about was having me a leg of lamb. I think I could eat a whole leg all by me-self. I hope that's what you're serving tonight."

"I think we will be dining with my parents tonight, Michael. I am going to run to the hacienda for a quick moment. Now you get out of the tub, and be waiting for me. And do not get dressed!"

"Oh, me beautiful wife. I do love you so."

Chapter XXII
The Arrival

Magdalena and Michael passed the days of June with much love and fondness in their lives. Molly was now walking, and speaking in her own tongue. She smiled all of the time, and people would remark on how happy a baby she was. She was the pride of the Sandoval family. Her hair was turning thicker and curlier. It was a shiny dark black, and it set off her green eyes. She had a round chubby face, with dimples in her rosy cheeks. For Magdalena these were the happiest days of her life. She had much to look forward to. Her days were kept busy not only with Michael and Molly, but making preparations to go to California. Her mother-in-law, and sister-in-law would be arriving any day, and Dona Sandoval was occupying herself planning a big welcome party. Then, there was to be a wedding. The date for the wedding was still not set; it was pending on the arrival of Liam's family.

One day early in June, Olivia came to visit Magdalena. The two were visiting in the parlor of the hacienda when Don Sandoval entered the room.

"Olivia, I have decided on a price for your services on the trail, and I would like to know if it is acceptable with you. I will pay you two hundred dollars; one hundred in advance, and one hundred when you arrive in San Diego. What do you think of those terms?"

"Sir, I find your terms more than acceptable. In fact, you are very generous, and I thank you very much."

"Good then, it's settled. I understand that the wagon train will leave the first of August. I hope that you will be ready."

"Sir, I am ready to leave at first sunlight!"

They all laughed, as they knew how excited Olivia and Magdalena both were. It was all that they had spoken of in the last few weeks. Suddenly, their visit was abruptly interrupted by a frantic knock on the door. It was Fanny Sullivan.

"The stage is here with Michael's mother and sister! Liam is with them now at the mercantile. I've come t' let ya know that I'll be takin' them to the rooming house in a short moment. Hurry along! Where's Michael?"

"He is out in the round pen trying out the new horses with Cotton. I will go fetch him. We will see you shortly Fanny, and thank you!" Magdalena replied.

"Well, this is good news!" said Don Sandoval. "I was hoping they'd arrive before the wagon train left. Now we will have time for a wedding and to get to know Michael's mother and sister before you have to leave. You better run and tell Michael, and hurry!"

"I am already going, Papa. Please watch Molly for me? I shall be right back for her, and we can walk together down to the mercantile."

Magdalena rushed though the door and ran all the way down to the round pen, calling Michael as she ran.

"What is it, Maggie? What's th' matter?"

"Your mother is here! She is at the mercantile now! Hurry!"

Michael jumped off the horse he was riding and handed the reins to Cotton. Cotton watched with envy as together, Michael and Magdalena ran to the parlor where Don and Dona Sandoval were waiting with baby Molly. They did not bother with the perambulator. Don Sandoval carried Molly as they walked together very quickly toward the mercantile. As they approached the store, Michael could no longer stand the anticipation, and broke into a run.

"Ha! Look at him go," said Magdalena. I have never seen him so excited before. I must admit, I myself am a little bit nervous to meet his mother and sister."

"Do not be nervous," said Dona Sandoval. "I feel quite sure that Michael's mother is much more anxious than you are."

When they caught up with Michael, he was embracing his mother with tears rolling down his cheeks. His mother and sister were both weeping as well. Even Fanny pulled her handkerchief from the sleeve of her blouse and wiped away the wetness from her face. Magdalena stood back and watched the reunion. She studied Michael's mother and sister. Neither appeared to look anything like she had imagined. Michael's mother was short and slightly portly. She was probably about her own mother's age, but time had been hard on her. She had black wavy hair like Michael's, but with a hint of wispy gray. There were deep lines etched around her eyes and mouth, and the corners of her lips drew slightly downward. Her clothes were very plain, but probably the best that she owned. She wore a gray wool skirt and a simple, but proper, white blouse. Michael's sister looked nothing like him. She was approximately five feet tall, perhaps a little more, and very thin. Her face was narrow and her cheeks were sunken. She had long red hair that she wore in a braid down her back, and a few freckles on each side of her nose, but just a few. Her lips were thin and her skin was even whiter than Fanny's. Magdalena wondered if she had ever seen the sun in her entire life. Why, even baby Molly had more color in her skin the day that she was born. Just looking at her made Magdalena pity her. Finally, Michael started to make the introductions. He grabbed Magdalena by the hand and pulled her inside of the circle of his family.

"This is Maggie, Mum. And these are her parents, Don and Dona Sandoval. And this, this is our baby, Molly."

Michael took Molly from Don Sandoval and handed her to his mother. While Magdalena looked on with a smile, she was suddenly filled with apprehension. What if they were sick? Caitlin looked so frail and ill, and Michael's mother did not look well either. What if they brought some strange disease from Ireland? What if they gave it to Molly? Michael's mother handed baby Molly to Caitlin. Again, Molly's apprehensions overwhelmed her. What if Caitlin did not have the strength to hold her? What if she dropped her? She watched as Caitlin spoke to Molly in her thick Irish accent. Caitlin smiled at Molly and Magdalena saw that she had the most beautiful smile and perfect teeth. She knew that bad teeth were a sign of bad heath and felt a little bit better at the sight of her healthy teeth. It was still early in the day, so Dona Sandoval invited everyone to dine at their home that night. Six o'clock sharp. It was settled, and the Sandovals, along with Magdalena and Molly, headed back to the hacienda to make the preparations. Michael stayed behind. He wanted to see the look on his mother's face when Fanny showed her the apartment that was to be her new living quarters. He knew that the efficiency was much grander than any place that his mother had ever resided in Ireland. Together, they all walked to the grand barn, with Fanny leading the way. Liam had a great smile on his face as he anticipated what was about to unfold. He and Michael kept exchanging glances of approval. They entered the barn, and Fanny turned to speak to Mrs. Malone.

"I hope that the stairs won't be too much for you t' handle."

"Oh, not at all," replied Mrs. Malone. "I might be old, but I'm capable."

They climbed the stairs together. There was a door at the top of the steps that kept the draft and the smell of the horses from the apartment. Fanny opened the door and led the way inside. Once inside, Mrs. Malone could hardly believe her eyes. She gasped, and looked around at the furnishings with her mouth wide open. How could this be? She was in a barn afterall.

" I thought fer a moment there that I was t' sleep with the beasts like the baby Jasus."

They all laughed.

"Let me show you your room, Mrs. Malone."

"Me room? There's more? But this is so much more space than I've ever lived in before."

"Well, just come and see then," said Fanny. She opened the door to the largest room, and led Mrs. Malone inside. Michael's mother looked at the big bed with the brass headboard. She looked around the room at all the other fancy furnishings.

"Who would have believed that there was a palace above the barn?" she said. "I just can't believe this. This is where I'm to stay until I find me own home?"

"No Mum," said Liam. "This is where you'll be living now. This is your home. Yours and Caitlin's."

"Come Caitlin, I'll show you your room," said Fanny.

"I'll be havin' me own room?"

"Aye, your own space all t' yerself dear." Answered Fanny.

Fanny opened the door to a smaller room, but impressive just the same. For a moment, Caitlin stood in shock.

"Oh, Mum, can you believe it? Just look around! Look at the stove, and look at the view out th' windows!"

Fanny walked around the room and opened the windows to let the breeze cool down the room.

"It does tend to get a wee bit warm up here in the summer, but if you leave all the windows open at night, and close them, and the curtains in the mornin', it helps t' keep the apartment cooler. And if it ever does get too warm, you can come into the main house. Or you can always visit Liam at the mercantile, or take a walk through town. You can put your feet in the river and cool off, too. I would suggest not wearing wool in the summertime here, though. You will find that it gets a wee bit too warm for that. Now, we'll leave you to rest a bit before we go t' dinner at the Sandovals. I'll have some lemonade and a morsel brought up to ya in a bit. You must be starvin' and exhausted from your trip."

"Aye," replied Mrs. Malone. "That was the longest journey I've ever taken. You know that I've never been away from Ireland before now?"

"Well, I hope that you'll not be missin' it too much," replied Fanny. "I am hoping that you will stay around and see your grandchildren born, and make Santa Fe your home just as we have."

"Well, there's a good chance that I'll be stayin'. I know that I don't want to be gettin' on any ship for a long time, anyway. Anyway, Ireland has nothing more for me these days. Here, I have me family about me."

Fanny smiled, and started for the stairs with Liam close behind.

"Liam," called his mother. "I like Miss Fanny." She said in a whisper. "Did ya marry her yet?"

"No Mum, we've been waitin' fer you and Caitlin. We'll be married soon, though. Caitlin, there are many fine men here, all for the choosin'. Females are scarce here, and I'm sure that you'll be quite popular. The men will all be talkin' 'bout ya soon."

Caitlin blushed, and for a moment Liam saw a hint of color in her cheeks.

"Everything is goin' t' be alright now, you'll see. You already have family here, and you will make friends fast. Everything will be alright."

I'll bring some food up in a moment."

Liam turned to leave, and closed the door behind him. He felt satisfied that his family was finally together, for the most part.

He felt happy that he and Michael were able to take care of his mother. And yet, there was a sadness about them. Were they missing Ireland, or perhaps Christina? He shook it off, and thought to himself that they would adjust and be happy in time.

That evening at dinner, the plans for the wedding were discussed. There would be no time for an introduction party for Michael's mother and sister. The introductions would be made at the wedding. There would be a grand reception at Fanny's house. Invitations were already addressed, waiting to be delivered. They would have to go out the next day. Most would be hand delivered. A birthday party for Molly would be held in the church gardens on the fourth of July. The family would spend as much precious time together as they could that July, before the wagon train departed on the first of August.

As the end of the month drew near, so came the emigrants in wagons. They were coming to join the wagon train west. Most camped by the Santa Fe River, waiting to hear the news that the train was ready to leave. Don Sandoval's supply wagons for the trip were being prepared. There were ten in all, filled with provisions for the new store in San Diego. There were guns and ammunition, slickers and sheets of India rubber, and uniforms for the Army. There was also a variety of other supplies, such as tools, dry goods and boots, yardage, cooking utensils, as well as an assortment of food staples such as flour, sugar, and coffee. Michael and Magdalena also had two covered wagons for themselves. Most all of the furnishings they needed from their casita was in one of the wagons. The other was to be their home on wheels while they were on the road. Each of the wagons had two yoke of oxen, and there was one yoke tied to the back of their supply wagon to be used in case something happened to one of their animals, or to alternate teams so as to keep the animals fresh. They also took a buckboard with a team of two mules, and again, two mules tied to the back. Michael's horse Blaze was also tied to the back of one of the wagons, as well as Magdalena's little red roan, Ginger. The buckboard carried a cage made of willow branches that contained seven good laying hens and one rooster. Magdalena would drive the buckboard, and Michael would drive the wagon that was used for their sleeping quarters and immediate personal belongings. Olivia would drive the chuck wagon that contained flour, coffee, tea, sugar, beans, apples, jerky, ham, bacon, and salt pork. On the last day of July, all of the wagons were loaded and ready to roll. There was much anticipation in the air. It was a mixture of emotions; some sadness, some excitement, and some fear.

Tomorrow they would start their journey.

Chapter XXIII

Wagons West

On the eve of their departure, there came a knock on the door of the hacienda. It was Captain Brooks, the leader in command of the wagon train. He was shown into the parlor for a conference with Don Sandoval.

"I assume that your wagons are ready to depart, sir," he said.

"You assume correct, Captain. Everything is ready to leave at first light."

"Then I am afraid that I may disappoint you with the news of a delay. It will be only a short delay, however. Some of my men just arrived in Santa Fe from El Paso, and I promised them a lay over to rest, and some good food before they were dispatched again. I am giving them two days. Also, I would like to speak with you about purchasing some fresh horses. I will need at least a dozen."

"I have some good saddle horses to spare," replied Don Sandoval. "My ranch hands have been working to ready them for the saddle for the past few weeks, and I have some fine horse trainers, as you know. So, you say a two day lay over?"

"Yes," replied Captain Brooks. "No more. I am as anxious as you to move this train to California. Mr. Brown and his family did not receive the news well. I am afraid that he has decided to take out on his own and not wait for the wagon train. I tried to discourage him, but he would not listen. The Natives along the Gila Trail are not at all peaceful at the moment. I am hoping that we can catch up with them at Las Cruces, but we have almost one hundred and fifty wagons enlisted, and most drawn with oxen. It will be a slow moving train. We will be lucky to make twelve miles in a day, and if I know Mr. Brown, he will drive his animals into the ground."

"Perhaps I can talk some sense into him," replied Don Sandoval.

"I'm afraid that its too late for that. He and his family have already set out. His wife was none too happy about it, either."

"Then I'm afraid there's nothing that either one of us can do at this point, except hope that the train catches up to them. Now let's go look at those horses, shall we?

The news of the delay was a disappointment to Magdalena, but Michael was happy for another two days with his mother and sister. Dona Maria was quite happy about the delay as well. It would give her more time to enjoy her granddaughter and go over last minute details that might have been overlooked.

The morning came at last, and the wagons were assuming their positions. Michael's wagons and buckboard were close to the front to the train, as was the chuck wagon driven by Olivia. They were heavily flanked by Cavalry, which was of some comfort to Dona Sandoval. She said one last tearful goodbye to Magdalena and Molly, and gave Magdalena a small leather bound book. It was a journal, filled with blank pages.

"I thought that you might want to keep a diary of your travels, like Susan Magoffin did."

"That is a splendid idea, Mama. I will do that. Thank you so much. I shall miss you. I love you, Mama!"

The morning was passing quickly, as the wagons took much time to get organized in all of the confusion. It was nearly ten thirty before the call of "wagons ho!" went echoing down from front to finish of the line.

Magdalena was in front of Michael driving the buckboard, Molly sitting next to her on the seat. She looked at Michael driving the covered wagon and smiled at him. He knew how excited she was to get started on their journey, and to see new places. She hadn't slept in nights, tossing and turning and talking constantly about California and their adventure west. Their route on the Gila Trail would take them along the Rio Grand for a substantial distance, guaranteeing them water, and grass for the cattle and horses for most of the way. At two thirty, the wagons were called to halt. They had traveled less than seven miles, but now that the wagons had taken their positions, Captain Brooks was confident that they would be able to make better distance the next day.

The train came to rest, and at once men were unhitching their stock to allow them graze. Women were busy collecting firewood and kindling; anything that would serve as fuel for their cooking fires. The children were happy for the chance to run and play amongst each other. Older children were enlisted in the chores of unpacking cooking utensils, and gathering wood. Olivia was busy preparing a meal for the many hands that she had to feed. Salt pork and beans with biscuits would be the dinner tonight. Some of the men took their guns and went hunting. Game birds and deer were plentiful in this area, and if they were successful, the next night they would be treated to a decent meal. It was still early in the day, and warm, so Magdalena took Molly to the river to bathe and wash out her diapers. She took off her boots and Molly's shoes, and Molly played in the wet sand on the banks of the Rio Grande while her mother rinsed out the soiled diapers. Michael was watching from a distance. He admired his wife so much. She had the traveler's spirit. Being raised with servants, cooks, and privileges all of her life never spoiled her or made her weak. She was so determined to be equal to the other folk on the train. It seemed to Michael that she even took delight in the toil and chores. He was to witness this in an even greater capacity as future days came to present. After Magdalena was finished with her little bit of washing for the day, she went to Olivia to see what she could do to help. Michael announced that he was going with two other men and try to find some game. While on the trail they would depend much on the natural resources, and it would not hurt to over-stock fresh meat, as there were many families on this particular wagon train that could benefit by their spoils. Some were very poor and had no firearms, or ammunition. Some were women with children traveling alone, all of what they owned on their single wagon. Some were even single women without food or shelter, going west where men out-numbered women ten-to-one. They were alone in the world, and hoping to find a man to settle with and make a family. Some were without wagons at all. Some were even without horses, having to walk the entire distance.

As the fires were lit, and the smells of biscuits, beans, and bacon cooking wafted through the camp, things seemed to settle down and become quiet. The quiet did not last for long, however. Women were cleaning up the pots and children were running about the camp. The line of wagons was more than half a mile long. From a distance, Magdalena could hear music. There was singing and fiddle playing, and laughter all about. She felt a sense of contentment, much the same as she had experienced sitting in front of the fire at Michael's camp site. As she and Olivia sat by the fire, Michael and one of the soldiers came riding into camp. Michael was on Blaze, and he led Ginger. There was an antelope on Ginger's back. Magdalena thought at the sight, "What a good little horse that I have, that she will pack a dead animal on her back without protest." Michael and the soldier dismounted and pulled the antelope off of Ginger's back. They turned their horses out to browse and water, and went straight to work skinning the animal that had been already field dressed. Michael, like Magdalena, felt a sense of satisfaction in his accomplishments. He thought back fondly of the time that he lived on the banks of the Santa Fe. They fed the offal to some dogs of the wagon party, and when their work was done, Michael and the soldier took a place by the fire, as while the women served them dinner that had been waiting for them.

"I could roast a small portion of that antelope now if you'd like, Michael," said Olivia.

"We'll save it for tomorrow," answered Michael. I'm much too tired to eat a big dinner tonight. Thank you anyway. I hope that you don't mind me inviting Andrew to eat with us."

"Not at all, there is plenty enough for one more mouth," she answered. "My mother always said, if there is enough to feed two, there is enough to feed four."

Magdalena was watching and listening as the conversation transpired. She could not help but notice Michael's new friend Andrew, watching Olivia and her every move. Olivia was also watching the young soldier, but not so noticeably. Magdalena understood what was happening. There was a magnetism between the two. She studied Olivia in the fire's glow. Olivia hadn't the time to go to the river to wash up like the others. Devoted to her agreement with Don Sandoval, she went right to work preparing dinner for the hungry emigrants as soon as they settled in camp. Olivia was stunning in the firelight. Her hair was pulled back, but wisps of wavy hair framed her wholesome face. Magdalena had never noticed before, but her friend was beautiful in a simple sort of way. Olivia was strong, and healthy. Her features were pure and plain. She had full lips, and almond shaped eyes. Her skin was slightly olive in color. She appeared darker in the light of the campfire, than she did in the sunlight. Again, Magdalena caught Andrew staring at Olivia. Baby Molly was sleeping peacefully in Magdalena's arms, and growing ever heavier by the moment.

"Olivia, if I put Molly to bed in the wagon will you listen for her? I would like to take a walk with Michael if that is agreeable with you."

"Of course I will listen for Molly. Go on then, you and Michael take your walk, but don't be too late. We will have to rise at first daylight tomorrow."

Magdalena laughed. "Of course Olivia. We shall not be long. Come Michael, I have something to discuss with you."

Magdalena took a pail that was tied to the side of the wagon. Together, she and Michael walked to the river a short distance away.

"The mosquitoes are horrible here," Magdalena said, as she swatted her arm.

"Is that what you wanted to discuss, Maggie?"

"No, of course not Michael. Tell me about your friend Andrew."

"There's nothing to tell, Maggie, except that he seems like an upstanding sort o' fellow."

"Will he be dining with us often?"

"Not if ya don't approve, Maggie. Why do you ask?"

"Haven't you noticed? He's attracted to Olivia."

"No, I hadn't noticed. Is that a bad thing?"

"No, Michael, it is not a bad thing. You may invite your friend Andrew to sup with us anytime. I like him. I think he would be good for Olivia."

"Now, Maggie, I think that we should mind our own business."

"Of course, Michael. We will see how things transpire. For now, I only wanted to give them some time alone together. You know, so that they might get acquainted."

Magdalena dipped the pail into the river to draw water. Together, she and Michael walked slowly, hand in hand, back to the campfire where Andrew and Olivia were still sitting and sharing a conversation. Magdalena poured the water into a pot and set it on the hot coals.

"I thought you might like some warm water to wash up in," she told

Olivia. "Since you didn't have time earlier."

"I would like that very much, Magdalena, but you mustn't fuss over me. I am your father's employee, and I should be taking care of you, not otherwise."

"Do not fret about it, Olivia. It was an excuse for Michael and me to have some time alone together. And besides, Michael needs some warm water to wash in as well."

Captain Brooks came riding up to the campsite and announced that the wagon train would be leaving at eight thirty in the morning, sharp. Anyone not ready would lose their place in line.

"We'll be ready," announced Michael.

"Private Anderson," said Captain Brooks, addressing Andrew, "Ride down the line and tell the other soldiers that we will be leaving at eight thirty sharp, and to spread the word."

"Yes sir," answered the soldier, arising to follow command.

Magdalena looked at Olivia. She wanted to visit with her for a while, but Michael told the ladies to hasten with their business and get some shut- eye. They would have to get up early the next day to have breakfast ready and move on. Most all of the cooking utensils were left out for the morning's meal. Olivia had already prepared extra biscuits that would be served with fresh butter and preserves for breakfast in the morning. Their big meal would be in the afternoon, when the wagons laid over.

As Michael and Magdalena lay in their covered wagon with baby Molly asleep in the corner, they spoke of the day's events. They had only traveled a short way, but it was a sample of life on the Gila Trail. They lay holding each other in total contentment. Michael thought of his antelope, and the good meal that it would make the next day. Together, they fell asleep holding each other to the sounds of music and singing. Magdalena stared out the small opening in the back of the wagon. She took to the stars, and the glow of the campfires, and they seemed to blend together. As her fatigue overcame her, she dozed to sleep thinking of the stories that her father told her when she was a young girl. Stories of the gypsies in Spain.

Chapter XXIV

Rattlesnake Stew

Morning arrived much too quickly, and Magdalena's rooster crowed his alarm that the hens were hungry and the cow needed to be milked. She nursed and changed Molly, and went straight to work finding her cow. Olivia, in the meantime, was brewing coffee and warming the biscuits for the morning meal. When Magdalena was finished milking the cow, she set the pail aside to let the cream come to the top. When it separated, she scooped the cream and put it in the butter churn and began to work it.

"Why do you waste your time?" asked Olivia.

"So that we might have fresh butter with our meal tonight. Why is that a waste of time? Do you not think that it would be nice to have on your biscuits, Olivia?"

"Of course I do," she replied. "But if you just hang the churn on the side of the chuck wagon, the bouncing of the wagon will do the work for you."

Magdalena stopped her work and gave Olivia's advice some thought.

"Does that really work?"

"Well, I guess we will find out, but there's work enough without making extra, so let's try it, shall we?"

At that moment, a gun shot rang out from the direction of several wagons behind. There was much commotion, horses nickering and women's anguished voices screaming. Magdalena scooped up Molly and ran to see what it was all about. She made her way through the crowd, and discovered the cause of the uproar. There, laying on the ground next to a wagon, was the largest rattlesnake that she had ever seen. She quickly tried to count the rattles, but a man bent down in front of her, and rapidly skinned the five or six foot snake. A woman approached the man and asked "What are your intentions for that snake, sir?"

"My intentions are to cure this skin and sell it for a nice price."

"But the snake itself, sir, what are you going to do with it?"

"I'll leave it for the coyotes. I have no use for such a thing."

"May I have it?" asked the woman. "I could use it in the stew pot tonight to feed my children. They are very hungry, and I have nothing else to offer them."

Magdalena studied the woman. She was young, but looked quite haggard. Her hair was loosely pulled into a bun on the back of her neck, with wispy locks falling loose in her face. Her skirt and blouse were filthy, and torn in places. Her waist was tiny even beneath her skirts and apron, and she appeared emaciated. She was holding an infant in her arms about the age of Molly, and had a little girl by the hand. The child looked to be about the age of five. A young boy about ten years old was standing behind the little girl. The lot of them looked like orphans from a Charles Dickens story; dirty, ragged, and starving. The boy had no shoes, and his trousers were much too short on him. The baby was lethargic, and the little girl was fussy. Magdalena had heard stories from the ranch hands about eating rattlesnakes. Although she had no desire to taste such a disdainful looking creature herself, she knew that it would provide this woman's family with meat for the night.

Magdalena approached the woman as she bent to pick up the dead snake. "Excuse me, Ma'am. My name is Magdalena."

The woman stared at her and waited for Magdalena to speak her business. She looked as though she was in no mood for meeting people or making friends.

Magdalena continued. "I am curious about the snake. How do you prepare it?"

"I throw it in a pot of boiling water with lots of carrots and potatoes and onions, and some barley to thicken the broth, that's what I do."

"Oh, that sounds wonderful. And is the meat tasty? Does it compare to anything?"

"It's very tasty, especially when I actually have carrots and potatoes and onions to add to it. It will provide my children with some broth and nourishment, and that is as much as I can expect for our dinner tonight."

Magdalena gave it some thought. "Well, Ma'am," she started.

"The name is Duncan, Eliza Duncan," the woman interrupted.

"Oh, may I call you Eliza?" There was no reply, only a long, uncomfortable silence. "Well, Eliza, I have always wanted to try rattlesnake, and never had the opportunity. Perhaps I can trade you some carrots and potatoes and a very large onion for a cup of your stew tonight?"

The woman let out a hearty laugh. "You mean to tell me that you want to trade good vegetables for snake stew?"

"Well, yes, I do. Would you be interested in the trade?"

"I'll be happy to take your food for a cup of my snake stew."

"Good then. Please follow me. Our wagon is just a short way up the line."

Together, the women walked to the chuck wagon without conversation. Magdalena instructed Olivia to give the woman twelve carrots, six potatoes, and a very large onion, while she fetched a tin cup to give her for the stew. As she approached the woman with her cup, Magdalena noticed the children looking at the pail of milk hanging from the chuck wagon, and the pile of biscuits and preserves on the tailgate.

"Would you like some?" asked Magdalena.

The children scattered toward the biscuits but were abruptly halted by their mother. "As much as it appears that you have more than you need, I will not accept charity, and we have nothing more to trade."

"We have thirteen wagons on this train, and many hired hands to feed. That is why there is so much food here. But yes, we can spare some. I wish that you would not look at it as charity, though. We must all band together on this wagon train and take care of each other."

Magdalena took a linen napkin and put half a dozen biscuits in it and a jar of her mother's preserves. She neatly brought the four corners together and tied it at the top. "Here. Please take it so that I may feel free some day to call on you if I need a favor."

The little girl was pulling on her mother's apron. "Take it Mama, please. I'm hungry."

Reluctantly, Eliza held her hand out and received the napkin from Magdalena. "Well, since you put it like that, I will. My daughter will give me no peace if I don't accept the biscuits, but only if you promise to come see me if you need anything. I can help with your baby."

"Oh, I promise. I am looking forward to getting to know you and your family. And, my cow gave me a good amount of milk this morning, so when you send your children back with my linen, tell them to bring their cups and I will give each one a cup full of milk to wash down Olivia's dry biscuits with."

The woman left and went back to her campsite. She had only one scrawny horse, and another scrawny burrow, that carried what little supplies they had. The two older children would ride together or take turns on the horse while Eliza led it, while she carried the infant in a shawl in front of her.

The children sat down on a blanket that was spread in front of a measly fire and devoured the biscuits and preserves, while their mother, in the meantime, put the snake in a skillet and fried it in some beef suet. After they had eaten the snake with their biscuits and preserves, the two older children, feeling much revived, ran back to Magdalena with the linen and their cups. They drank as much milk as they could, filling their cups over and over again. Their mother had remained behind with her infant. Had she gone with them, she would have had to protest their mercenary behavior, and she did not have the heart to deprive her starving children of the much needed nourishment. Magdalena took the linen and cut a large roast from the leg of the antelope. She wrapped the meat in the linen and sent it back to Eliza with the two small children. After filling each of their cups one last time, she instructed the children that they must save that milk for their baby sister.

When the children arrived back at the campsite where their mother was waiting, they gave her the meat and the milk. Their mother drank down one cup so quickly that the milk was streaming from the corners of her mouth, leaving a track of dirt and trail dust on each side of her drawn face. After wiping her mouth with the back of her hand, she took a small sip from the next cup, and then offered it to the starving baby. Her own milk had almost completely dried up from lack of nourishment, and she had very little to offer her infant. That night she would make a fine stew. She would cut up some antelope meat in very tiny fine pieces to trick Magdalena into believing that she was eating snake stew, since the snake had already been consumed by her ravenous children.

As Olivia was cleaning up after the morning meal, and Michael was hitching up the cattle and mules, Magdalena took a pail and walked down to the river where she had seen wild black currants growing the evening before. She picked one and ate it to test its readiness. It was sweet and ripe. She hurried to fill her pail as full as she could before the wagons started to roll again. Molly played along side of her as she picked and sampled the wild currants. If the train halted early enough in the day, she would bake pies in the small portable iron stove that she had brought along. She would have to bake four or five to feed all of the hands, and she could only fit one in the stove's small oven at a time. But given the time and a little luck, she would have them all ready by the time dinner was over. It would be a special treat. She heard the call of "wagons ho in ten minutes!" and ran quickly to take up place upon the seat of the buckboard with Molly beside her. Before long, the wagons were moving again. This day, everything was far more organized.

As the train moved slowly along, Magdalena took in the beauty of the New Mexico Territory. It was a wondrous place that she was leaving, but still, she had no reservations about seeing, and settling in a new place. She let her mind wander and daydream about the future. She thought about what the Captain had told them earlier. He didn't want to stop the train until they had gone at least fifteen miles. They needed to average ten miles a day or more to meet their schedule. Magdalena knew that in order to make fifteen miles, it would cut into her pie making. If need, she could put it off for one more day. Then she remembered when her mother taught her how to make a strudel. If the big pans would fit in her little oven, she could make two or three strudels in less time than four or five pies. It would all depend on the size of the little oven. She remembered something else the Captain had said. They might see Indians this day, but not to be alarmed. They were not the type of Indians that would cause any threat, more just a nuisance. He said that the Indians who lived in these parts where beggars, and at times horse thieves, but not hostile. Magdalena kept her eyes peeled. Just as her daydreams were taking her away, she heard the sound of a child calling to her.

"Mrs. Malone!" She looked down to see Eliza's young son.

"Where is your little sister?" inquired Magdalena.

"She's ridin' on the horse. It's my turn to walk," he responded. "It's almost always my turn to walk. Mama says because I'm older, and I'm a boy, and that means I'm stronger."

Magdalena called back to him. "Can you climb up here while the cart is moving? I do not want you to hurt yourself, but there is room for one more here next to Molly and me."

"Yes ma'am!" he replied with enthusiasm.

In spite of his undernourished self, the young boy was nimble and riding next to Molly before Magdalena ever had a chance to tell him to be careful. Molly knew that the wagons would not stop for a noon meal. They had been instructed to eat well in the morning because there would only be time for two meals a day, if that. In anticipation, she had packed some cheese and bread and ripe green apples for Molly and herself. She reached down to the floorboard and brought the basket up to the seat.

"Are you hungry?" she asked the boy, not knowing if he had eaten anything that morning.

"Well, yes ma'am, I sort of am, but my mother told me not to be beggin' or making a pest of myself. She said that we will eat good tonight."

"Ah, yes indeed," replied Magdalena. "Rattlesnake stew."

"Yes ma'am," the boy replied in a sheepish manner. He knew the truth of it, that the rattlesnake had already been eaten, but he would keep his mother's secret.

"Well, there is some cheese and bread, and a couple of apples in that basket if you want any, and you are not a bother to me if you have a little. What is your name boy?" she asked.

"Seamus," replied the boy. "But sometimes my mother calls me Shameful instead. She's just foolin' really, but sometimes when she calls me that, she's really very mad at me. Mama is mad most all the time though."

"Why is that?" asked Magdalena.

"I don't know. I guess she's mad at my father for runnin' off. He went to California over a year ago to find gold. He said that he'd send for us. He said that he'd send money. But he never sent nothin' all this time, and the money my ma had all ran out. She took in sewing for a while and made a little money, but then she ran out of thread and needles. She had to decide one day to buy thread and needles, or eggs and soup bones to feed us. She says hateful things about my father all the time. I guess because I'm the only boy, I remind her of him. Those are some of the times she calls me Shameful."

"Well Seamus, you are not shameful at all. It is no fault of your own anything that your father has done, or your mother for that matter. And besides, maybe something happened to him. Maybe he could not write. Maybe he came down sick, or something. Anything could have happened."

"That's sort of what I was thinkin' too, ma'am," he said as he reached into the basket and produced a ripe green apple. He looked at the apple then held it out toward Magdalena as to offer it to her. She looked at his filthy hands and almost declined, but then thought about it again. Taking the apple from him she rubbed it on her dress. "Don't mind if I do," she said, taking a bite and giving the boy a wink.

Seamus pulled another apple from the basket and followed Magdalena's example, wiping it on his filthy shirt, and then taking a large bite from it. "Mmmm, I ain't had an apple in as long a time as I can recall. This is almost as good as eating apple pie."

Magdalena admired the spirit in this young urchin. He had so much to be angry for, and yet, his attitude was admirable. He seemed so carefree. He took another bite of his apple and noticed Magdalena staring at him with a smile on her face. He flashed a huge grin in her direction. She laughed at him and said "you remind me of the Cheshire cat in a story I recently read."

"What's a Cheshire cat?" he asked.

"It is a cat that has a smile so big, that when he smiles the rest of him seems to disappear, and all that you see is his big happy smile."

"Sometimes I wish that I could disappear," he replied.

"Me too," answered Magdalena, with a concern for the boy.

Molly was growing sleepy, and ready for her mid morning nap. She crawled down on the floor board of the buckboard where she curled up on her blanket and went to sleep. Magdalena had decided that the next day Molly would ride with Michael in the wagon. It would be much more comfortable for her, and she could play and move around more.

The train kept a slow and steady pace on the well worn trail, and Magdalena wondered how many miles they had gone. Her back was starting to stiffen, and she was anxious to stretch and move around. She had enjoyed the company of her little companion, Seamus. It was a nice diversion. She looked to the sun and knew that it was past noon. Then she looked all around to see if she could spot any signs of Indians.

"Do your chickens give you eggs?" asked Seamus. "Or are you going to eat them?"

"Heavens no!" said Magdalena. "They are layers. When we get to California I will let the eggs hatch so that we can have even more layers, and maybe a few fryers. There is no need for more than one obnoxious rooster after all. How old are you, Seamus?"

"I think I'm eleven, but maybe I'm twelve. I can't rightly remember when my birthday is, and neither can Ma."

"I see," said Magdalena, noticing his small stature.

Just then she heard the Captain's command. "Wagons halt!" The command was echoed down the line.

"Thank goodness," she said. "I doubt that my back would have taken another hour on this trail."

"I best get back to my mother before she comes a lookin' fer me. She's gonna bring you some snake stew tonight, so I'll be seein ya later if she lets me come with her. Thank you again for the apple, ma'am!"

"I will be seeing you later then, Seamus. I cannot wait to try rattlesnake stew! Tell your mother that I look forward to it!"

Magdalena took Molly down to the river, and took a pail for water with her. Michael went right to work unhitching the animals to turn them out. He noticed Seamus leading the poor old horse and burrow to the river for water. Neither animal was traveling to well, and both were so emaciated that their ribs were showing. After he was finished with his teams, he walked back to Cotton where he was just finishing turning out his teams as well. "Cotton, do you think that you could have Charlie look at that woman's horse's feet? I think they should be trimmed and shod. Just look at how that old horse travels, poor thing."

"I'll have Charlie look at them, but I'd advise you not to be too charitable. Before you know it, that woman and her children will be latched to you like a bunch of ticks, sucking the life out of you."

"If her animals go lame, then what? Will we just leave her and the children on the trail?"

"Well, I suppose you do have a good point there."

"Anyway, my wife would never turn her back on those hungry children. She'd go t' bed hungry herself before she'd let a child go to bed hungry."

"Well, that is one of your wife's many good qualities, Michael. I'll see to the woman's horses straight away."

Magdalena put the water on to boil. She would make tea, and with the rest of the water she would sponge herself and the baby off. Her eyes and nose were full of dirt, and so was her hair, but that would have to wait until they laid over longer. Olivia was busy roasting large cuts of the antelope. She had a feeling that with the way that Michael and Magdalena were inviting dinner guests to feed with them, she'd be needing extra. If it wasn't eaten that night for dinner, it would go in the baskets on the wagons for snacks and be eaten cold the next day in bread with butter. She rubbed the meat with olive oil and garlic, and stoked the hot coals to break them down. Then she skewered the meat and hung it over the coals on two forked poles stuck in the ground, turning it occasionally while she boiled beans in a pot that she placed directly into the fire. She added onions, tomatoes, and green chilies to the beans. Magdalena offered her a cup of tea, and after she washed up, she started on her black currant strudel. She noticed Eliza walking her children down to the river. She was cleaning their hands and faces with her linen napkin. Soon, the camp was filled with the smell of wood smoke and dinners cooking. The children seemed to take everything in stride. To them it was one big adventure; a church picnic, or camp out. They were running and laughing and climbing trees while their parents took care of whatever needed to be done. Cotton and Michael approached the chuck wagon.

"Will your friend Andrew be joining us for dinner tonight again, Michael?" Magdalena inquired.

"I haven't asked him. Should I?"

"You had better ask Olivia first, do you think?"

Olivia had already been keenly listening, but displaying no interest. "Go ahead and ask him if you like. What is one more mouth? It is nothing to me, and anyway, I put on a healthy portion of meat and beans."

Michael smiled, and was about to say something, when he noticed Charlie walking toward them.

"I've done the best that I can with that woman's horse. The old mare has one hoof cracked clean to the coffin bone. It's a wonder it can walk at all. The horse's feet show signs of a bad diet, too, but I did some corrective shoeing and we'll just have to see what happens. The hooves are very soft and they might not even hold a shoe. The burrow wasn't so bad; I just trimmed him up a bit.

"Did Eliza offer you any resistance?"

"Not a bit. She was very grateful. In fact, she invited me to dinner tonight, and I accepted."

"Oh really?" Magdalena and Michael looked at each other. "Did she tell you what they were having?" asked Magdalena.

"Stew," replied Charlie.

~*~

Around the chuck wagon, dinner was just finishing up when Charlie and Eliza strolled up together with the children. Eliza had a change of blouse on, and had removed her apron and combed out her hair. She looked much improved from earlier that morning. The children also had been washed up.

"We brung you some stew like I promised," said Eliza.

"Oh! I cannot wait to try it. Thank you so much."

"I think you're gonna like it," said Charlie. "I thought it was quite tasty, myself."

Magdalena dipped her spoon in to the cup. Reluctantly, she brought a small taste up to her mouth and blew on it as to cool it down, and then she tasted it. "Mmm, you are right, Charlie. This is delicious! Eliza you have turned a rattlesnake into a tasty stew. It is just wonderful! Well, please sit down and have some coffee. I hope you have brought your cups with you."

"Seamus, run back to the campsite and fetch the tin cups!" demanded Eliza. The boy was off like a dart, and soon he returned. Magdalena was just finishing up her stew, and Olivia was cutting the strudel. While they ate their strudel and drank their coffee, the children finished off the milk and devoured their servings of dessert.

"If I had known my kids could have eaten so well on a wagon train, I would have signed up months ago," said Eliza.

"We are only too happy to share," answered Magdalena.

They sat around the campfire enjoying their new found friends. There was talk of dreams for the future, and they listened to the gypsy music coming from further down the line. Everyone seemed content, especially Eliza. She was a different woman. In the course of a day, she had changed from angry and suspicious, to happy and affable. After some time had passed, she announced that she needed to get back to her camp and bed down the children. Charlie offered to walk her to her campsite, and she accepted.

"I just want a moment to speak to Magdalena," she said. "In private."

"Of course," said Magdalena. Together they walked a short distance and paused under a stand of cottonwoods.

"I want to say thank you for bein' good to me and my children. I think you're right, we all need to take care of each other on this train. I know that you've done most of the caring so far, but I'd be proud to call you my friend. Thank you for sending Charlie over to take care of my horses today. He's wonderful. And the Captain gave me a small tent so my kids and I don't have to sleep out in the open. My little girl Annie is so afraid of the wolves."

"And rightfully so! Well, Eliza, I am proud to call you my friend, also. I hope that we shall be friends for years to come." She took Eliza by the arm and began the walk back to the campfire. "I am so happy that this day has been good for you. It has been good for me as well. Your son Seamus kept me company for a good part of our trip today. If not for him, I think I would have died of boredom! He is quite the young man."

"Yes, well, he's quite smitten with you as well, I'm afraid. Now don't let him eat all your provisions. He has already eaten more today than he normally eats in a week!"

Eliza and Charlie disappeared into the night with the children. Molly had worn herself out playing, and was already sleeping in the back of the wagon when Magdalena returned.

"Thank you for putting Molly to bed," she told her husband. "Now I think we should retire as well. We have a big day tomorrow, and I am stuffed! I ate two dinners tonight, did you realize that? The rattlesnake stew was not at all bad, either."

Michael gave a hearty laugh. "Well," he said, "I have it from a good source that the rattlesnake was their breakfast this morning. What was in that stew was the antelope you gave her, and a bunch of carrots and potatoes and one very large onion."

"No! Do not tell me! Well, I am relieved in about that, Michael, and I think that I shall sleep much easier knowing. The thought of eating that disgusting reptile almost made me lose both dinners. Thank you for telling me."

"Well, you have to keep it a secret that I told you."

"I promise. Michael, have you noticed that Eliza's baby girl acts nothing like Molly? She is so small and lethargic. Do you think that she is sick?"

"I do not know, Maggie, but perhaps she just needs some better food than she has been getting. We will see to that. Now get some sleep. I heard the Captain say that we would try to make another fifteen miles tomorrow.

Her kissed her good night, and in another moment, they were both sleeping soundly.

Chapter XXV

The Layover

In the next two days, the wagon train began to fall into a steady routine. Folks on the train were becoming acquainted. There were emigrants from many parts of the country, as well as from other countries. Magdalena was fascinated by the Gypsies from Spain, after hearing her father's stories about them since she was a little girl. They were very resourceful, and grateful for all that they had, even though their possessions were meager. She admired that greatly, and decided that she herself, wanted to be more like them. She noticed how they loved their families and bound closely together as a community. They seemed to relish and appreciate everything, no matter how small or insignificant, like a bird singing, or a colorful sunset. In the evening after a long day on the trail, they would gather together and sing and dance and rejoice in another fine day.

After their chores were finished, and Molly was put to bed in the back of the wagon, Michael and Magdalena would wander down the line of campers. They would introduce themselves to the others on the train, and see how they were managing. They took note in what they were eating, and how they were tolerating being the trail. Magdalena recalled Susan Magoffin's journal, and how she spoke very little of distressful situations, even though there must have been plenty. The poor young woman had miscarried, and contracted Yellow Fever on the trail, which would years later claim her life. When she and her husband became stuck in Mexico at the start of the Mexican war, Susan Magoffin took care not to reveal too much in her journals, lest they be ceased by the enemy. Magdalena admired her greatly, and followed her example of writing in her own journal almost every night.

The wagon train was marking good time on the well traveled Gila Trail, charting fifteen or more miles each day. One afternoon, when the train stopped, Captain Brooks announced that they would lay over the next day, and afford the travelers a restful Sabbath. He would preside over Sunday services for anyone who cared to attend. This would also allow the animals time to rest and feed, and the people on the train time to bath and wash clothes, or tend to any other chores that needed attention. Magdalena was looking forward to the break and to having time to socialize, as were the others. That night at dinnertime, things seemed more relaxed. Nobody was in a big hurry to get things cleaned up or put away after dinner, because they knew that they would be laying over the whole next day. The water here was good, and there was plenty of grass for the cattle and horses. By Monday afternoon, they would be in Albuquerque. There, the people on the train would be able to buy any provisions that they might need from the villagers. Magdalena was looking forward to it. She still held out hope of finding her brother, even though she had finally accepted that his death was probable.

Sunday morning came, and Molly mercifully slept a bit longer than she normally did. Magdalena took advantage of the break, and slept in herself. She awoke much refreshed. Michael had already milked the cow and set her loose again to feed. She had lost weight in the short time they had been traveling, and he knew that she needed good, rich fodder to keep up her milk supply. Olivia had gathered the eggs and prepared breakfast, so that when Molly and Magdalena emerged from the wagon, all that was left to do was enjoy the food that Olivia had prepared. After breakfast, Andrew called on Olivia, and together they walked toward the river. A romance between the two young people, appeared to be in full blossom. Charlie also was showing an interest in Eliza, but it would never be more than a friendship.

Eliza was still married, and although she had little interest in rejoining her husband, she needed to find out what had become of him before she would entertain the idea of a new man in her life. Still, Charlie took her under his wing, and helped her as much as he possibly could with the daily routines of being on the trail.

Magdalena was just finishing up her breakfast when Seamus came running up to their campsite.

"Something's wrong with the baby, and Mama's acting strange! Can you come, Mrs. Malone?"

"Of course!" she replied.

"I'll go with you," Michael said.

Michael picked up Molly, and together they hurried to Eliza. She was sitting on the blanket, clutching the bundle in her arms and looking straight ahead, never acknowledging their presence.

Magdalena bent down to address her. "What is it, Eliza?" There was no reply.

"Eliza, give me the baby."

"No! No! No! You are not going to take her away from me. She is mine! She is sleeping now. Do not disturb her!"

"Eliza, give me your baby," Magdalena said in a stern yet steady voice. "Let me take care of her while you tend to your other children."

Eliza reluctantly handed the baby to Magdalena. "There is nothing that you can do for my baby now."

Magdalena received the baby from her mother and knew instantly that Eliza was right. It was too late. The tiny baby girl had passed away in her sleep that night. Magdalena handed the bundle back to her mother. "I am very sorry Eliza, but you must say your goodbyes. Michael and the men will prepare a grave for your baby. Seamus, you and Annie come with me. You will have some breakfast at our wagon this morning.

"Is the baby dead, Mrs. Malone?"

"Yes Seamus, I am sorry, but I am afraid that she is. She was just too weak, but she will be happy now, and never have want for food again."

She sat Eliza's children down with a plate of food, and walked over to where Michael was standing with Cotton and Charlie. Charlie started running toward Eliza's camp when Michael told him of the news. When Magdalena had caught up to Michael, she buried her face in his chest and began to sob. He was still holding baby Molly. A tear came to his eye as the three of them clutched one and other. Then Molly's little voice said "Mama," and Magdalena cried even harder.

"Oh, Michael, I could never bear it if anything happened to our baby."

"Neither could I, Maggie, but we have a healthy happy baby, and nothin' will happen to her. Now, I have to go help the men make a grave. You pull yerself t'gether, and go to Eliza with her children in an hour. Charlie is with her now. We will all be there with her when she lays the baby to rest.

"Alright, Michael."

Magdalena cleaned up the plates when the children had finished their breakfast. Then she took the little ones to the river and washed them up. She looked in the direction of where the men were making a grave. She could see a crowd gathering, and she knew that there were many people tending to Eliza, and that they would be there for her support when they put the baby in the ground.

"It is time to go now. We will have a funeral for the baby," she said to the children. "You know, I did not even know her name."

"Mama never named her," Seamus said. "She was born after Pa left, and she said she would let Pa name her when he came home. We just called her 'baby'."

Magdalena took Eliza's little girl by the hand. She carried Molly, and together she and the children walked toward the grave site. Captain Brooks said a few words, and Michael placed the baby in the grave. She was bundled up in her blanket, but there was no coffin. The Captain knew that they could take the baby to Albuquerque the next day and give her a proper burial, but that would put the train behind and require donations from the already poor emigrants. It would be better this way. Eliza began to wail as they shoveled dirt on the baby's little body. When the hole was half filled, rocks were placed in it, and then more dirt. Charlie drove the modest wooden cross that he had made into the ground, and two soldiers trampled the grave with their horses. In doing so, it was the hoped that the wolves or coyotes would not discover, and disturb it, but there was no guarantee. Someone began to sing. It was a low, melancholy, yet melodious voice, in a language not understood by most nearby. The song however was understood. It was a sendoff. It was a welcome. It was comforting. The gypsy women cried as though the baby was one of their own. Eliza and the children were invited back to the chuck wagon to sit for a while, but Eliza refused, wanting to be alone with her children. They went back to where her tent was set up. For the rest of the day, people from the train stopped to pay their condolences and bring food to the impoverished mother and her poor children. What had planned to be a enjoyable Sunday for Magdalena and her family had turned out to be a sorrowful day. Magdalena spent the rest of the day with Molly and Michael down by the river. They sat quietly and talked until Olivia came to fetch them for the afternoon meal. They would eat a little earlier this day, and prepare for and early start again in the morning.

The next morning the camp began to bustle quite early. Magdalena went to check on Eliza and found her sitting next to her baby's grave. She had been there all night.

"Come and have some coffee with me, Eliza."

Eliza stood. She went to the little tent and woke up her children. "Seamus, go fetch the horses. We have to leave soon."

As the child obeyed his mother's instructions, Magdalena looked around Eliza's campsite. All of the food that had been given to her the previous day had been left out all night. It had been pillaged by varmints, and her meager provisions were scattered all about the site. Annie crawled out of her nest in the tent, and Eliza went straight to work taking the tent down. Magdalena gathered up their belongings and laid them neatly by the pack saddle. She then took the little girl by the hand and started walking toward the chuck wagon, Eliza following with her tin cups. They shared some breakfast, and Seamus came with the horses just in time to join them. Before long all were regrouped, and headed out on the Gila Trail once again. Molly rode in the wagon with her father, and Seamus rode with Magdalena. Eliza led her horse and mule with Annie perched on the back of the horse.

Magdalena and Seamus rode for a long period in silence. Now, whenever they passed a grave marker along the side of the trail, it held new meaning for Magdalena.

That afternoon, around two o'clock, the wagon train was called to a halt at the edge of the town of Albuquerque. Town's people in arrived to greet the wagons in an effort to peddle their wares. Some sold bright red rebozos, and multi-colored serapes. Others sold leather zapatos, belts, tooled spur straps, and gun holsters. There were baskets, and pots, and ristas of dried red chilies.

"Michael, can we walk to town and have dinner there today? I think it might be nice to get away from the train for a little while, and I would not mind shopping. Would you mind if I spent a little of our wedding money?"

"Of course not, Maggie, you know you don't need to ask me that. Wha' tis it that you want to buy?"

"Seamus told me that he does not know when his birthday is. He said that he has never had a birthday party. I thought that I might buy him and Annie some new clothes, and perhaps a couple of toys. One night when we lay over, we can throw them a birthday party, and invite everyone in the camp."

"I think that sounds like a wonderful idea, Magdalena. I'll just go get Molly's perambulator and we will go."

Magdalena put a fresh diaper on Molly and wrapped her in a clean blanket. She told Olivia not to expect them for dinner. They were planning on having some good Mexican food in town. She was missing her mother's cooking. In town she and Michael bought Annie two little dresses of calico, and some undergarments, and ribbons for her hair. They bought her some good sturdy boots and stockings, and a doll that the local Indians had made. They purchased boots and stockings for Seamus, and two blouses and two pair of trousers. They also bought him a tooled leather belt, in case the pants were too loose in the waist. After they were finished shopping, they went to a small café. It was plain on the inside, with dirt on the floors. The shutters on the windows were all open, and the air was warm and a bit stifling. Flies were buzzing all around, yet the wonderful smells still attracted them. They ate enchiladas stuffed with cheese and pork with a savory green chili sauce, and frijoles, and they drank lemonade. When they were ready to take their leave, they ordered four dozen tamales to take back to the trail hands. On the way back to camp they came upon a man selling ponchos and serapes, and Magdalena bought a brightly colored serape for Eliza. They put it in Molly's perambulator, along with all of the packages wrapped in brown paper, and Michael carried Molly the rest of the way on his shoulders.

When they arrived back at the camp, people were settled into their normal nightly routine. Olivia was putting up the pots and utensils that she used that evening. Magdalena gave her the tamales to disperse, and she and Michael took Molly into the wagon and readied themselves for bed. The weather was growing increasingly warmer, and the canvas over the wagon held in the warm air and blocked the breeze. Michael loosened up the canvas in the back of the wagon to let the breeze in. As the sun started to fade, the flies left the wagon and mosquitoes assumed their positions.

"I wish that we could replace this canvas with Spanish lace," Magdalena said. "It would be much cooler, and we could keep it all tied up to keep the flies and mosquitoes out."

"Maybe you can invent it," said Michael. "It sounds like a good idea, but I doubt it would last long out on the trail. Hurry up and finish in your journal, Maggie, and come to bed."

Chapter XXVI

The Browns

The next day the wagon train set out on time, and Captain Brooks expected that they would accomplish a few good miles that day. He knew that on this particular day, they would enter real Indian Territory, and that the Indians were not at all friendly or content at the moment. It would be a dangerous stretch. The next town they would come to would be Socorro, with only a few small villages in between and along the way. It would take a week to get there, by the Captains calculations. He passed the word around to the men folk on the train, and told the soldiers to be especially aware of their surroundings from this point on. They would be relatively safe in the towns and Forts along the way, but in between they would have to be ready for anything, at anytime. Captain Brooks reminded the soldiers that they were there to protect the wagon train, and he wanted the troops spread out evenly from the front of the train to the back. He told them not to worry the women folk about the Indians, but to stay especially close to women and children traveling alone.

About twelve miles into their journey that day, a wagon was spotted on the side of the trail. Captain Brooks sent two sentries ahead to check it out. A short while later they rode back at a gallop.

"Indians!" one of them cried out. "They killed the emigrants!"

"Keep your voices down, men!" commanded Captain Brooks. "I do not want you arouse the wagon train into a panic."

"Yes sir! There are a man and a woman dead, sir, and the man is badly mutilated and stripped naked. Their wagon has been ransacked."

"Are there any survivors? Did you check inside the wagon for children?"

"Yes sir! There are no survivors, sir!"

"Well then, there is nothing that I can do for them. When the train reaches them, we will stop the head of the train there, and let it stand by long enough for us to bury the dead. There is no way that we can keep the situation from the women folk now. They will all be edgy, but maybe it is better to have more eyes watching for those red skinned heathens."

Just before the wagons reached the massacre scene, Captain Brooks called for a halt. He ordered one of the soldiers to pass along the train that they were going to rest for an hour or so. He then dismounted, and took a detail to survey the situation closer.

"It is Mr. Brown, and his wife," said Captain Brooks. "They haven't been dead very long. They had three young daughters with them. I will need a detail to go find the Indians that committed this atrocity, and bring back the girls."

He organized a detail and instructed the soldiers that time was essential.

"It was a small band of Indians who committed this heinous act, but they will soon be reunited with their tribe. It is important that you overtake them before they reunite. The lives of those girls depend on it, as well as your own. I won't hold the train up for you, so when you find those girls and return them, and you will find them, head South toward Socorro."

As the soldiers were preparing the graves for the two adults, the curious emigrants began to mill about, and talk among themselves. In the rear of the train, only the soldiers knew of the situation. The emigrants had no idea what was happening, only that the procession had come to a halt. Michael and Magdalena's wagon was stationed in the forward section of the train. They were able to see the Brown's wagon on the side of the trail. Clothes and provisions were scattered about. They decided to take a closer look to find out what was happening. The first body they sighted was a woman's. She was lying face down with an arrow in her back. Magdalena gasped and turned her head. The Captain approached them.

"She must have seen us coming and tried to run for it," said Captain Brooks. "The Indians must have seen us, too, it appears that they left in a hurry. They can't be too far from here. I only hope that my soldiers catch up to them quickly. The Indians have taken their little daughters."

"How do you know this?" asked Magdalena.

"It's Mrs. Brown, Ma'am. Her husband is over there a few rods away, but I do not suggest you go over there; it is an ugly sight what they did to him. I see that the soldiers are taking his body to be buried now. I would like to get this wagon train moving as soon as possible. There will be no formalities I'm afraid."

Mr. Brown's body had been stripped naked, and horribly mutilated. He had been sliced from his chest cavity to his pubic bone, and disemboweled; his genitals shoved into his gaping mouth. There were slices in the skin of the entire length of both his arms, and legs. The poor man's organs were strewn around him, and from the look on his face, his eyes bulging, the heinous deed was most likely committed while he was still alive.

Magdalena was horrified. She knew the Browns well. They were friends of the family, and Mr. Brown conducted business with her father. She stared in disbelief at the body of Mrs. Brown who laid close by. The soldiers were coming to retrieve her corpse for burial. One soldier put his boot on her back and pulled the arrow from her lifeless body, so that she could be turned over and buried face up. When they turned her over, Magdalena screamed at the sight. Tied up in Mrs. Brown's shawl, against her chest, was her infant daughter. The Captain ran to the baby and picked up the tiny bundle.

"Had we arrived just a short time sooner, she may have been saved," he said. "She has suffocated under her mother's weight and there is nothing that we can do for her now." He looked in the direction that his soldiers were traveling, and silently offered a short prayer that they return with the two remaining daughters. Magdalena spotted something lying underneath the wagon. At first glance she thought that it may be a child's body, but instead it was only a doll. She picked it up in hopes that the girls would be returned, and that it might bring some comfort to them if they were. The mules that pulled the Brown's wagon had been stolen by the Indians, so the Captain ordered one of his soldiers to hitch up a team of Army mules to the wagon and bring it along. The girls would be needing it when they were brought back. It was in fact, the only remainder of their past. The infant was buried with her mother, and when the task was completed, Captain Brooks wasted no time in rolling the wagons. They traveled another four miles before he halted the train. He had wanted to put more miles behind them, but he knew that the animals and emigrants needed to rest. Four miles was nothing for Indians to ride at a speedy pace on their Mustangs, but the wagon train moved much more slowly, and the animals were greatly taxed. He called a meeting with the soldiers at suppertime to discuss strategies and appoint pickets. He ordered the emigrants to be silent this evening. There was to be no music, no dancing. He wanted everyone bedded down early, and they would leave at first light. No campfires that night, and no breakfast in the morning.

The night passed without incident, with the exception of Eliza's old mare giving out, and dying. Captain Brooks bound to Eliza's aid.

"There will be no time for dressing out that animal I'm afraid. Tie up your burro to the Brown's wagon and put your children and provisions inside. If you can drive, I will appoint you to drive that wagon for now."

"I can drive," she replied.

To her, the mare dying was a God-send. She would not have to walk this day, and hopefully, ever again on this journey. It would make the journey much more comfortable for the children and herself. It was a very fine wagon that the Brown's had had, and it was roomy inside. If the Indians had not seen the emigrants coming, they would have burned it. There were still many provisions inside of it; furniture, a small stove, and fine warm feather mattresses. Eliza was sympathetic to the loss of the Brown's and the kidnapping of their little girls, but still, their misfortune was to her benefit.

The wagons began to roll out in a slow and somber manner. The quietness was making Magdalena anxious. Occasionally, a cry of a baby, or the barking of a dog, would break the silence, but nothing more. It was windy, and the weather was quite warm. The livestock had not been unhitched to eat or drink, the night before. As the wagons rolled slowly over the Gila Trail, the animals were tiring. The tongues of the oxen were hanging from their mouths, and their noses and eyes were filed with dust from the trail. Dust storms were common in this part of the country, and things seemed unsettling to Magdalena, as though the sky would break open at any moment, and it's fury would rein down upon the travelers.

They passed many crude grave markers, and Magdalena noticed every one of them. Once, she looked back at Michael behind her, and noticed him cross himself as they passed three makeshift graves. She missed the company of Seamus, but was thankful that Molly slept in the wagon most of this day. She looked down at the basket that she had packed with cold food, but was not in the mood for it. Eventually, the wagon train came to the edge of the town of Socorro. Captain Brooks did not want to leave the wagons in the rear vulnerable to attack, so he pulled the train into town and halted it dead in the center. He sent word that the train would halt for an hour or two to recruit and water the livestock. The emigrants needed to take their pails to the river and carry them one by one to their thirsty animals. Over and over again they made their way to the river and back. While Magdalena was carrying her pails to the river and back, it suddenly occurred to her that this was the location that the supply train that her brother was on had been attacked. Socorro, yes, that is why the name sounded familiar. This was where her brother had died. As the town people came to greet the wagon with their goods to sell, Magdalena began to ask questions. She wanted to talk to someone who knew something about the attack. She approached a man and asked him "Sir, do you remember a supply wagon coming here a few years ago that was attacked by Indians?"

"Yes," he replied. "I remember it well."

"Were there any survivors?"

"No, there were no survivors. Not a one. What the Indians did to those men was an abomination. No one lived to speak about it. The people in town could hear the commotion from their homes, but we were all too afraid to come out of our houses. Afterward, it was very, very quiet, but we were still afraid to come out. The next day, when we thought it was safe, we ventured out. The Apaches were gone by then, probably many miles away. Every person in town went to see. The men from the wagon train were all scattered about, dead on the ground. They were all naked and mutilated. Their boots and uniforms had been stripped from them, and stolen. There was nothing much left in the wagons, and most were still smoldering from being set afire. Now, the Apaches are all pissed off. First the Spaniards pissed them off, and then the Mexicans, but it is the white people who piss them off the most, and they are out for revenge. You people best be watching for them," the old man said while shaking a feeble finger at Magdalena. "Where is this train going, anyway?"

Magdalena did not answer. She was still assimilating what the old man had told her. The pain was apparent on her face.

"What happened to the men? Did you bury them? How did you identify them?" she asked.

"We could not identify them. We sent word to Albuquerque that a small supply train had been attacked. It was very hot, and by the next day the bodies were stinking in the hot sun, and their blood was drying on the ground of our village. The coyotes were coming, and the buzzards. We buried them in one big grave and held a service at the church for them. Many candles were lit. Many women of the village cried for them.

"Where is it? Where is the grave?" she demanded.

"It is right on the south edge of town," answered the old man as he pointed his boney finger toward the west. "You will pass right by it on your way out of town. There is a boulder that marks the spot, but that is all. Sometimes the women in town place flowers there, but not so much anymore. People tend to forget with time. You will see the mound though. Would you like to buy a God's Eye? For the grave perhaps?"

Magdalena did not answer the old man. She watered the mules and started back to the river for more water. Michael was watering the cattle, and the ranch hands were caring for the horses. The animals all appeared to be spent, and exhausted, and Magdalena thought about Eliza's old horse. It was spared this dreadful leg of the journey. Magdalena offered her mules more water and started for the river again. She met up with Michael.

"Where is Molly?" she asked.

"She is with Eliza and her children. She is fine."

"I do not want her around them. They might be sick. Eliza has lost a baby already, not to mention her mind! What if they have the lung disease, Michael? Why did you not wait for me, or find

Olivia?"

"Maggie, what has gotten into you? Eliza has been around the family already and you never said a thing. In fact, you welcomed her."

"Michael," she interrupted, "my brother is here. He is buried at the edge of town. I heard the whole story from an old man who lives here in this village. He said that they put all the men in one grave at the edge of town where the Apaches attacked their wagons. He said the grave is right by the trail and we would see a mound. I want to go there. I want to go there now and see for myself."

"We have t'stay t'gether Maggie. We have t'stay with the wagons. I will ask the Captain if we can take five minutes to stop when we see it. The old man may have been crazy, or lyin' to' ya anyway. You cannot take his word for it."

Michael approached the Captain.

"Are you ready to roll?" asked Captain Brooks.

"Aye, Captain, but I have a question for ya. Can we make a short stop at the edge of town? Magdalena has it in her mind that her brother is buried there. Some old man in town told her that some Apaches massacred a supply train there, and she thinks that it may be the one that her brother was on."

"It is true, it happened. I remember it well. I know right where the grave is. I will give her five minutes, no more. We still have five miles before we camp for the night. Tomorrow, we will go fifteen miles and lay over for a day to let the animals recruit. We have some hard traveling ahead of us."

"Is it safe?" asked Michael.

"We will not be safe until we reach Fort Craig, but we must rest regardless or we will never make it, especially the animals. At Fort Craig I will ask for more soldiers to go on with us to California."

On the way out of town, sure enough, there was a burial mound. The Captain halted the train as promised, and Magdalena spent only a minute or two before climbing back on the buckboard.

They traveled another five miles before the wagons came to a halt. The emigrants were effete, and discouraged. Captain Brooks knew that the animals would need to be well fed, watered and rested before moving on, hence, he permitted them to be unhitched this night. He posted many pickets, and many of the emigrants also volunteered their watch of the animals. The Captain ordered no fires, or music once again, but the travelers were too exhausted from the past two days to give it much thought or care. Olivia rationed out cold beans, and biscuits, and apples, and they ate what they could before getting some much needed sleep. That night in the wagon, Magdalena clutched her baby daughter and held her tightly all through the night.

Chapter XXVII

The Bosque

The emigrants arose fresh and renewed the next day. Captain Brooks announced that they would travel seventeen miles that day to a Bosque. There, there would be rich fodder for the animals, good water, and plenty of fire-wood. The wagons would lay over for a day there before heading out to Fort Craig. Again Captain Brooks ordered quiet on the trail. Again there would be no fires, so another cold breakfast. Most of the travelers were running short of food without the benefit of a fire. Not having to cook, Olivia milked the cow that morning herself. Magdalena gathered the eggs. She did not separate the milk, but mixed raw eggs with the heavy milk and gave some to her husband and daughter and then indulged herself. Eliza's children came to the wagon very famished that morning, so Magdalena shared the milk and eggs with them as well, sending them along with some for their mother. She also gave them six ripe green apples. Olivia came to Magdalena and told her that there was still some boiled ham left, and that it should be eaten soon before it spoiled in the heat. Magdalena instructed her to give it to the men, and have some herself. She would wait for dinner that night to eat again. She took a small piece of ham and gave it to her baby daughter, who was now thirteen months old and enjoying solid foods.

About the time that Captain Brooks called for the wagons to roll, the detail that was sent to find the Brown children approached. They had two small blond headed girls with them, each riding in front of a soldier in his saddle. Hannah was age seven, and Emma was age five. The girls appeared to be in shock. They had witnessed their parent's massacre, and had been in fear for themselves during their time with the Apaches. They appeared ragged, dirty, and weak. Captain Brooks ordered the soldiers to take the young girls to Eliza, and have her look after them. Magdalena walked to the Brown's wagon with a pail of water, and bathed the girls. Her heart went out to them, and she wondered what was to become of them. She produced the doll that she had found underneath their wagon at the massacre site.

"I wonder who this could belong to?" she said.

The girls just looked at her for a moment, and then Hannah slowly took the doll from her and handed it to her baby sister. Eliza gave the girls some water to drink, and Magdalena took an apple out of her apron pocket. She cut it in half and gave each child a piece. Neither child spoke a word, and soon they were fast asleep in the comfort of the familiar wagon, a stranger at the reins.

Magdalena approached Captain Brooks and asked what was to happen to the girls. He told her that they would go to Fort Craig with the wagon train, and the girls would stay there until they could find some relatives.

"Mrs. Brown has a sister in Santa Fe," said Magdalena. Her name is Mrs. Stockholm. She lives on Second Street."

"That is good information. We will send word to her about her sister and see if she will take the children. If she refuses, they will go to an orphanage unless other relatives will take them."

"She will not refuse," answered Magdalena. "She is a good woman. I hate to see those babies go all the way back on the Gila though. It will be hard on them."

"They will be in good company of many soldiers," answered Captain Brooks.

"How did the soldiers get them back?" asked Magdalena.

"They waited until night time and rushed the Indians

encampment. There was no use trying to find the mules. The gunshots spooked the animals, and they all scattered. Now, we must get these wagons rolling."

The wagons rolled along quietly. The emigrants were well rested, and that night they would have fires, and lay over. It was encouraging to the weary travelers. The hour was three o'clock when the Captain finally called a halt. They had reached the Northern Edge of the Bosque. People went to work immediately, unhitching their animals, building fire rings, and collecting wood and water in their pails. Magdalena pulled the small iron stove from her wagon. At first, the emigrants were quiet and afraid to talk, but after some time, they felt more at ease.

"Olivia, I will help you to put salt bread out to rise tonight, and tomorrow we will bake all day! I am so hungry, I think I could eat Eliza's old horse, raw!"

Olivia laughed. "Me too!"

The Bosque was a little bit of paradise to the travelers. There were exotic birds by the thousands, and artesian springs with sweet, cool water. The Captain had mentioned to Magdalena that there was also warm springs nearby where the ladies could bathe. The higher elevation, forty five hundred feet, offered relief from the heat of the hot desert floor. There was good grass and tulles for the animals to feed on. There was pheasant, quail, grouse, geese and ducks, as well as rabbit, deer and moose. The captain encouraged the people to hunt and stock up on meat while they could.

"But Captain," said Magdalena. "Won't the sound of gun report bring the Indians? And what about our fires?"

"This is a sacred place to the Indians. They will not attack us here. They would be afraid of leaving ghosts here. As much as they do not like us camping here, we are only ten miles from Fort Craig now, and it is a big deterrent to them. I am not saying to let your guard down though, and I will still expect quiet in the camp tonight. No music, I am sorry to say. Tomorrow we have an easy ten miles of trail to Fort Craig. Once we are there, you may have all of the music and dancing you like, inside the walls of the Fort.

Michael did not want to wait for morning to go hunting. He was hoping for some fresh meat to put on the fire that night. Olivia was busy making corn cakes and boiling beans. The fresh vegetables were scarce now, they wouldn't have any more until they came upon a farm or town to buy them. Magdalena had been too distracted in Socorro to think of it. Olivia took some dried chilies from a rista and ground them up to flavor the beans. Then she added two onions, which had kept well on the trail. Magdalena put water on to boil. She would use some of it to sponge off her baby, and some of it to clean herself. She was looking forward to taking a bath in the warm springs the next day, and wash the trail dust from her ears and hair. The rest of the water was used to boil the eggs that her hens had never failed to give her on the trail. There were almost three dozen in all, and once boiled, they would make convenient snacks. She looked up to see Eliza walking toward her dragging the two Brown girls, one in each hand. She was walking briskly and did not appear to be at all happy.

"What am I supposed to do with these girls? They don't say a word, and the little one wet herself all over one of the perfectly good beds in the wagon."

Magdalena could not believe that Eliza was being so impatient with the young girls, who had just lost their parents and been kidnapped by Indians.

"What are you supposed to do with them? Clean them, be patient with them, feed them and take care of them, for a start. You could try loving them also, if you can find it in your heart. And remember, Eliza, the bed that Emma soiled is her own, as is the wagon that shelters you and your own children. Try putting your children in their place, and then find some compassion deep within yourself. You can start by bathing all the children, then bring them to our chuck wagon, and you all shall have super here with us tonight."

Eliza turned away dragging the little girls along. She mumbled under her breath as she briskly walked away, "I cannot even take care of my own children. How am I supposed to take care of two more?" As she dragged them along, little Emma kept looking back at Magdalena.

In a little more than an hour's time, Michael and Andrew came riding back to camp, each of their horses pulling a make shift travois behind them. They had already killed two elk and field dressed them both. Magdalena and Olivia grasped each other by the arms and danced round and round. Michael dismounted, and Magdalena hugged him with all of her strength.

"Oh Michael! You are such a good hunter and provider! How did I get so lucky? Can you slice some thin pieces of meat off that animal for Olivia to put in the fire now? I don't think I can wait for supper."

"You do not have t' ask me twice," he answered. "Andrew has t' take the other animal t' the Army, but he will be back to dine with us tonight at supper."

"Splendid!" said Magdalena. She looked at Olivia and saw the smile on her face, and wished that they could spend more time at the Bosque. It was so pleasant here.

"Oh, and one more thing," said Michael. He walked over to little Ginger and removed two very large geese from her pack saddle and held them up. "Sorry t' be makin' so much work for ya, Olivia."

"Oh, I do not mind at all Michael. It will make up for the days that I had to do nothing. I will smoke those both over the spit tonight when I roast some of the elk, and we shall feast!"

Magdalena took Molly by the hand, and she teetered along

beside her mother. In her other hand, she held a pail and together she and her baby went for a walk along the river to look for edible flora. There, she found crabapples, and wild plums, and filled her pail to the brim. Others were doing the same. The sun was starting to set, and Magdalena took in the beauty. The livestock was browsing on the tall grasses near the water. Some woman were washing out their clothes, others washing their children. Just then, Seamus appeared.

"Hello, Mrs. Malone."

"Hello yourself, Seamus. I have missed you."

"Mama has been in one of her moods. She was happy when we got the wagon, but since those girls are with us now she's mad again."

"What do you think of the Brown girls, Seamus?"

"They are all right, I supposed. They don't talk. The big one whispers to the little one in her ear, and that is all."

"The poor things have been through an ordeal Seamus. We must all be patient with them."

"Mama says that they are going to sleep in the little tent tonight. She does not want them in the wagon with us. She does not want the little one to wet herself again."

"What do you think that I should do, Seamus?"

"I don't know, ma'am. I feel sorry for the girls, and Mama is mean to them, but you can't tell her that I told you so."

"Where do you want to sleep, Seamus? In the wagon or in the little tent?"

"I'm a boy, I can sleep anywhere, even on the ground under the stars."

"You are not a boy Seamus, you are a young man, and quite a good one at that. So if you had to go back to sleeping in the little tent, it would not bother you?"

"No ma'am. The tent is much better than we had it before,

sleeping on a blanket with not enough to go around and being cold all night."

"What is your mother doing now, Seamus?"

"I dun'no. I think she is washing Annie. She found some dresses in the wagon that fit her and she wants to put one on her. She says that she won't give them back to the girls, they are for Annie now."

"I see," said Magdalena.

"And she took the doll you gave Emma away from her and gave it to Annie, too."

"Seamus, I have to go help Olivia with supper now. You and your family have been invited to eat with us tonight. Tell your mother there are wild plums by the river. She should collect some. They are very good for growing children."

Magdalena took a plum from her pail and gave it to Seamus. Then she went directly to the campsite and found Michael with Andrew and some of the hands, while Olivia was busy roasting elk and geese. She told Olivia what Seamus had told her about the girls.

"I can take them in the chuck wagon with me," said Olivia.

"No, it is far too small, and besides, that wagon belongs to them. It is all they have left that is familiar to them. Why should they be displaced? But I do not want Eliza's children to suffer for it, either. I must speak to Captain Brooks."

Magdalena picked up Molly, and walked quickly to find the Captain. She told him the whole story, and together they made a plan. They would keep their eyes closely on Eliza, and when they caught her mistreating the Brown girls, she would be on her feet and walking again, and back to sleeping in the little tent on the ground.

Evening came around, and Eliza came to the chuck wagon

with her children. She no longer seemed too proud to accept charity. She was acting as though it was her right to dine with the Sandoval's party. Magdalena was not going to spoil their supper and good fortune with criticism. There would be time for that later. She noticed Annie all clean and well dressed, holding Emma's doll. She wished that she had given her the gifts that she and Michael had purchased in Albuquerque. She had been waiting for the perfect time to throw a birthday party for Annie and Seamus, and with the adversity on the trail the perfect time had not yet come. She would still throw them a party, but when they reached Fort Craig where they could have music and dancing.

"I see that Emma is letting you play with her doll, Annie," she said.

"Mama gave it to me," replied Annie.

"Well, you must return it this night, and her dress too."

"That is Annie's dress, and so is the doll," said Eliza.

"Eliza, you know that I took that doll from the Brown's wagon and gave it back to the girls when the soldiers brought them into camp."

"That was another doll. This one is Annie's."

Just then Hanna spoke out. "The doll is Emma's! It was my doll and I gave it to her. That is Emma's dress she is wearing, too. She took all of Emma's dresses and shoes and gave them to Annie."

"That wretched little girl is lying," said Eliza.

"Who is lying?" asked Magdalena.

"Let us remember, you are ladies," interrupted Andrew. "The doll and the dresses must be returned to the girl. It's all she has left, and that is the end of the story, Eliza. We all know that you came on this wagon train with nothing. Magdalena has taken you and your children under her wing. Where is your humility?"

Eliza rose to her feet. "Come, children," she commanded.

"We do not want to go with her," said Hannah.

"Neither do I," said Seamus. "I'm hungry."

"Stay here then, and finish your dinner," said Magdalena.

Eliza stormed off, dragging her protesting child, Annie, by the hand.

"I do not want to go yet Mama," cried Annie. "I'm hungry!" She dropped the doll in her path as to return it to Emma, and Hannah ran to fetch it. She handed it back to Emma, and Emma clutched it close to her.

Magdalena put a pot of water on the fire to warm. She would clean up the girls herself, and the next day she would see what clothes they still had in the wagon, and put clean dresses on them, and wash and mend the ones they were wearing. She allowed Seamus and the girls to stay with them until the hour was late, and then she instructed Seamus to take the little girls back to their wagon. They protested, but Magdalena told them not to worry. She told them it was only for one more night, the next day they would be at Fort Craig, and everything would be alright. Reluctantly, they went with Seamus.

The camp grew quiet as the night grew late, and around ten o'clock, wolves nearby began to howl. Screams came from a few wagons behind Michael's and Magdalena's, and Magdalena knew that it was the Brown girls. She started to get up to go to them, but Michael held her back.

"Let Captain Brooks take care of this, Maggie. He promised me that he would."

They saw the Captain and a several soldiers walk past their wagon and to Eliza's campsite. There, they found the two little girls in the tent, huddled in the corner crying in fear of the wolves. There was no blanket in the tent, they were sleeping on the cold earthen floor. The Captain went to the back of the Brown's wagon and found Eliza comfortably sleeping in a feather bed. Her little girl was resting soundly beside her. Seamus was in a corner feigning sleep. He knew what was about to happen would not be pleasant.

"Mrs. Duncan!" the Captain called out in a stern voice. "Why are those little girls in that tent all alone with no blankets?"

Eliza stirred and rubbed her eyes.

"Oh, did I forget to give them a blanket? Well, here then, give them this one."

"I don't think so," replied Captain Brooks. I think you need to get out of that wagon, and bring anything that you'll be needing to get you through the night."

"What?" said Eliza. "What is this all about?"

"It is about humanity, Mrs. Duncan. You need a lesson in it. Get out of that wagon, now."

She climbed out of the wagon, cursing under her breath, and the soldiers put the little girls inside. They climbed onto the bed that was still warm from Eliza's body heat, and covered themselves up. Emma was still whimpering in fear.

"Don't be afraid, Emma, we are alright now," her older sister reassured. And then, from the corner where Seamus was situated, he said in his most manly voice, "Don't worry, I will watch over you, even if I have to stay awake all night long."

Eliza was instructed to sleep in the little tent. Captain Brooks told her that she could drive the wagon onto Fort Craig providing she could be civil to the little girls. Otherwise he would appoint a soldier to the task of driving and Eliza could walk the last ten miles to the Fort.

"And then after we leave the Fort? What about then, Captain?

Are you giving me the wagon?"

"No ma'am. The wagon is the property of those girls. It will go back to Santa Fe with them. You will be left to your own devices, so I suggest that you be affable to the other's on this train. You will need them at some point."

The Captain turned and walked to the Malone's wagon. He told them not to worry about the children, he would have the soldiers looking after them throughout the night.

In the morning, there was milk and eggs, and meat, and beans, and Olivia and Magdalena were already making bread and biscuits with the dough that had been left on the warm rocks by the fire to rise. When the children rose from their slumber, they ran to see what was for breakfast. Eliza's children had grown accustomed to dining at the Malone's chuck wagon, and it was now their routine. Eliza was not to emerge from her little tent for many hours after the children were fed and bathed. After breakfast, Magdalena took all of the children and the laundry to the hot springs to bathe. From a pocket in the side lining of her wagon, she produced a bar of lilac soap that had been neatly wrapped in brown paper. Back home in Santa Fe, she would bathe almost daily with her perfumed soap. She had never realized what a special pleasure that it was. She took Molly by the hand, and the girls and Seamus all carried their own laundry and followed behind her. The children played in the warm but malodorous water, and enjoyed it immensely, while Magdalena cleaned their clothes and diapers on the rocks. Molly played beside her wading in the warm water. She hung each article on tree limbs to dry, and then she took her naked baby, and waded into the odoriferous waters to bathe herself with her lilac soap. The children were having much fun in the water, and they all looked clean and fresh, and renewed. Other emigrants were doing the same in other springs nearby, and Magdalena knew that there must be others still, awaiting their turn for the spot that she occupied with the children. When the garments were close to being dry, she instructed the children to dress, and bring what was theirs back to camp.

Back at the camp, Magdalena was informed by Olivia that the wagon was to lay over another day at the Bosque before heading to Fort Craig. Magdalena was delighted. Her husband had gone out with a hunting party to secure more game for the Army, as well as for themselves. Olivia and Magdalena took a walk with the children down the line. They introduced themselves to folks they had not yet met. When they returned, they set about doing chores that they hadn't had time to do previously. Magdalena mended the girls dresses, and pinafores. She penned a letter to her parents, informing them of the past events on the train, including information about the Browns, and the girls. Once she was at Fort Craig, the letter would be carried by soldiers to Santa Fe, and reach her parents in no time. Most likely, the Brown children would be delivered to their aunt at the same time. She penned a few lines in her journal, and later she and Olivia baked bread for most of the afternoon. If it came down to eating cold food again, at least they would have biscuits and preserves. When the men retuned several hours later, they paraded the spoils of their hunt. They had elk and deer meat, duck and goose, pheasant and grouse. It had been a bountiful day at the Bosque for hunting. Magdalena told Michael of the emigrants that she and Olivia had met on the train that day. Some were very poor. Some spoke no English. Most had no guns.

"Michael, I think you should take some of those birds and share them with the starving emigrants on this train. Think of them as your neighbors. And since we are going to lay over another day here, you can hunt again tomorrow. I have heard that the fishing here is good, also. Perhaps, since Olivia and I have gotten so much done today, she and I can go fishing tomorrow."

"T'is a splendid idea, Maggie!" he replied, and was off riding down the line to share his spoils.

"Michael!" called Magdalena as he rode off, "Those at the end of the train are in the most need."

Michael waved an acknowledgement back to Magdalena as he and Blaze rode down the line, leading Ginger behind with plenty of grouse, and pheasant, and geese, to feed the population.

"You have a good man, Magdalena," said Olivia.

"Indeed."

Michael went straight to the end of the train, passing out birds all the way back to their own chuck wagon. There were no birds left when he returned, as the emigrants were more than grateful to accept his offering. When dinnertime approached, Eliza showed up at the chuck wagon for her meal. She was fed, but conversation between Magdalena and herself was minimal. When Eliza had finished her dinner, she rose and started to walk away.

"What about your children, Eliza?" asked Magdalena.

"What about them?" replied Eliza.

"Well," said Magdalena. "Today I bathed them, I fed them, and I mended their clothes. What did you do?"

"Well," began Eliza. "I just relaxed a bit. I think I needed it, and since you think that you are a better mother to my children than I am, I really had nothing much to do."

"You could have bathed yourself, Eliza, you need it. Or you could have fished, or collected plums, or berries. You could have done something productive. And you call your son Shameful! Who is Shameful now? I told you before that I was proud to be your friend, but for the first time in my life, I have to say that you are no friend of mine, Eliza. Now you go back to your tent with your stomach full and have a nice nap, but do not be showing up here tonight at our campfire, unless you are bathed and want to pull your share of the chores around here."

"Who made you camp boss, Miss High and Mighty?" replied

Eliza.

Eliza walked up to Magdalena and put her face inches away from hers, staring her straight in the eye. Magdalena did not give her the satisfaction of an answer, but she knew that suddenly, she was in charge of five children, when she had started out just a few weeks earlier with only one. She smelled the foul stench from Eliza's mouth and turned her head.

"That's what I thought," said Eliza.

At that moment, Magdalena knew in her heart that this women was pure evil. She knew now why Eliza's husband had left, but could not understand him leaving his babies. For a moment, she thought on it. She wondered if Annie and Seamus's father was still alive. She wondered if he could be found, and if he wanted his children. What was to happen to them?

Chapter XXVIII

Fort Craig

After two days of rest and nutritious grass, the animals were much recruited, and Captain Brooks announced that the wagons would roll in the morning. Since it was merely ten miles to Fort Craig, there would be ample time in the morning to prepare a hearty meal. The men had been abundantly successful in supplying the Army and the wagon train with fresh meat, and the morale of the emigrants was greatly elevated.

In the morning as the men were busy hitching up their wagons, the women were packing the last of their supplies. Eliza had still not emerged from her tent, nor done one single thing to tend to her children's needs. Magdalena was growing increasingly impatient with her, but decided to turn the matter over to Captain Brooks. She would feed and tend to the children that day, but once at Fort Craig, the Army would have to take charge of them. The wagons began to roll out, and they rolled right past Eliza, sleeping in her tent. When she finally emerged, she could see the last wagon about a quarter mile away. She quickly dismantled the tent, and hastened to catch up with the travelers. Seamus had tied the burro behind the buckboard and rode along with Magdalena, while a soldier drove the Brown's wagon with the girls inside. Magdalena surmised that Eliza had just lost her mind. As much as she hated to think of the children being sent to an orphanage, she was in no condition to assume responsibility for them herself.

The wagon train advanced six miles, and Captain Brooks called a half hour break to rest the animals and let people stretch. This was still hostile territory, so he did not want to pause for long. Eliza had caught up to the line, and when the wagons paused to rest, she raced from the rear of the line up to the Malone's wagons. She was coughing and sputtering, and was about to give Seamus the beating of his life, but her condition prevented her from doing so. She was thin and pale, and looked more haggard, and dirty than she had the first day Magdalena had met her. Andrew, standing nearby, had seen her approach. He poured some water from his canteen into a cup and offered it to her.

"Your lungs must be full of trail dust from walking behind the train," he said.

She took the water down quickly, and asked for more before offering the cup back to Andrew.

"No, you keep it," he said, fearing that she may have consumption. "Tie it up in your apron strings and keep it for later."

"Seamus, take your mother some biscuits and plums," Magdalena said to the boy.

"Yes ma'am," he replied, and hastened off to do as he was instructed. When he retuned, he told Magdalena that his mother wanted to resume the duty of driving the wagon.

"It is not up to me, Seamus. You must take it up with Captain Brooks."

Captain Brooks took a few moments to think about it. If the woman was truly ill, it would be cruel to make her walk. However, she had brought punishment upon herself and needed to learn a lesson. It was only another four miles to Fort Craig on a nice flat road. She would have to walk. Once at Fort Craig, Captain Brooks would check her into the infirmary where she could rest for as long as she desired.

The wagons commenced to roll out, and when the train arrived at Fort Craig there was still plenty of daylight. The animals were turned out, and went directly to the flowing waters of the

Rio Grande. The emigrants made their campfires inside of the protective walls of the fort. Here, they were no longer restricted to the line of the wagon train. Their fires were spread out amongst the common area of the fort, and it was a far more social atmosphere.

Michael noticed seven wagons with families on the outside of the walls. He asked Captain Brooks why they would not come inside, with the rest of the emigrants.

"Those are Rebs from Arkansas," was his reply. "They say that they do not wish to live amongst the Feds, and they do not need our help. They also said that they would not eat and sleep amongst the Buffalo Soldiers. There are a large population of them at this fort.

The Confederate-minded emigrants from Arkansas had discussed leaving the train, and traveling on alone. However, after being witness to the Brown massacre, the woman folk had persuaded their men to follow the train with the Cavalry escort.

"Are they in any danger of Indian attacks there outside o' th' fort?" inquired Michael.

"We have not had any trouble with the Indians here since the battle of Val Verde in sixty two," replied Captain Brooks. "But, they are still out there, and there are no guarantees. I will not post any men out there to protect them, seeing as they are adamant against it. I will, however, post men to watch the livestock."

Eliza was seen by the doctor at the fort, and he determined that she had an advanced case of walking pneumonia. He ordered her to bed rest, and prescribed her some laudanum to help her sleep. She was shown to a private room next to the infirmary. It was a small room with a cot, a chair, and a small table with a candle on it, nothing more.

That night, there inside the walls of Fort Craig, there was music and dancing, and plenty of food to eat. It was a warm summer night, and with all of the smoke from the campfires, the mosquitoes had been kept at bay. Magdalena decided that they would have a birthday party for Eliza's children, even though Eliza herself would not be able to attend. Olivia was making a plum pudding, which would have to suffice in the place of a cake. She waited until dinner to tell the children, and they were very excited. Emma had grown very attached to Seamus, and was constantly his shadow, which was a comfort to Magdalena. It was hard to keep her eyes on so many children, and she knew that Seamus would take good care of her. Many of the emigrants joined the birthday celebration, making the children feel very important. It was festive for everyone. As people were singing, and clapping to the music, Eliza emerged from the shadows, lurking like a predatory animal.

"I have come to put my daughter to bed," she announced in a slurred tone.

"But I do not want to go to bed, Mama. It's my birthday and we are having a party."

"You must come to bed with me now, Annie. It is late, and I do not want you to get sick like me."

She took the little girl by the hand. In Annie's other hand, she clutched her new doll. As they walked back to Eliza's room, little Annie looked back toward her surrogate family. Seamus watched as they disappeared back into the night. Eliza gave her little girl a drink of water, and put her to bed in her cot. Then, she took the bottle of laudanum that the doctor had given her, and drank down a good portion. Together, they lay in the cot, never to wake again. In the morning, the doctor discovered Eliza and little Annie, dead from an overdose.

Chapter XXIX
Arizona Territory

Captain Brooks held the train at the fort for six days to rest and prepare for the next leg of the trip, as well as to fortify the Cavalry escort with more men. He knew that the next two hundred miles would be more difficult than the first part of the journey. There would be less shade, less water, and the weather was becoming warmer. There was also the question as to what would happen to Seamus. He had been staying with Magdalena and the girls, sleeping in the girls wagon. On the day that the train was preparing to pull out, he ran to Magdalena and threw his arms around her.

"Please take me with you, Mrs. Malone. I won't be no trouble, I promise. I can do chores, help with the animals. I can learn to hunt with Michael. I don't want to be an orphan. Please!"

Tears were streaming down his face, and Magdalena had to choke back her own tears.

"It is not that easy, Seamus. Michael and I have a hard road to face ahead of us." Magdalena looked up at Michael. They both knew that there were too many orphans in Santa Fe already, and that would be where he was bound. The orphanage might not even take him, since he was already close to being thirteen. Magdalena had an idea. She would send him to live with her parents. Their big hacienda was empty now, and Seamus would help to fill the void. Quickly, she penned a note to her parents and gave it to Seamus, hoping that her parents would not decline her plea.

"Carry this with you all the time, Seamus, do not let anything happen to it." She told Captain Brooks to instruct the General at the fort to deliver Seamus to her parents when they reached Santa Fe. All that she could do now, was hope and pray that her plan would come to fruition. In her heart she felt confident that her parents would be comfortable with the idea. They could always set him to work with the livestock, and bed him in the bunkhouse with the other hands. Perhaps, he would not look like the urchin he was with the new clothes that Magdalena had purchased for him in Socorro. Perhaps they would see in Seamus, what she herself saw in him. A loving boy, eager to please and be a part of a family. She looked at him lovingly. There he stood, for once with clothes that fit him, and shoes on his feet. Magdalena had grown very attached to Seamus, and she would miss him sitting next to her on the seat of the buckboard.

"Give this letter to my parents when the soldiers take you to their house. They might be able to help you find a good home, Seamus, and you and I will meet again. I promise."

She turned, and quickly walked to the buckboard where Michael was waiting to help her up. From her perch she clicked for her team to move forward, and briefly looked back at Seamus, standing all alone in the world, staring back at her.

"Git up!" she commanded her mules, not daring to look back again. In another moment she disappeared into the cloud of dust on the Gila Trail.

~*~

The next days passed slowly. Life was monotonous on this leg of the trail. At times they passed through little villages where Magdalena and Olivia would shop for supplies, mostly in the way of fresh vegetables or fruit, potatoes, and bushels of un-husked corn to supplement the livestock. The heat was oppressive, and Magdalena felt dirty all of the time. The trail was littered with the bones of dead animals that had spent themselves and could not continue. They had given out, and their owners had left them to fend for themselves. Magdalena made sure that her chickens were fed every day, and that her milk cow was the primary recipient of their corn. Her cow was worth ten times it's weight in gold, and she knew it. Often, emigrants would come to her and try to buy milk or butter. When she could spare a little, she would give it to them without charge. She had no use for their money, but plenty of need for the milk. Sometimes the train would pass graves along the trail. At times they would run into cowboys, herding their beeves to Arizona, or California. Once, they came upon three Argonauts on their way to the California gold fields. All three were on foot, leading their pathetic little donkeys with all of their worldly possessions strapped to their pack saddles. They reminded Magdalena of Eliza.

The Gila trail was commonly used by cowboys to herd their livestock from Texas to Arizona and California. Therefore, although good fuel was abundant in the form of cow patties, the grass and fodder was often well devoured, or spoiled by the forerunners. At times, the emigrants were forced to travel a distance from the trail, leading their animals to better grazing. This was slowing the train down, sometimes by several miles a day. It did afford the women more time for cooking and mending, however. It took over two weeks to travel from Fort Craig to Las Cruces, but there was no loss of animal or human life. They held over for a few days there to rest and recruit the animals. Shortly after leaving Las Cruces, dysentery began to travel through the train. Magdalena had been warned by her father that the most common cause of sickness on the trail was due to bad water. She was always careful to drink tea or coffee, or milk, and almost never drank the water straight from it's source unless it was directly from a sweet, deep artesian spring. Fortunately, Olivia followed her example, and they escaped the malady. Once again, the wagon was held up for three days to allow the sick to rest. After three days, Captain Brooks rolled the wagons out again, and those who remained ill had to make the best of it. Now the wagons were headed west, traveling along the Mexican border toward Arizona Territory. The next eight days proved to be the hardest and most monotonous. Then, one day, the Captain announced that they had crossed into Arizona Territory.

The terrain here was much like prairie. There was tall grass for the animals, but it was yellow this time of year. Still, it was good nourishment. Although small, there were creeks with good, clear water that ran over stones, with a sandy bottom beneath. Some soldiers rode out from Fort Bowie to intercept the emigrants. They told of good hunting in this area. There was deer and antelope, and wild pigs, if one was so inclined to eating them. Quail, wild turkeys, and grouse were also plentiful.

Captain Brooks decided to lay over the wagon train for two or three days so the animals could refresh. The grass and water were good, but there was little or no fuel for camp fires here, other than what cattle had produced, and a few scrawny mesquite here and there. After they were situated and the livestock were turned out to browse, Olivia and Magdalena took Molly and the three of them set out to collect fuel for their camp fire. Some of the women on the train refused to use the cow pies, saying that it would contaminate their food. Magdalena trusted her ranch hands and had no problem with it. In fact, after using it the first night, she told Olivia that they would spend some time the next day collecting plenty for their future fires. It was easy to light, and burned clean and hot giving out little smoke. There was just enough smoke to keep the mosquitoes away, but not so much that their clothes and hair would reek for days, the way the wood smoke did. Andrew joined the Malone's for dinner that night. He and Michael made plans to hunt antelope the next day. Andrew had been through these parts many times, and was well familiar with the territory. He stood pointing in every direction. "Fort Bowie is that way, and Camp Supply is that way, and from there if you go a little south, there is Turkey Creek, and, Fort Huachuca is that way one hundred and thirty miles, and over there is Texas Canyon. Those mountains right close, those are the Chirichahuas, and those over there, those are the Dragoons, and yonder are the Whetstones."

"Whoa! Whoa there, Andrew!" said Magdalena. "You are going too fast. Why are there so many Forts around here?"

"Oh, this is Injun country to be sure. Those red devils are all around us. But do not worry, ma'am, we are safe out here on the prairie where we can see all around us for miles. Safer, I guess I should say. Anyway, we have a lot of soldiers now, so I would not worry yourself too much about it."

There was silence for a long pause. Magdalena was thinking about what Andrew had said, perhaps a bit to deeply. Others must have been thinking the same thing. Nobody was talking, and they had contemplative looks on their faces as Magdalena studied them in the fire's glow. Her eyes met with Olivia's, and they stared at one another for a moment. Finally, Olivia broke the silence.

" Shall we tell them, Andrew?"

"It's your call, Olivia."

"Oh, do tell," said Magdalena. "Now you have me in suspense!"

"Andrew has asked me to marry him! And I want you to be my maid of honor Magdalena, and Michael will be our best man."

"Michael! How long have you known about this?"

"I just found out today."

"Well, when is all of this going to happen?" asked Magdalena.

"We have no ring yet," answered Olivia.

"I do not think you need a ring to get married Olivia. You can take care of that later. Why, I think that you should do it now. Why waste another day?"

"I like how you think, Magdalena," said Andrew.

"Here comes Captain Brooks now. Shall we ask him to marry the two of you this night?" asked Magdalena.

Olivia and Andrew looked at each other.

"But I don't know," said Olivia. "Spending our wedding night in the chuck wagon just doesn't sound appealing to me."

"Michael, did you pack the canvas tent that you used to stay in when you lived on the river?"

"Aye, 'tis in the wagon with our furniture."

"Well, we are going to be here for a couple of days, why don't we set it up and the newlyweds can honeymoon in the tent?"

"Sounds fine to me," said Andrew.

"No," replied Olivia. "I would rather wait and do it tomorrow. I think I would like to clean myself up a bit and find something nice to wear in my trunk. I want it to be special, Andrew."

"I think you are right, Olivia," said Andrew. "What is one more day? That will give Michael and me some time to hunt antelope in the morning, and we can have a wedding feast and invite the whole camp. Then I can get cleaned up as well. We will ask Captain Brooks to marry us tomorrow night, then."

Michael and Andrew spoke with Captain Brooks, and then they found the canvas tent and set it up. Olivia could use it to dress in the next day, and sleep in it that night. They set up a cot inside for Olivia, as she refused to sleep on the ground where serpents might attack her in her sleep. The next morning, Magdalena woke up early and milked the cow and fed the chickens. She changed Molly's diaper and nursed her back to sleep. After she had started a fire with their efficient fuel, she began to rummage through her trunk. When she found what she had been looking for, a periwinkle taffeta dress, she removed it from the trunk. Then she found a hat that was adorned with some dried flowers and peacock feathers. She began to removed the flowers and feathers, and tied them up in a purple ribbon. Olivia and Magdalena were about the same build; however, Magdalena was a tad bit taller. It would take a couple of hours to take up the hem in the dress, but she thought it would be perfect for Olivia to be married in. She would make a gift of when Olivia awoke. When the others started stirring from their wagons, Magdalena already had the cream separated from the milk and hanging in the churn on the side of the chuck wagon. She had a big pan of scrambled eggs cooking, and biscuits with preserves waiting. There would be much to do this day. She would assume all of Olivia's chores while Olivia prepared for her wedding night.

After breakfast was finished and the pans were wiped clean, Magdalena offered Olivia the dress and bouquet that she had made from the dried flowers. Olivia was delighted to be the recipient of such a gift. Right away she tried on the dress, then went about taking up the hemline. Magdalena took Molly and began collecting "prairie fuel" until she had several bushels. Andrew and Michael went looking for antelope, and were gone for several hours. When they returned with a good supply of meat, Magdalena began roasting it right away. She would serve roasted antelope, and fried potatoes with onions, for dinner that night. She also would slice up apples and put them in the Dutch oven with browned sugar and fresh butter. It was the best that she could do under the circumstances, and in the end she was rather proud of the outcome.

That evening, Olivia and Andrew were married, and there was music and dancing and festivities, and all ate until they could hold no more. Afterward, the married couple retreated to their tent, and Magdalena went about the cleaning detail. When she and Michael were just about ready for bed, a family approached them. There was a husband, a wife, two small children and a baby in the woman's arms. They asked if she had any milk to spare, as their baby was hungry and the woman had stopped producing her own milk. They had a small copper pail with them, so Magdalena obliged them with the milk, even though her cow was not producing as well as it had in the beginning of the journey. She also gave them some roasted meat, leftover from the wedding dinner, and some potatoes, and six boiled eggs. There were no more baked apples, but she gave them four ripe green apples and some wild plums. She then told them that she had several ranch hands and a family of her own to feed, and that she would give them milk when she could afford to, but could not make it a daily routine. Magdalena's naïve outlook of humanity was beginning to take a turn. Eliza started it, but the emigrants were reinforcing it. At Fort Craig, when she strolled about the commons of the enclosure, she would hear people talk. These very people who came unprepared on this wagon train, and begged food and milk from her almost daily, were the same people who used horrible descriptives when speaking about the Irish, the Mexicans, and those filthy heathen Inguns. They would carelessly throw out insults, assuming perhaps, that everyone felt the same about these races. They cut her to the quick. Her mother was Mexican and Indian, and her husband was Irish, and her baby was all three. She recalled a conversation that she and Michael had had when they first discovered that they were going to have a baby. "Be proud of who you are," Michael had told her. She wondered if these poor pilgrims would even want her food if they knew she was not Spanish, as everyone had assumed.

In the morning, the wagon train rolled right after breakfast. In the afternoon, when it was preparing to halt, a late-in-the-season monsoon blew in a thunder storm. Magdalena wrapped the reins around the brake handle and let the mules continue unchecked. She turned around to cover her chickens with a sheet of India rubber that she kept handy for just such a situation. But then the lightening cracked, and the thunder boomed, and her mules spooked. She was pushed back into her seat by the sudden bolting of the mules. Two soldiers on horseback came rushing to her aid as the mules ran away with the buckboard, the reins now dragging on the ground.

"Maggie!" she heard the desperation in Michael's voice. He was not close enough to help her, and he had his own team to drive. She struggled to grasp the reins, and knew that she was in trouble when she saw that they were no longer at her reach.

She asked God to deliver her from this situation, and thanked him that Molly was riding with her father in the schooner. The Cavalry soldiers were trying to steady the mules from the front of the buckboard, and eventually they were successful, but it was a hard lesson for Magdalena. She sat driving the mules in the pouring rain, and Michael called to her.

"Maggie! Don't you want to' put on a slicker?"

"No!" was her reply. "The mules are still flighty. I just want to keep going."

The train moved along in the downpour for another long hour. Although the air was warm, the flesh on Magdalena's arms had goose bumps. The wind blew hard, and it made the mules even more skittish. Finally, Captain Brooks called the train to a halt, but the animals were left harnessed to their wagons until the storm passed and they were able to settle down. Turning them out now would be risky. They storm might spook them, and they might run off, causing a delay in their progress.

That night, Andrew and Olivia had little choice but to sleep in the chuck wagon. Although the canvas tent was fairly waterproof, it had no floor, and the ground was saturated. Everything was saturated. The air was thick and heavy. The spirits of the travelers had been drowned. The wetness of earth, and the clothes on their backs, was uncomfortable. There was little to burn, and even the mesquites were dripping with water. Magdalena was proud of herself for being prepared. She and Olivia built a camp fire in no time, and unlike others on the train they would have a hot meal that night. Soon enough, the beggars began to arrive at their campsite.

"No!" said Magdalena. "I collected fuel all day while all of you rested, and played your music. I have none to spare."

"Maggie, this is not like you," sad Michael.

"They had the same opportunity as I did," replied Magdalena. They could have collected fuel, but they are lazy. They just want charity. God helps those who help themselves. I am tired of hearing about the lazy Mexican, or the worthless Irish, when it is we who those come to for help when they need it. I am done with them, Michael, done! We will not go without on their account. We have men and women, and a child to take care of. Those others are not our responsibility. I get no return favors from them, other than insults when I offer our provisions. I will never let a child go hungry, but for the lazy and judgmental parents of those innocent children, I say to the devil with them!"

"Maggie, this journey is making you hard."

"No, Michael, it is making me smart."

After that night, nobody came around asking for milk, or food, or fuel, or anything from the Malone campsite. The talk around the wagon train was all about those high and mighty Malones. How quickly they had forgotten about the milk, and food, and medicine, that had been dispensed so freely by Magdalena to those in need. How quickly they forgot about the birds and meat, that was delivered to them by Michael. In some way, Magdalena felt relieved, but in another she felt guilty. Her mother had always taught her that in a community there will always be those who have, and those who have not. Yet, in a community, everyone has something to offer. Did not these poor pilgrims who wanted food or milk for their babies offer entertainment and music which lifted the spirits of the weary travelers? Magdalena's mother had learned this communal lesson from her own mother. Living in the Apache society, one knew that every person had a station, and that the tribe on a whole depended on the contribution of each person, no matter how rich, or how poor they might be. She took a few days to think about it, enjoying the break from the beggars, and then she began to humble herself. She walked down the line one morning to the family who once approached her for milk. She inquired about their baby, but could see for herself that the infant was growing weak without nourishment from her mother. Magdalena held out the pail of milk, fresh from her cow, and not yet separated so as to contain the rich cream that was used for their butter. At first, the emigrants refused her charity.

"I do not wish to see you bury your baby along the Gila trail somewhere, and I am sure that you do not wish to bury your baby, so please, take this milk for your children."

The father of the family stepped up and reluctantly accepted Magdalena's offer. He poured the milk into a pail of his own, and his hungry children ran to it with their cups, thirsty for it's nourishment. Some was poured into a glass bottle for the infant, but the infant was too weak to take the offering. Her mother started to force the fluid into her mouth a tiny bit at a time, and eventually the baby fell asleep, exhausted from the effort of swallowing. Magdalena's heart sank. She needed to take care of her own baby, but the thought of an infant dying on the trail of hunger when she had the means to save her was too much for her to bare. She thought about what her mother would do, and decided that she would take some milk to that starving family every day, and when she could, she would feed the rest as well. She would adopt one family; just one. That would be manageable, and feed them the best that she and Michael could. Taking care of all of the starving emigrants on the train had proven to be too much of a burden, but taking care of just one family would be manageable.

In the morning, the wagon train started rolling again, but the earth on the Gila had turned to sticky muck. The animals slipped and struggled to pull their heavy loads through the deeply saturated ground. Along the wagons rolled, inch by inch, and then something glorious happened. Magdalena remembered that it was Sunday, but there had been no time for prayer services that day. She said a prayer of thanks to the Lord for the sun that beat on their faces. She knew that although it was hot and uncomfortable, that the sun would soon dry up the trail and make it hard, and easier to traverse. She began to sing. She sang "Onward Christian Soldiers, marching as to war. With the cross of Jesus, going on before...".And then Olivia joined in, and then Michael, and Andrew, and the soldiers, and one by one all the way down the line, the travelers were all singing. At the end of the line, the emigrants were singing along with the start of the line, with no delay in beats. Each beat of the music was right together, and they sang verse after verse. Magdalena paused for a moment to listen, and a smile came to her face. This time, it had been her turn to provide the music. When the hymn was completed, there was a long silence, and then she started to sing again, and so did the travelers.

Chapter XXX
Wild Turkeys

Again, the monsoons blew in rain, wind, thunder and lightning. The water-laden wagons struggled along in the weather. The animals, although somewhat unsettled by the storm, welcomed the relief that the rain brought. It saturated their hides to the skin, and cooled their bodies. Captain Brooks announced that when they reached the San Pedro river, he would call a halt to the wagon train. There was an abandoned homestead there, with a small adobe dwelling, and a very large barn. Some of the emigrants would be able to find shelter from the rain in the barn. He told the Malones a story of the family who once lived there. They had been cattle ranchers, but some Mexican cowboys slaughtered the entire family, women, children, and all. They stole their livestock, taking all of the chickens, beeves, and horses. All that had been left behind were the cattle dogs, and the dogs had turned feral and had begun to hunt as a pack. Captain Brooks warned that if anyone saw them to be wary, as wild dogs could be more vicious and dangerous than a pack of wolves.

"How do you know that it was Mexicans that killed this family?" inquired Magdalena.

"The beeves with their brand were spotted in Mexico on a cattle ranch, and some of their horses, too. I suppose that it was just assumed. That poor family never did get any justification."

The wagon train arrived at the homestead. Magdalena thought what a peaceful place that it was. The small adobe dwelling was built close to the San Pedro river, and the huge barn stood several rods away. The rain ceased, and the travelers settled in, some opting to rest in the spacious barn. As Olivia and Magdalena were preparing their campfire with the fuel that Magdalena had collected, Magdalena noticed some movement from a copse of cottonwoods down by the river. As she surveyed the area to find the source of the movement, something caught her eye on the left side of the copse. She turned her head and looked some more, but saw nothing. Eventually, she went back to her work helping Olivia prepare an evening meal. As the women worked together, a great commotion erupted from the trees where Magdalena had thought she had seen something move. Out from the low laying chaparral scattered a large flock of wild turkeys, followed by two dogs. Another dog joined them from one side, and then another from the other side. The lead dog caught a very large turkey and the pack disappeared as quickly as they had appeared.

"Did you see that?" asked Andrew to anyone who was listening. "Did you see that dog catch that turkey? He looked like one of those wild spotted dogs from Africa."

Captain Brooks answered him. "That dog is a Catahoula, and you do not want to be messing with him. They can be very mean. We should have shot it while we had the chance, and taken the turkey for ourselves, but it all happened too quickly."

"It may not be too late to shoot a turkey or two," answered Michael. "I'm goin' t' get me scatter gun and try to find them. They cannot have gone too far."

Michael climbed up onto the seat of his wagon, and reached behind the bench seat where he kept his hunting guns. He placed his foot on the steel rimmed wagon wheel to step down, but his feet were muddy and the wheel was slippery. He lost his balance and began to fall. As he started to go down, he dropped the gun and it landed on the butt of the stock, causing it to discharge. Hearing the sound of the gun report, Magdalena looked up and saw Michael laying on the ground. Without realizing it, she screamed, and started out to run to him. When she reached

Michael, she knew that it was much worse than him just falling from the wagon. He had taken the full charge of the gun to his upper right side. There was even some shot in his face. She began sobbing uncontrollably. This could not be happening. Captain Brooks ordered his soldiers to carry Michael into the adobe. He asked Magdalena which wagon contained their bed, but she was too distraught to answer. Olivia pointed it out, and the bed was erected inside the adobe in a matter of minutes. Olivia filled her apron with cow fuel and put it in the wood burning stove inside. Quickly, Andrew lit the fire in the stove. A pot of water was put on to boil, and the Army surgeon went right to work extracting the small pellets from Michael's face and body. Magdalena was in shock. She held Michael's hand and sobbed until she could cry no more. Olivia went back to work on the dinner and watched over baby Molly. This unforeseen accident was a horrible tragedy to the whole wagon train. Michael was a good hunter and provider to not only his own family, but to many of the hungry emigrants as well. She prayed for a speedy recovery, but inside the small adobe the surgeon had no good news.

"He's been gut shot," the doctor announced. He blurted it out in the most blatant way that he could. There was no use covering up the facts that should be made known. "There is nothing I can do for him. His insides are most likely torn to shreds. It is only a matter of time now before he bleeds out." Magdalena stared at the doctor in disbelief. She would never allow Michael to leave her. They had promised to be together forever, and it was just too soon to be forever. She lay down on the bed next to him, and very gently put her arm over him, avoiding the wounds to his side. The others in attendance left the adobe to give Magdalena some time with her dying husband.

"Maggie," said Michael in a whisper. "I am sorry t' let you and Molly down."

"You have not let us down Michael. We will hole up here until you are well, and then we are going to California."

"Maggie, take off me boots," he weakly instructed her.

Magdalena jumped to her feet and as gently as she could she pulled off Michaels left boot. As she pulled it off a large roll of paper notes fell out.

"What are you doing with all of this money Michael?" she asked. "Where did it come from?"

With whatever strength that he could muster Michael told her that in one boot was money to start the new supply post. Her father had entrusted him with it. In the other boot was his life's savings. He told Magdalena to take and hide the money. He told her not to tell anyone, and she obeyed. Inside of their wagon was also hidden their gold and silver coins, given to them at their wedding. There was a small fortune here, and as much as it made Magdalena nervous, she did not want to have to think about it at this moment. She put the paper notes in the deep pockets of her skirt, keeping both rolls separate in two different pockets, and covered Michael back up. She resumed her place next to him, and in a short while Olivia entered the room with Molly.

"Molly is asking for you, Magdalena," she said. "Can I bring you some stew in a while? It is almost ready."

"No thank you, Olivia, just leave Molly here with Michael and me. We want to be alone for a while."

"Alright then, Magdalena. Molly has already been fed. We will see you in the morning."

Magdalena, Molly and Michael fell asleep together in the little adobe dwelling, in their own bed. The bed where Molly was conceived in love one beautiful, happy night two years before. In the morning, Magdalena awoke to find Michael had passed in his sleep. She didn't move for a very long time. She stared at the ceiling of mud and straw that was caving in from the heavy rain. She watched the water and mud drip steadily from the sod roof.

She listened to the sound of Molly breathing, and thought what a glorious sound that it was. If only she could hear that sound from Michael. This could not be the end of their life together. It would not be. She had loved Michael with all of her heart, and the most wonderful handful of years in her life had been spent with him. They had so many plans together. His family had finally come together in Santa Fe. There must be more. There just had to be more.

Chapter XXXI

The Departure

The next day, Captain Brooks knew that the wagon train would most likely not be able to travel the thirty two miles to Fort Huachuca that day. They would let Magdalena and Molly have a little more time with her husband while the soldiers dug his grave, and then move out later in the day. He came to Magdalena to speak with her about the arrangements.

"Mrs. Malone, we need to bury your husband. We can try to take him to Fort Huachuca and bury him in the cemetery there, but it may not be a good idea given the weather and the two day trip, and, well.... We could bury him in the family plot here where the homesteaders are buried."

"No!" cried Magdalena. "I will not see my husband buried with a family of strangers and souls who were murdered. I will find a place for his grave myself."

She went outside to find the sun shining. Mercifully, the rain had ceased. She surveyed her surroundings. Behind the adobe dwelling was a bluff, a single little hill standing alone. She climbed to the top and looked around. She could see the valley all around her. She could see the Dragoon Mountains to the north, the Whetstone mountains to the west, and the Chirichahua Mountains to the east. Mexico was about ten miles to the south. There were big, white, puffy clouds in the sky, and behind and between them a deep blue sky. "Michael would have loved this day," she thought to herself. "This is where I will have him buried, and I will put a bench here next to him, so I can visit him, and talk to him. Together, we will enjoy the view."

The soldiers buried Michael, and Captain Brooks read a few words from the bible. Magdalena did not cry a single tear. When it was time for the wagons to prepare to roll out, Captain Brooks came to Magdalena and told her to ready herself for the move.

"I am not going anywhere," was her reply.

"But, you cannot stay here," said Captain Brooks.

"That is exactly what I intend to do," she answered.

"Mrs. Malone, come with us to Fort Huachuca and you can remain there for as long as you like. Decide later if you wish to go on to California, or back to Santa Fe, but you cannot stay here."

"I am not leaving here," said Magdalena. "I promised Michael even before we were married that I would never leave his side. I will remain here with my husband, Captain Brooks."

Olivia was standing close by, and she interjected.

"Captain Brooks, I think that you are wasting your time. If Magdalena says that she is staying here, then she is staying here. Magdalena, I still have a commitment to fulfill to your father and to the mission in Los Angeles. I need your instruction now. Shall I continue on with the chuck wagon? Are the supply wagons still going to California? I am sorry to put this upon you at a time like this, but we must make a plan."

"I will hold the supply wagons here until my father can find another person to run the post in California," she answered. There is no use sending them all the way back to Santa Fe just to have them sent back to California. I think that my father will want the chuck wagon. Captain Brooks, do you think that you can have the wagon sent back to Fort Huachuca once Olivia is delivered to San Diego?"

"That will be no problem. Are you sure about this, Magdalena? I hate to think what your father will say when he finds out that I left you out here in Apache country all by yourself with a baby. Do you want us to take Molly to Fort Huachuca?"

"No, she stays here with me," answered Magdalena. "We are a family, and we will remain together, Michael, Molly, and me."

Magdalena helped Olivia to transfer the wagons, and they said their goodbyes. She wished Olivia and Andrew a long happy life together, and she gave Olivia a hug. Olivia tried to hide her tears as Magdalena then went to Andrew and gave him a hug, also.

"I will send some soldiers out from Fort Huachuca to check on you in a few days, Mrs. Malone. God be with you," said Captain Brooks as he rode off with the wagon train.

After they passed, there were only the supply wagons and Magdalena's buckboard remaining, along with the wagons containing her provisions. She called a meeting with the men who were traveling to California with them.

"I will need volunteers to ride back to Santa Fe and inform my father of the situation. Those who wish to go on to California may take horses and catch up to the wagon train. Any who wish to remain here with me until I hear back from my father may do so, but nobody has to do anything that they do not wish to do. I deeply regret to put you men in this position. Without the wagons you can make good time on horseback, either back to Fort Craig, or onto Fort Huachuca, the choice is yours. I only ask you to help me put my cow and my horses in the stalls in the barn, and put my chickens in one stall as well. Also, I would like to house as many of the wagons as I can in the barn, if you don't mind. Molly and I will sleep in the adobe for now."

There were twelve wagons and a buckboard to secure. The cowboys parked them side by side, very close together in the barn. They managed to fit them all in, even the buckboard. They put them all in the center of the barn, leaving an aisle on either side so that they could access the stalls. Then they placed all of the chickens in one stall and closed the Dutch door that had iron bars on the top. The chickens seemed much relieved to be freed from their willow prison, and the rooster made quite a fuss. Cotton collected yellow grass and used it to line their makeshift coop. He gave them scratch and water, and then the cowboys put up the horses and mules in the stalls. Most of the animals were doubled up two to a stall in order to accommodate them all. They were given corn, water and oats. The oxen were turned out to graze, and Magdalena's milk cow was put in a stall by itself. She was watered, and given an ample amount of corn, oats, and grass.

After all of this was completed, the men closed the doors at one end of the huge barn, and left the doors at the other end that faced the adobe partially opened. They built a small fire close to the river, and sat around it devising their plans. Cotton had always been Don Sandoval's lead man, and he felt an obligation to protect Magdalena and Molly, so he volunteered to stay on and help her with the animals. He asked for one more volunteer, and Charlie also agreed to stay on. "This was good," thought Cotton. Charlie was a good and strong man, and the two of them worked well together and thought alike. It would be better for the rest of the men to stay together and travel together through Indian country. In the morning, the twelve men would ride out together. The rest of that afternoon they gathered food and provisions from the wagons, chose the mules or horses that they would ride, and gathered their bridles together. Once they knew which animals they would take, they made sure that those animals were fed and watered well. They would waste no time riding back to Fort Craig where they would ask for a military escort back to Santa Fe. It was a good plan, and it would work. One of the cowboys had chosen Blaze to take, but the others knew that Magdalena would never hear of it. Blaze and Ginger would stay with her. They were part of the family, and she would need her horses and a good team of mules to remain with her, and so it was.

Magdalena thanked Charlie and Cotton for staying with her. She made all of the men dinner on the stove inside the adobe, and again expressed her gratitude to all of them for their loyal service. After their meal, the men retired in the barn, and

Magdalena and Molly went to sleep in their own bed where Michael had taken his last breath. Again, the rain came. By the candlelight, Magdalena stared at the ceiling of mud and straw. The rain was dripping through, and little pieces of mud were dislodging and falling through. Magdalena drifted off to sleep as she fretted about Michael's grave and what all of this water might do to it. She was awaken suddenly in the night to a loud noise. She could not make it out. It was a barreling sound and it grew louder and louder. It was coming closer and closer. All at once the water from the San Pedro crashed through the little adobe taking with it parts of the walls down river. The roof was caving in all around Magdalena and Molly. Swift water was rushing into the vulnerable structure. There had been too much rain. The adobe had been placed too close to the river, and now the river was swollen, and the long neglected structure gave away. The river had risen to the point where the adobe was actually in the river, and Magdalena was in the adobe with her baby. The rapidly moving water kept taking bits and pieces of the adobe with it, and the water was rising rapidly. She had to get her baby out of there, and she had to do it now! She picked up Molly and wrapped her in a soaking blanket and started for the door, thankful that she had never undressed that night before going to bed. Slowly making her way through the rapidly rising water, she positioned her legs and braced herself. One tiny step at a time, through the swift flowing current, she made her way, until finally she reached the edge. She collapsed, and held her frightened baby in the heavy, water laden blanket. It was unusually dark outside, and the angry river rolled and rumbled. Magdalena looked up at the sky at the swiftly passing clouds. At times, the clouds would part enough to reveal the millions of stars in the heavens.

"Do not worry, Molly. We are fine. Your Papa is watching over us, and he will not let anything happen to us."

She rose up to her feet again, and followed the tiny glimmer of light that came from the campfire near the barn. Finally, she arrived at the barn and stood at the door soaking wet from head to toe, holding her baby. The few men who sat near the fire just inside the barn door sprang to their feet in disbelief.

"The river washed away my house," she said. Then, she found the wagon that stored her belongings from the casita in Santa Fe. She and Molly climbed in. Finding a small opening of space, she undressed Molly and herself, and they laid down and fell fast asleep under the warmth of a fresh blanket. In the morning when she awoke, then men had already left for Fort Craig. Cotton and Charlie had coffee on their campfire, and were tending to the animals. Magdalena went to the fire and poured herself a cup of coffee.

And so began the first day of her new life in Arizona.

Chapter XXXII

The Catahoula

Two weeks passed and Magdalena began looking for her father to arrive. She felt like a real gypsy now, squatting on someone else's homestead, living in a barn, and eating off the land and the small supplies that Olivia had left her from the chuck wagon. She still had her tiny portable stove. Olivia had left that as well. The adobe was all but gone, and the feather bed had been ruined, but she saved the headboard. The river had finally receded. Charlie and Cotton were taking fine care of the livestock. From time to time, Magdalena would catch a glimpse of the wild dogs. The Catahoula frightened her.

"Doggy!" Molly would say in her innocent little voice.

"You keep away from those doggies, Molly," commanded Magdalena. "Those are bad doggies, do you hear me?"

One sunny day, Cotton took an old lariat that he had, and threw it over a tall, strong limb of a cotton tree growing close to the river. Molly loved to play in the cool sand in this spot, so he went about constructing a swing for her there. In the evenings, she could see the javalinas playing in the mud holes nearby, and watch the deer browse.

"Doggy!" she would proclaim.

"No, Molly! Those are not doggies. Those are mean piggys. You must keep away from them. They do not like people. Let us go talk to Papa for a while, and when Cotton is finished making your swing, we will come back and try it out."

And so they hiked to the top of the little bluff where Michael was laid to rest. Cotton had made a wooden cross for a grave marker, but Magdalena had plans to some day replace it with a better one made of granite. She sat on the log that Cotton and Blaze had dragged up the hill. Cotton said that one day soon, he would split the log in two and make a right proper bench of it. But it would do for now, just the way that it was. It reminded Magdalena of Michaels camp by the river in Santa Fe. She spoke to Michael, just as though he was sitting right next to her on that log, and it confused baby Molly.

"Where's Papa? I don't see Papa. Where is he Mama?"

"You cannot see him, Molly, but he is here and he can see you and hear you. Is there anything that you want to tell your Papa?"

"I wuv you, Papa," she said.

"Your Papa says that he loves you too Molly. He loves you more than anything in the world, and even though you cannot see him, he will always keep loving you. You are his precious little girl. And I am his precious wife, and we are one big precious family. Magdalena tried hard to hold back her tears and compose herself. "Look, I think Cotton has finished your swing. Do you want to go and try it?"

"I want sweeen!" answered Molly.

Magdalena smiled and took Molly by the hand. They walked to the big cottonwood tree, and Magdalena lifted Molly up to the seat and placed her upon it. She gave her a little push, and Molly giggled.

"Thank you, Cotton. This will help break the monotony of Molly's day. I really do appreciate it. It is a wonderful gift."

"Well, that just makes it all worth it," said Cotton. "But you know that it's my pleasure. I love Molly, too, you know."

"I know, Cotton. You are part of the family. Come now Molly. We need to get supper started."

Magdalena felt a chill in the air, and she knew that fall would soon be upon them. She wondered how it would be living in the barn when the cold weather came.

In the entrance to the big barn where the little stove sat, Magdalena started a fire and put some tea on to boil. When the stove was much hotter she could put the grouse that Charlie had shot in the little oven, and a Dutch oven with biscuits on the top. Just outside the barn and around the corner, she could hear Molly talking in her tiny voice. She assumed that she was talking to her doll.

"Papa loves us. Papa takes care of us. Come here, doggy. Mama is cooking dinner. Come eat dinner, doggy!"

Magdalena paused. "Molly?" she called. "Who are you talking to out there?"

"I talking to my doggy," she answered.

Magdalena jumped up and ran outside. She looked around and saw nothing. Molly must have been pretending.

"You scared my doggy, Mama," she said.

"Well, it was time for your doggy to go home anyway Molly. You have to come inside now. It is getting cold and your dinner will be ready soon."

"My doggy hungry, Mama."

"Your doggy can find his own food. Now come inside the barn."

~*~

A few more days passed, and Magdalena kept a constant vigil for her father's arrival, but still there was no sign of him. She decided to take Molly down to the river and wash some clothes and diapers. As she preoccupied herself with her wash, Molly played by the water.

"Do not get too close to the water, Molly. You have not yet learned to swim. I do not want to have to get in that cold water to fetch you out, do you hear me? Are you listening?"

"I hear you, Mama," she answered.

Magdalena hung the wet laundry on branches to dry, and she and Molly started back toward the barn.

"I want to sween, Mama," said Molly.

"Oh, Molly, not now darling. I have so much to do still. Maybe later when we come back to get the laundry after it dries."

There was no protest, and Magdalena kept walking, and talking to Molly.

"Tonight after dinner, I will read to you from your story book, Molly. Would you like that? Molly? I asked you a question, Molly. I said, would you like me to read to you from your story book tonight?"

Magdalena paused, and looked down. She did not see Molly. She looked around, and spotted her daughter heading back toward her swing in a full run. She had almost reached her destination, when Magdalena saw the Catahoula. Her heart sank. She screamed for Cotton to bring a rifle, but had no way of knowing if he had heard her or not. She did not even know where he was at the moment. The Catahoula was running at full speed toward her baby. Magdalena started running toward Molly, screaming as loud as she could to scare the animal, but it was no use. She would never outrun the wild dog. She was running, and screaming, and crying.

"Molly! Molly!"

And then, she saw another dog from the other direction, running toward Molly at full speed. She remembered the turkeys. This is how dogs hunt in a pack.

"Not my baby! Molly! Molly! No, no, no!" she screamed in terror, all the while running. But the Catahoula overcame Molly, and then ran right past her. He ran toward the other dog at a full charge. Magdalena watched, her heart beating hard as she still worked her way toward her baby. The other dog was large, and gray. It was not a dog at all, but a Mexican wolf! The Catahoula charged the wolf, and the two met with full impact. A dogfight ensued. The sound was horrible. By the time Magdalena had reached her baby, she was close enough to hear teeth gnashing, and guttural, demonic sounding growls, emitting from the dogs. Magdalena was out of breath. She bent down and scooped up her baby and started walking as fast as her feet would carry her toward the barn. Halfway there, exhausted and stunned, she turned to watch the dogs. It felt like forever but it was over in moments. The wolf lay dead, and the Catahoula, badly injured, limped over to Molly's swing and laid under it.

"Oh, my doggy! He's hurt, Mama!" The dog lay bleeding badly from his neck and hind leg. "My doggy. Poor doggy. Mama will make you all better," the child called out.

Molly wiggled from her mother's arms and ran toward the injured animal.

"No, Molly!" her frantic mother called out to her. "Do not touch that animal!"

It was too late. The child reached down to pet the dog, and he whimpered. His tail was wagging weakly. Magdalena started to protest again, but she knew at that moment that the Catahoula had saved Molly's life, and that it had been a conscious, thought out decision on the dog's part. The dog had protected her baby from that wolf. As Magdalena finally caught back up to her daughter, the dog curled it's lips back and growled at her. Then he laid his head down on Molly's feet and closed his eyes. Magdalena reached down and cautiously felt him.

"He is still alive," she said. "Come Molly."

"But, my doggy!" protested Molly.

"We are coming right back to take care of your doggy, Molly. I have to get some medicine, and I need your help. You want to help your doggy, do you not?"

Magdalena picked up Molly, and walked as quickly as she could back to the wagon that had been her home for the past few weeks. She quickly put her hands on the box of medicines. Then, she took a needle and thread from her sewing kit. She and Molly returned to the dog, still laying on the ground bleeding. She could feel eyes watching her, and she knew that the other dogs were lurking in the brush. Although she was afraid, she tried not to think of it. She would do what she could for the Catahoula, and if he survived, she would show her appreciation to the dog for the rest of his life. If he did not survive, then so be it, but she had to try. She took some brandy out of the medicine box, and poured some into the wounds of the dying animal. He let out a whine in protest. Magdalena cleaned the wounds and sewed them up the best that she could.

"I am sorry, doggy, but I must do what I must do to make you better. I hope that you know that I am trying to help you. I do not know what will happen now, Molly, but I have done all that I can to make your doggy better."

Cotton rode up on Blaze, and Magdalena told him what had happened.

"I don't think that you ought to be touching that animal," said Cotton.

"Molly touched him before I did," she answered. "Perhaps you should quarantine us."

They both laughed, and for the first time since Michael had died, Cotton saw the life in Magdalena's eyes again.

"Will you hitch up a travois to Blaze and take this dog back to the barn, please, Cotton? I intend to bring him back to life. I will try to do for this dog, what I could not do for my husband."

"But Magdalena," he started.

"Molly loves this dog, it is her doggy. He saved her life, and I must do what I can to repay the favor. If you would just help me to get him back to the barn, and then you can see what is left of that wolf hide."

"You're the boss," he said as he rode off to fashion a travois.

The dog was dragged back to the barn on the travois. Magdalena had her doubts that he would live through the night. Molly stroked the pathetic looking animal and spoke to him in her tiny voice. In the morning, Magdalena was surprised to see the dog laying on the blanket she had given him with his head up. She milked the cow and poured some of the milk in a tin pie pan, then added some stale biscuits. She then took the pan to the dog and placed it in front of him. This time, he did not growl at her. He sniffed the food and ate a bit of it, mostly lapping at the milk before laying himself back down.

Charlie's voice called out, "It's your father Magdalena! He has come, and he has soldiers with him!"

Magdalena scooped up Molly and started running toward the group of riders.

"It is your Grandpa, Molly! He has come!"

Don Sandoval jumped from his horse and embraced Magdalena, who was still holding Molly.

"I've come to take you home," he told her.

"No, Papa! I will stay here! This is my home now."

"What sort of a home is this for you, out here amongst wild savages? What sort of a home is this for your baby? Magdalena, be logical. You cannot stay here."

"Papa, I am making dinner now. I was not counting on so many, but we will manage." She looked around to take a quick head count. She hadn't noticed him before, but there sitting up on a very stout palomino, was Seamus. He had color in his face, and good clothes, and a fine pair of riding boots.

"Seamus! Did you ride here all the way from Santa Fe!"

"Yes Ma'am!" he replied, with a proud smile on his face. "I missed you so much, Mrs. Malone."

"He would not be left behind," said Don Sandoval. "He is quite a young man, and your mother and I have become very attached. In fact, she had a horrible fit when I told her that he was coming along with me: did she not, Seamus?"

"Yes she did!" he said as he climbed off his horse. He hugged Magdalena and Molly, and they hugged him back.

"Is that your horse, Seamus?"

"Yes, Papa gave him to me. Isn't he the most beautiful horse that you have ever seen?"

"Yes, he is indeed, Seamus. The most beautiful horse that I have ever seen. She smiled at the thought of Seamus calling her father Papa, and she knew that she had done the right thing by him. "Molly and I missed you so much."

"I'm sorry about your husband, Ma'am."

"Seamus, now that my parents have adopted you, that makes you my little brother. So, I was thinking that maybe you should call me Magdalena."

"Can I call you Maggie, like Mr. Malone did? It sounds much friendlier."

"Of course you can, Seamus; I would like that. Now let us go have some dinner."

Chapter XXXIII

The Homestead

In the morning, Don Sandoval thought for sure that his headstrong daughter would have come to her senses, but it was not to be so. She was adamant about remaining. She took her father to the peaceful place where Michael was buried, and together they sat on the log while Seamus played with Molly.

"I want to put a fine granite headstone here, Papa, and a real bench, and an iron gate around it. I will plant a couple of peppertrees for shade. Michael will rest in peace here, and I will live the rest of my days out in this place and be buried next to him. And some day, Molly will be buried next to us. I like this place, Papa. Look, you can see all around for miles. Maybe someday I will build a grand Malone monument up here.

"The soldiers tell me that this is a well used cattle trail. They say that it gets a lot of traffic. They also tell me that it is only thirty two miles from Fort Huachuca."

"Yes, that is true! And Captain Brooks has sent soldiers here twice to check on me, but I have not seen any cowboys bring their cattle through here yet."

"I was just thinking, this might make a good place for a supply post. A place that could supply wagon trains, and cowboys, and the soldiers from Fort Huachuca."

"I think that is a wonderful idea, Papa! And we already have twelve wagons with provisions for the supply post. That is, unless you still want to send them to California."

"I have resigned myself from that contract, Magdalena. I think I like the idea of establishing a mercantile right here, it's much closer to Santa Fe. Gather some things together for a trip Magdalena. We will leave first thing in the morning for Tucson. If this is a homestead, and the homesteaders are no longer here, then maybe we can file a claim on this property ourselves. We will put it in your name. Put together what we will need for a three day trip, and put it in the buckboard. I want to get an early start."

Magdalena packed food, clothes, and the canvas tent in the back of the buckboard. She was delighted by her father's support. Cotton and Charlie were left in charge of the livestock, but Molly and Seamus rode in the back of the buckboard and traveled to Tuscon with Magdalena and Don Sandoval. The children had a little nest of blankets where they could lay down if they tired, and a basket with biscuits, and wild plums. Her food stores were low, but they could stock up on a few items in Tucson. Don Sandoval drove the buckboard, and Magdalena sat on the bench seat next to him.

"I have your money, Papa," she told him as they made their way down the well seasoned trail.

"What money is that?" he replied.

"The money that you gave Michael to open the supply post in California. It was the last thing he made sure of. He had it in his boot. Before he died, he told me to remove his boots, and I found the money. It is in my purse now."

"Good, you hang onto it. We may need some things in Tucson. Remind me to post a letter to your mother when we get there."

"I will, Papa, but I think if you give it to the soldiers at Fort Huachuca it will get there much quicker. They come to check on me from time to time."

"That is good to know," replied Don Sandoval. "That is very good to know. I will make sure that I tell your mother that, also. She will be very upset with me when I return home without you and Molly."

"Papa, I want some beeves. If I get this homestead, I want my own beeves. Just a few, maybe forty or fifty to start. If Cotton will agree to stay on with me, I would like to keep him in charge of my livestock. I want more chickens, also, and some hogs."

"I see that you have given this situation much thought Magdalena, but I think that the store will keep you more than busy."

"It is the dream that Michael and I had, Papa. Please, will you stake me?"

"Yes my darling, ambitious daughter, you know that I will."

~*~

In Tucson, Don Sandoval sent the letter off to his wife. If the soldiers came to visit, he would send another letter, and see which one arrived home first. They were fortunate to secure the homestead in Magdalena's name. The man at the government office was more than happy to know that there were going to be settlers on that homestead again, and most especially a woman. The west lacked women, especially single women. Since the property had already been surveyed, the man at the office handed Magdalena a map of her property. One hundred and sixty acres in all, with the San Pedro River running directly through the middle. Then, she and her father went to register her a brand. Magdalena had already thought about it. It would be the Triple Bar M. Three bars, with the M in the middle. Nobody owned a brand like that, and it was issued to her without hesitation. It would be hard to disguise that brand with another, and Magdalena's father was very proud of her determination. While in town, they inquired about lumber to build a real home for Magdalena. The merchant told them that they could order it from him, or go direct for a better price. He told them that the lumber mill was on Turkey Creek near Camp Supply.

"Thank you, sir, I believe I will do as you suggest and buy direct," said Don Sandoval.

That evening, they rented rooms at the hotel, and the four of them ate dinner at the fancy hotel restaurant, which was not really all that fancy. Magdalena drew much attention in town, and it made her nervous to have so many eyes upon her. Did people think that her father was her husband? And why not, older men often married younger women to give them children. But that was not the reason. People stared at Magdalena because she was beautiful, and also because she had never been seen there in Tucson before. The town was curious as to who she was.

The family enjoyed a hot dinner, and ordered some tamales for the road, which they would pick up in the morning before they set out. Magdalena bought a dozen more chickens and they were all crammed into a tiny wooden crate for the journey back home. The back of the buckboard was quite filled with supplies now, and the children had less room, but did not complain. At times they would take turns riding on the seat next to Magdalena. Don Sandoval pushed the mules hard. He wanted to get back to the homestead. Magdalena was also anxious to return to what was now her homestead. She was not at all impressed with the town of Tucson. It was littered with trash on the roadsides, flies everywhere, dead animals left where they fell. She was only too happy to be on her way back to what she could now honestly call her home.

When they arrived back at the homestead, Magdalena was already calling it the Triple Bar M Ranch. Cotton and Charlie had taken good care of it in the time that it took to go to Tucson and back. The Catahoula was up and walking, and very much improved. Although Cotton had been feeding it scraps, the dog kept his distance, and was not too anxious to be friends with him. But when he saw Molly, however, he ran to her with his tail wagging and smothered her with dog kisses.

"My doggy! He's all better!"

"You did not tell me that you got yourself a dog Magdalena," her father said.

"I did not know I had a dog until just now, and anyway, it looks more like Molly's dog to me."

Magdalena had not told her father about the incident with the wolf, as she knew that it would only give him cause to worry.

"That pack of dogs has been lurking around here since the Catahoula made the barn his home," said Cotton. "Do you want me to shoot them?"

"No," said Magdalena. "I think I will just start feeding them. Perhaps they will gentle down and be useful when I get my beeves, since they have already been working dogs."

"Beeves?" repeated Cotton.

"Yes, beeves. I am going to be a cattle baroness," said Magdalena with a laugh. "My father has already agreed to stake me forty, or fifty head."

"How are you going to manage this place all by yourself?" inquired Cotton.

"Well, Papa is going to the lumber mill to buy lumber for a house, a chicken coop, a mercantile, and a bunkhouse. I will need to hire myself at least two good ranch hands. Can you recommend anyone?"

"Well," he started.

"Oh, by the way, I have chickens that need to be let out of their tiny cage. Will you put them in a stall in the barn please, Cotton?"

"I am already on it," said Charlie.

"Oh, and Charlie, please do not mix them with my hens. I want to use these new hens as layers, and I will let my old chickens hatch some eggs to increase my stock."

Magdalena looked up and saw a trail of dust to the west. Although she could not yet see riders, she knew that was what it meant. People were coming, and she was hoping that it might be soldiers from Fort Huachuca. Almost an hour later, Captain Brooks rode up with eight soldiers. They greeted Magdalena and her father. Magdalena invited them to some tamales and coffee, and they readily accepted. They were on their way to Camp Supply to bring back more Cavalry soldiers.

"What good fortune," said Don Sandoval. "Do you mind if I ride with you? I have to go up to the lumber mill on Turkey Creek to buy lumber for Magdalena's new house."

"So," said Captain Brooks, "You really do intend on staying here."

"This is my homestead, Captain, all one hundred and sixty acres of it, and it is all mine, legal and filed for. I even have a map of my boundary lines. I call it the Triple Bar M. I registered my brand in Tucson the other day. Papa is also opening a mercantile here, which I am to over-see for him."

"Too bad it is not opened yet," said Captain Brooks. "There is a wagon train coming from El Paso, it should be here in a few days. I will send word ahead that they cannot lay over on your homestead. Will you give them passage rights?"

"Of course I will, Captain. That is how I intend to make my money in the future."

"It is good to see you in better spirits, Mrs. Malone, and looking forward to your future. It is a good sign that you are healing."

Cotton had still not answered Magdalena's question about acquiring some good ranch hands. He was not quite sure how to take it. Was she telling him that he was to return to Santa Fe with her father? He wanted the position of running the ranch, but was not sure if she wanted him. Also, it was very remote, and Cotton was still hoping to meet a nice woman and be married. How would he ever meet someone out here in the middle of nowhere?

A gust of wind blew through, and a chill was in the air. The aspens and ash trees by the river sounded like rain as their shedding leaves rustled, and Magdalena noticed that they were turning yellow. She pulled her shawl tighter around her shoulders.

"We will be leaving in the morning at first light, Don Sandoval: will you be ready?"

"Yes, I will be ready. I think I better hurry up and get a house built for my daughter. It is promising to be a cold winter."

Chapter XXXIV
The Log Cabin

Eight days later, Don Sandoval retuned with four very large, flat wagons loaded with split logs. Driving the wagons were four, very large lumber jacks, happy to go out for delivery and get away from the mill for a time. The men unloaded the wagons, and Don Sandoval, Cotton, and Charlie went to work straight away. Magdalena's log cabin would be the first structure to be built. The area would be twelve feet by forty feet. They would divide it in two. One half would be the kitchen and living area. The other side was divided again, into two smaller rooms. One for Magdalena, and one for Molly, or guests. Don Sandoval was planning on visiting and bringing his wife in the future, and they would need a place to sleep. Molly would share a room with her mother until she was older. The floors were made of boards, while the sides of the cabin were made of split logs, the cracks filled in with plaster. Originally, Don Sandoval considered constructing the house from boards, but the logs would be much stronger and safer, and better insulated. Before placing the floor boards, a spacious cellar was dug out. Here, Magdalena could store fruits and vegetables. The trap door on the top was disguised, and after the house was finished, a Navajo rug would be placed over it.

"Here you can hide if you ever see Indians coming," instructed Don Sandoval.

"I have not seen one single Indian since I have been here, father."

Don Sandoval did not tell Magdalena what he knew. Captain Brooks had told him that the Apaches had been causing some trouble with settlers in the Sonora desert between Mexico and Tucson. It was only a matter of time before Magdalena would see them, and he wanted the log cabin to be fortified. It was cause for much worry for Don Sandoval.

He installed windows on the south and north side of the house, two on each wall. Shutters were placed on the outside, as well as the inside. The shutters had latches that could be locked in place. There were also two very small windows placed on both walls, with the same shutter design. These tiny windows would be used mainly for guns in case of an attack. They would also provide some degree of ventilation during the hot summer months. The log cabin would have an exterior porch that would wrap around the entire perimeter. Magdalena loved the outdoors, and she could do her washing, sewing and reading from a rocking chair on the porch. But the bunkhouse needed to be constructed before the porch on the cabin. The bunkhouse was a smaller dwelling with only one room. The dimensions would be ten feet by twelve feet. There would be a stove in the center, and two beds, one for each man. It also had a floor constructed of boards, and the same shutter design, although Don Sandoval knew that the inhabitants would all fair much better if the men were in the main house with Magdalena, should they fall under attack. It was merely a precaution. The bunkhouse had no cellar, and no porch, and if needed it could house an additional two men on small cots. When the bunkhouse was complete, the chicken coop and the outhouse came next. Both structures were finished in a day. The chicken coop was a very fine housing for chickens, thought Magdalena. The new chickens that Magdalena brought from Tucson were moved to the coop, but the others were left in the stall in the barn to hatch their chicks. Next, the finishing touches to Magdalena's house. The porch, the stove, the basin, the furnishings. Her wagon of furniture from the casita was unloaded, and she decorated the best that she could. She was still missing a bed, so she and Molly had to sleep on cots until one could be purchased. She dreaded another trip to Tucson, and decided that the cots were plenty good for Molly and herself. She had already adapted to the pioneer way of life, and it suited her well. The log cabin was beginning to fee like home.

Next, the mercantile needed to be built, but there was not enough lumber, and Don Sandoval would need to return to Santa Fe before his wife grew too anxious.

"I will be leaving for home in the morning," he announced to Magdalena. "When I return, I may bring your mother, and I may even bring Michael's mother. She expressed a desire to visit Michael's grave. I think I may bring Liam out to help you with the mercantile."

"No!" Magdalena interrupted. "Please do not bring Liam, Papa. I can handle the store by myself."

"Well, I need someone to help me drive these wagons back."

"Just not Liam, Papa, please!"

"What is your problem with Liam, Magdalena? I thought that you liked him."

"I do Papa, it is just that he reminds me of Michael. They look so much alike."

"Alright then, I will bring some of the cowboys, they can help me. But eventually you will have to let Liam come and visit his brother's grave. He is family, you know; you cannot avoid him forever."

"I know, Papa, I am just not ready yet. Papa, will you bring me a headstone for Michael? Something nice, made of stone?

"I think I can manage that. I will bring some regular beds, as well. When I come back, I will purchase the lumber for the mercantile. Until then, you will have to work from your barn. I am leaving Seamus here with you for now. He can help around your homestead, and learn some things from Cotton. I can travel faster without him, and, well, it is just not a safe trip for the two of us alone. I will go to Fort Craig and hook up with an attachment going to El Paso or Santa Fe. I hope to see you around Christmastime. That is a little over two months from now.

"You will not be able to get close to the lumber mill that time of year Papa. I have heard that they close for two or three months during the winter. The mill will reopen the first sign of Spring thaw, so please, do not try to attempt to go there first. What about Cotton and Charlie? Are you not taking them with you to Santa Fe?"

"And leave you and the children all alone out here? No, they have both agreed to stay on and work for you. I upped their salary a little, but when you have your ranch established, and get on your feet, you will have to start paying them yourself."

"I will, Papa."

"There is no use in me bringing you any beeves in the dead of winter. There will not be enough good fodder on the trail to deliver them; you will have to wait until Springtime."

"Papa, the Gila is a cattle trail. Perhaps I can purchase a few head from some cowboys when they come through."

"That, my daughter, is a splendid idea. Now go light that stove and warm this house warm of yours, will you?"

Chapter XXXV

Annabelle

The next morning, Magdalena's father said goodbye to Magdalena and the children and rode off quite early. Later in the day, Magdalena spotted the wagon train from El Paso in the distance. She was always happy to see visitors, and always just as happy to see them leave. From the time that she first spotted them until they arrived at the Triple Bar M, took exactly an hour. She walked down to the trail to greet them.

"Are you Miss Sandoval?" asked the trail boss.

"I am Mrs. Malone," replied Magdalena.

"Oh, I see. Well, we passed a man on the trail who told us that his daughter had a homestead on the San Pedro, and that she had a supply post. He identified himself as Sandoval."

"Yes, that would be me, and Sandoval is my father." she answered. "But I do not have many supplies that a wagon train might need. I have no food to sell you, other than some jarred preserves, but I do have some tools, and dry goods, canvas and India Rubber."

"Would you by chance have any horse shoeing supplies? My Ferrier has broken his rasp on a hard headed nag."

"Yes, I believe that I can help you with that, if I can put my hands on it. I really am not quite ready for business yet. Where are you camping tonight?"

"Well, we were planning on camping right here, where we always camp."

"No sir, you cannot camp on my homestead. I have to put a halt to that. You see, I am planning on ranching cattle here, and I need the good water and grass for my own livestock. You will have to pull your train up the river a mile or two. You will still have water and fodder for your livestock there."

"Well, do you mind if we just stop here for a piece and let these pilgrims buy some goods from you?"

"No, of course not."

"We have some wagons to mend, and horses to shoe," said the trail boss.

"Those things can be done two miles down the trail," replied Magdalena. "You can halt your train here for an hour, but make no mistake, this is my home and I do not want it defiled."

"Yes, ma'am," said the trail boss as he road back to the train to give the travelers instructions.

Magdalena sold the Ferrier a rasp, and some horseshoe nails. She sold some of the travelers on the train pails, and tin cups. One traveler who had a very poor wagon bought a large sheet of India rubber to cover his rotting canvas at nighttime and during the rain. It was an uncommonly cold fall, and turning colder by the day. Since the weather was much colder than usual, blankets were also in great demand. The travelers purchased what they could from Magdalena, and proceeded another two miles westward. The last of the wagons had just crossed the San Pedro, when one seemingly straggler halted to rest under a stand of cottonwoods below the old barn. Seven women in total emerged from the wagon. They went straight to work building a fire, and unhitching their thirsty mules. Cotton started toward them. "I will take care of this, Magdalena."

"No, Cotton, let me," she said.

As she approached the wagon of women she greeted them.

"Hello there," she called out. They all looked up at her approaching, and just as quickly went back to their chores without so much as a word of greeting in reply.

"You cannot stay here," said Magdalena as she approached the campsite.

"Says who?" asked an older lady of large stature. The portly woman placed her hands on her hips, and puffed up her chest.

"Says I," replied Magdalena. "You are on my homestead, and you cannot stay here."

"We were told that this homestead has been abandoned. How is it that you can just take it over?"

"I have done it legally in Tucson; I have the papers to prove it. Are you with that wagon train which just passed through?"

"Yes, I guess you could say that," answered the puffed up lady. "They don't want us too close though, so we just sort of hang behind a piece."

Magdalena looked around. The women were all still working on their chores, fairly unconcerned about Magdalena.

"Where are your men folk?" inquired Magdalena. The women all laughed.

"Why, they are waiting for us in the goldfields of California," replied the woman in charge. "And where is your husband?"

"Oh, he is here, but I would not count on seeing him if I were you." Magdalena had figured out who, or what these woman were. She looked around again, and noticed one young girl who appeared to be out of place. She must have been about sixteen years of age, maybe seventeen at the most. She had long blond hair that she wore in a braid down her back, and was wearing a plaid traveling dress with an apron over it. It was very proper attire. The girl was busying herself with food preparations. She picked up a pail and started toward the river.

"So, you are pulling out with the wagon train in the morning?" asked Magdalena.

"First thing," replied the older woman.

"I suppose that it will be alright if you spend one night here. It looks as though you are already settled in anyway."

"Very neighborly of you," replied the woman in a half sincere, half sarcastic tone.

Magdalena looked around for the young girl with the braid, but had lost sight of her. Perhaps she was going to the river to freshen herself, or fetch water. Without further conversation, Magdalena turned and walked back to her cabin. As she reached for the door she heard a voice call out to her in a whisper.

"Ma'am! Ma'am!"

She turned toward the direction of the voice. There stood the young girl with the long, blond braid.

"What is it?" ask Magdalena. "What are you doing up here? Should you not be down by the river with the rest of your companions?"

"No, I should not!" replied the girl, still whispering.

Magdalena could see that she was frightened or distressed.

"Can I come inside?" pleaded the girl.

"Well, my children are in the house, and I do not think that it would be a good idea to invite a stranger in. I always tell them, never let a stranger in the house."

"Please!" begged the young girl. "Just for a moment! I would like a word with you."

"Well, just for a moment then."

Reluctantly, Magdalena opened the door and gestured as if to invite the girl in. She pointed to a chair. The girl sat, and Magdalena pulled a chair up next to her. Seamus and Molly were sitting at the table in the kitchen, eating cornbread with fresh butter.

"Is that butter they are having with their corn cakes?" asked the girl. "I cannot remember the last time that I tasted fresh butter."

"Just what is it that you want to tell me?" asked Magdalena, growing impatient.

"I want to work for you," replied the girl.

"Work for me? There is nothing here for you to do," said Magdalena. "I have men working here and I do not need the distraction of a woman on my ranch. And, anyway, as I have already said, there is nothing for you to do here."

"But I just cannot go to California with those women. I just cannot!"

"Then why are you traveling with them?" asked Magdalena.

"I have made a mistake. That is all. I am human, and I have made a horrible mistake in a moment of desperation. I was deceived! You see, I was living in Albuquerque with my mother and father. My father left to fight in the war. One day, my mother received a telegram that he was not coming home. She about went crazy. She would not eat, she would not talk, she would not even bathe. She just sat in a chair looking out the window day after day, watching for my father to come home, but of course he never did. Then, one day she just up and left and she never came back. I waited and waited. For four months I waited. Then the men from the bank came. They told me that I had to leave. They gave me fifteen minutes to gather up my things. I did not know what to take, so I just put some clothes and a few necessities in my trunk, and I stepped outside. The moment that I was outside of the house, they boarded up all of the doors and windows. They wasted no time about it, and would not let me go back in. They would not let me take anything other than what I was carrying. I was so frightened. I did not know what to do or where to go. I knew at that moment that I was all alone in the world, with no place to go, and nobody to call family. I sat on the stoop of the only home that I had ever known, and I began to cry. I cried for an hour, or maybe longer. Eventually a girl came by, her name was Ruby. She asked me why I was crying. I explained, and she told me that she knew a lady, Miss Delilah who would give me work and take me in. I followed her to Miss Delilah's house, which was a very grand house with many rooms in a very busy part of town that I had never seen before. She offered me a job scrubbing floors and emptying chamber pots, doing laundry, and being a servant to many other girls. These girls who I catered to, worked on their backs all night and slept for most of the day. They smoked cigarettes and drank whiskey. I never had met any women like these women in my life before! That was two months ago. Now we are headed to California, where Miss Delilah is going to buy another house, and her best girls are going with her. I was under the impression that she was taking me to be a house servant in her new place in California, but I heard her talking one night to the girls when she thought that I was sleeping. She told them that she could auction me and probably get three hundred dollars for me in San Francisco, since I have not yet been spoiled. I do not want to go. I am not that sort of person. I am afraid! Please, please! You are a woman, have pity on me. Please help me."

"Annabelle!" A voice called out. "Annabelle, where are you! You best show yourself, and I mean it. I will take a strap to you girl!"

She looked at Magdalena with pleading eyes. There was a violent knock on the door. Magdalena rose and walked to answer it. She glanced at the rifle hanging over the door and contemplated taking it down, but then decided against it. She opened the door, but only a few inches.

"Yes?" she said. "What can I do for you."

"I'm lookin' fer my girl. Is she in there?"

"I do not want any trouble on my property. If you intend to cause trouble, you can take your leave now," replied Magdalena.

"Hand me over the girl and there will be no trouble. I know you have her in there."

"And if I do not?"

"Then you got some trouble on your hands Miss Fancy Pants, so jest hand 'er over."

"I will not," replied Magdalena.

"Oh yes you will," insisted Delilah. "She's my property and you will hand 'er over to me now, or pay me the three hundred dollars I plan to fetch in San Francisco when I sell her."

"Perhaps you have not heard, Madam, but slavery has been abolished in this country, and the selling of human souls is against the law. This girl of yours has a mind of her own, and she has decided that she will not go to California with you. Now you gather your girls and you get off my land!"

"There is no law out here, Miss Fancy Pants. I have an investment in her, now hand over the girl!" The brash woman produced a tiny pistol from her pocket and pointed it at Magdalena. Magdalena quickly tried to slam the heavy door, and the gun went off as she slammed it on the woman's arm. In the bunkhouse, Cotton and Charlie heard the gun shot and came running. They found the woman standing at the door, which Magdalena had managed to shut.

"What's going on here?" asked Cotton.

"I'm jest tryin' to git what's mine," answered the woman.

"Magdalena!" called Cotton. "Open the door, let me in!"

Magdalena cracked the door open, but just a bit, and Cotton pushed his way in, while Charlie trained his rifle on the buxom old woman. Magdalena was unharmed, the bullet had not found its mark. Instead, it had missed her and lodged itself in the log wall. Magdalena explained what had transpired, and asked

Cotton to escort the women off her property. If they refused to go, then Charlie was to ride out to the wagon train and fetch the trail boss. They would send word to Fort Huachuca for the soldiers to come and move these women off the Triple Bar M, and then the woman would see that there was indeed law out in these parts.

Charlie and Cotton stood over the women with rifles trained as they packed up their belongings and hitched up their team. As they drove past Magdalena's cabin, the old woman called out, "I'll be back fer what's mine, Miss Fancy Pants. I'll be back, and you best be watchin' over yer shoulder!"

Magdalena watched for a long while as Charlie and Cotton followed the wagon across the San Pedro and down the Gila. Then she went back inside. She put her copper kettle on the stove to boil some water for tea. It was growing late in the evening, and she needed to put dinner on. For a long while, she worked without saying a word. The children also were strangely quiet. She poured some tea for the young visitor, and instructed her to sit at the kitchen table. She placed the cup in front of the young woman. All the while she was thinking to herself, "What now? What am I going to do with this situation?"

Annabelle was the first to break the silence.

"Your cabin is so warm, and cozy," she said.

"Yes it is," replied Magdalena. "My cabin is very cozy. It is just big enough for the children and me. Any more would be a crowd."

"Thank you for saving me from Delilah," said Annabelle "She is an awful woman, and I truly am sorry to have put you in the middle. It is clear that you are unhappy, but I will figure out something soon. I promise you that I will not stay long."

There was another long silence.

"Do you have any suggestions?" asked Annabelle.

"I am trying to think!" said Magdalena. "You cannot stay here, we agree on that. I have enough on my hands without taking on more. I will have Cotton take you to Fort Huachuca tomorrow, and the soldiers there can decided what to do with you. Perhaps you can find work as a cook, or laundress there."

"But that is where the wagon train is heading. Delilah will be there. She will strap me and cuff me to the wagon so I cannot run away again."

Magdalena made dinner without speaking much. Finally, she sent Seamus to fetch Cotton and Charlie to eat. Together, they sat at the table and ate dinner without their normal light-hearted conversation. Finally, Magdalena spoke.

"I intended on baking pies today, but the events of the day kept me too preoccupied to do so, so I am afraid that there will be no dessert tonight. I apologize for that. Seamus, I would like you to get your cot and Molly's and put them in my room. You will sleep with me tonight. Cotton, will you please fetch another cot from the store's supply for Miss Annabelle? She will be spending a day or two with us. If we do not have any visitors from Fort Huachuca in the next two days, then I will have to ask you men to escort Annabelle to the fort, if you do not mind."

"I don't mind," said Cotton. "Not at all."

"I don't mind neither, Miss Magdalena," said Charlie.

"Good, then in the meantime you can make yourself useful around here," she instructed Annabelle. "Seamus, please fetch some water so Annabelle and I can wash the dishes. Charlie, tomorrow will you please bring a barrel up from the barn so we can store water here at the cabin? It seems so unproductive to be running to the river every time we need water."

After the dishes were washed, Magdalena showed Annabelle to the children's room.

"You can sleep here." She handed the girl two Mexican blankets. "I do not have any extra pillows; you will have to improvise, or do without."

At that moment, Annabelle realized that everything that she owned in the world was in Delilah's wagon. She did not even have a change of clothes, or a ribbon for her hair. She had been reduced to nothing more than a beggar. Still it was better than the alternative.

"We rise early around here," said Magdalena. Breakfast is at seven thirty." She left the room, closing the door behind her. She put Molly to bed, and she and Seamus stayed up a little longer. She had missed her conversations with Seamus. He was still a child, and yet so grown up. He always had a smile to share, and Magdalena found comfort in his presence.

"What are you going to do with that lady?" he asked.

"I have not thought that far ahead, Seamus. I do not yet know. Have you any suggestions?"

"Maybe you could build another room on the cabin and she can stay here and be part of our family," he replied.

"No, Seamus, I like our family the way it is. And besides, I have a secret. I will share it with you if you promise not to tell anyone."

"I promise! I can keep a secret," he said.

"I am expecting a baby, Seamus."

The boy's eyes grew very large and his mouth puckered up.

"A baby!" he echoed.

"Shhhh, now remember, you promised. You cannot tell anyone."

"A baby," he repeated in a whisper. "What will your baby's name be Maggie?"

"It will be Michael, of course."

"But what if it's a girl?"

"It will not be a girl, Seamus. It will be a boy, and his name will be Michael. He is the last great gift that my husband gave me before he died."

"Why is it a secret, Maggie?"

Magdalena smiled. She enjoyed hearing the name that Michael had given her.

"If Papa finds out that I am going to have a baby, he will never let me stay here, Seamus. Do you understand now?"

"Yes, I do."

~*~

Three days passed, and Magdalena had no visitors from Fort Huachuca, so she instructed Cotton and Charlie to take Annabelle to the fort and hand her over to the soldiers. By now, the wagon train would have moved along, and Annabelle would be safe from Delilah. The girl had been pleasant, and helpful, but Magdalena did not want or need another woman in her house.

"But Magdalena," protested Cotton. "Shouldn't one of us stay here with you at the cabin? I don't feel right leaving you and the kids all alone."

"We will be fine, Cotton. I am far safer here in my cabin than you are out there on the floor of the Sonora Desert. Leave early in the morning and try to make it in a day. Try to go twenty miles at least. The weather is not too warm now, and you will cross water twice on the way, so you can push the horses a bit harder than you normally would. You can take your time coming back, though. Stay the night at Fort Huachuca and get some good food and rest if you like. I will be fine. Turn out the livestock before you leave in the morning. They can take care of themselves. I can take care of the cow and chickens. You better keep Ginger in a stall; she will try to follow Blaze. She will nicker and carry on for a spell, until she can no longer hear or smell Blaze, and then I will turn her out."

~*~

The two men delivered Annabelle to the fort without incident. She was very sad to be passed off the way that she had been, but Cotton promised that he would come and visit her in two Sundays. He would pack a picnic and they would lunch together on the scenic grounds of the fort.

Annabelle was taken into the home of one of the officers stationed at the fort. The Captain's wife had been sick on and off for more than a year, and was too weak most of the time to do the regular chores and take care of the children. There was already had one servant that cleaned the house, and did the laundry. They also had a cook. Annabelle's primary job was to take care of the children. She would dress them in the morning, and walk them to the school on the fort, then pick them up in the afternoon and walk them home. There was a girl, ten years old, and a boy, eight years old in her charge. The Captain who she worked for was a kind man. He loved his family very much and was good to Annabelle. She thought of her own father, and how much she had missed being part of a real family. Her accommodations here were comfortable and pleasant. The Captain's wife referred to Annabelle as her "Godsend." The best part about it was, she was free to do as she pleased on Sundays. That would be her day off. She could go to church with the family, and dine with the family, or not. It was entirely up to her. At the end of each month she was to be paid a salary of twelve dollars. The situation turned out to be ideal for her.

Chapter XXXVI
The Cowboys

Weeks rolled past, and Magdalena was beginning to show her condition. Although nothing was said, Cotton and Charlie knew that she was with child.

One Winter morning, after she collected eggs and fed her hens, she walked down to the barn to milk her cow. Cotton was saddling up Blaze. Ginger had a pack saddle on her, and Magdalena knew that the men were going out to hunt.

"What day is it Cotton?" she asked.

"It's Thursday," he replied.

"No, I mean what is the date today?"

"Oh, it's January first."

"We missed Christmas?"

"Yup."

"I thought my father would be here before Christmas. Do you suppose something has happened?"

"I don't know, Magdalena, but don't fret too much. He's not all that late yet."

"You and Charlie are going hunting?"

"Yup. Need to get some fresh meat."

Magdalena shivered and hugged herself to keep warm.

"It's so cold, I bet my cow is going to give me frozen milk," she said.

"You ready yet, Cotton?" Charlie called. He was already mounted up on his horse and ready to go. With their rifles across their saddles, they promised not to return without some fresh venison or elk, and they rode off. Magdalena watched the two men ride off for a long time as she thought of her absent father, and the Christmas that her children had missed. She finished her chore of milking the cow and started back toward her cabin. From the east, she noticed the trail of dust that always meant somebody was coming. The men had ridden off toward the west, and Magdalena wondered if they had seen the dust. It would be an hour before the cause of the dust trail would arrive at her homestead, she knew this from experience. When the children woke, she scrambled eggs and gave them bread with butter and milk. The wild plums and berries along the river had long been exhausted, and the trees were barren. Two more months of winter, Magdalena thought. She pondered all of the things that she wanted to do in the springtime, and longed for the warm sun on her shoulders. She would plant a vegetable garden, and some fruit trees, and acquire some livestock.

After breakfast, she cleaned the dishes and went outside to check the progress of the visitors. She was always a bit apprehensive about Indians, but still she had not seen any. When she looked toward the east she saw a great heard of cattle. From a long distance she could hear the whistles and shouts of the coaching men driving the herd. Finally! The cowboys she had heard about. They were coming and they were bringing a large herd of beeves with them. She had not seen any travelers on the Gila for over two months, and was anxious to hear news of back east. Any news at all. On her homestead she had been very secluded from the outside world, although Cotton and Charlie made trips to Fort Huachuca every other Sunday. On occasion they would bring back newspapers, sometimes weeks old, and she devoured them. She read them over and over until she had nearly memorized them. She also entertained Molly and Seamus with them, by reading them aloud, and using them as teaching tools for Seamus.

"Quickly, children! Cowboys are coming, and they have many animals with them!"

Together, Magdalena and the children walked down to the river, followed by Molly's dog, which Molly now called Laz. Laz was her abbreviated way of saying Lazarus, which is what her mother had named him since he had been so close to death, and then recovered strongly. The other dogs also followed at a distance. They were not as tame as Laz, but they no longer posed a threat, and in Magdalena's mind they were actually a comfort, adding a degree of security for her. The small family sat by the river and waited until the herd arrived on her homestead. A leathered but good-looking man approached her on his horse.

"Hello!" he said. "You must be the woman of the house."

"Hello yourself!" answered Magdalena. "I am. I am happy to see you. We have been without visitors for weeks. Do you have time to rest your herd and have coffee with us?"

"Time is always an issue, especially since we got such a late start, but I'm sure the men would welcome the break."

"Are you the trail boss?" asked Magdalena.

"That, and the owner of these poor animals. I guess we should have waited a month or two, there's not much for these animals to eat on the trail this time of year. But I have a contract, and I need to get them to market. You really don't mind me pausing them on your land?"

"Not at the moment," said Magdalena. "Although, it may be different in the future. Anyway, like you said, there is not much here for them to damage. I will put a pot of coffee on while you get your men. I am anxious to hear any news that you can bring me."

The trail boss called in his men, leaving two to watch over the herd.

Magdalena fed them bread and butter, and again scrambled up some eggs which were plentiful. She produced some preserves from her pantry that she had been rationing, but the occasion called for it.

"Where are you coming from?" ask Magdalena. "And where are you headed?"

"We came from El Paso, have a contract to deliver these beeves to the Army in Tucson," he replied. "I guess they're getting hungry up there."

"Well, you are almost there," said Magdalena. "Will you be coming back this way?"

"Yes, but not right away. We plan on staying in Tucson for a week, maybe two. Uh, is your husband around?"

"Yes, he is around. He went out with our hands for a deer this morning early, but he should be back any time now."

"They say the Indians in these parts are on a war party. I don't think they should leave you and your kids alone out here."

"Well, thank you for the information, I'll let him know. I am expecting my father to come any day now with some more men. We are building a supply post here on my homestead. He is already a week late. I do not suppose that you saw anything on the trail did you?"

"No, ma'am, where is he coming from?"

"Santa Fe."

"They had an unusually hard winter this year, ma'am. The town was snowed in for over three weeks. If he could have been here, I'm sure that he would have been. Try not to worry too much."

"Sir, I do not suppose that you could spare any of those beeves that you are driving up to the Army, could you?"

"How many you looking for?"

"Thirty or forty, depending on the price. I do not have much money on hand now, but I have applied for my brand, and my intentions are to start a small herd of my own."

"That would mean competition for me. Why would the Army buy my cattle from El Paso when they could get 'um right here?"

"No sir, I only have one hundred and sixty acres here, not enough to support a large herd. Mainly I would be supplying the wagon trains that come through here."

"Well then, I will sell you twenty head, at twenty five dollars a head."

"Twenty five dollars a head! For those scrawny animals?"

The cowboys chuckled. "They will fatten up just fine come springtime," said the trail boss, "but you'll need to feed them until the grass comes up."

"If they do not die first," said Magdalena.

"She has a point there," one of the cowboys jokingly said.

The trail boss gave him a look of disapproval.

"I will pay you twenty dollars a head for twenty animals," she said. "It is all the money I have anyway, so I cannot offer you any more."

Magdalena was hiding the fact that she had a large sum of money on the premises. She glanced toward the window to see if there was any sign of Cotton.

"All right, you have a deal lady."

"I would like mostly heifers and cows, please. I will need them to start my herd and increase my stock."

The trail boss narrowed his eyes, and then told his men to cut out twenty beeves from the herd. They put the cattle in a round pen that had been left by the former homesteaders, and repaired and renewed by Cotton and Charlie. All parties satisfied, they bid their goodbyes as Magdalena's hands rode up with a deer across Ginger's back.

"Afternoon, Mr. Malone," the trail boss greeted as he rode past Cotton.

"Afternoon yourself," Cotton replied with a puzzled look on his face.

"Look Cotton! I am a rancher now," said Magdalena. "We will keep them in the round pen for now. Tomorrow we can brand them, and by that time the herd will be well on their way to Tucson and we can turn these beeves out without worry that they will follow the herd. Will you water them for me, please?"

"I'm already on it," said Charlie. "You can dress out that meat while I take care of these beeves."

"I will get the oven started," said Magdalena. We will have roast venison for dinner tonight, with mashed potatoes."

Cotton dressed out the deer and cut a roast from it's leg, before hanging it from a pulley in the barn. He pulled the dead animal up high enough to keep the dogs and varmints away from it, and took the large roast to Magdalena.

Supper was served early that day, and all present ate until their bellies could take no more, even the dogs.

Chapter XXXVII

The Apache

Over the next few days, the weather began to warm. Although it was still quite chilly when Magdalena milked her cow in the morning, she could feel that springtime in the air. Seemingly, the flora had changed overnight. The wild plum trees by the river were budding. Tiny shoots of grass broke through the ground. Birds were singing before she was out of bed in the morning, and she was thankful. Her beeves were thin and in need of grass, but it would take time for the new grass to mature and develop the nutrients that the cattle needed to gain weight. She still looked for her father every day, but two weeks had passed since the cowboys came through, and there was no sign of him.

"Cotton, I need you and Charlie to take one of the wagons to Tucson and buy some grain for the livestock and some chicken feed. I will give you a list of things to buy. I am running low on potatoes, and I need yams, and apples. I think you should go right away. Those poor animals look as though they are starving."

Magdalena had become comfortable being alone with the children on her homestead. Nothing unpleasant had ever happened since Michael's death, and she felt sure that her father would show any day. Ever since she had decided to stay on, she had a feeling that Michael was watching over her and Molly.

Cotton harnessed four mules to a wagon, and he and Charlie set out for the three day trip to Tucson.

Magdalena was starting to get that nesting feeling that comes in the last couple of months of pregnancy. She cleaned out the chicken coop and her cow's stall, and did her laundry before taking the children to the river to fish. They sat for a while on the banks of the river with nary a bite.

"I think that Papa will be here any day now," she announced to the children. "I think that I should bake some bread before he arrives. I hope that he brings some of Mama's blackberry preserves. It will dress the bread up so much finer than just butter. Come children, let us go back to the cabin."

"Can't Molly and me stay here and fish a little longer?" asked Seamus.

"Molly and I, Seamus, not Molly and me. Molly is still so little Seamus, what if she falls in the river?"

"I can swim, I'll watch her Maggie. I'll watch her really good."

"I wanna fish!" proclaimed Molly.

"Well, all right then, but just for a little while. And stay where I can see you from the window."

Magdalena went into the cellar and retrieved a ten pound sack of flour. She went straight to work preparing a huge amount of bread dough. She added yeast, sugar, salt and milk to the batter. After it was kneaded and divided into eight loaf sized portions, she covered the dough to let it rise. The day was warming up, which was good for rising dough. She then walked down to the river and found Molly and Seamus playing by the water.

"Look Mama! Pawywogs!"

"That is a good sign, Molly. It means the cold weather is going away, and now springtime is here. Soon we will pick wild currants and make pies!"

Magdalena looked around for any sign of trail dust. Her angst regarding her father's arrival was beginning to unnerve her.

"Bring your poles back to the house now," she instructed her children. I will make you a snack and we will read for a while from the big story book."

As Magdalena read to the children, Molly fell asleep, as her mother knew she would. Magdalena put her down in her cot, and Seamus took the story book and retreated to his own cot. Although Magdalena was trying to teach him to read, he still had not grasped it, but he enjoyed looking at the paintings in the book. Magdalena checked the fire in her oven, and checked the dough. It was ready. She put four loaves in the oven, which is all that it could hold, and an hour later she put the next four in. The cabin was starting to feel quite warm, so she opened all of the windows, and a refreshing breeze drifted through the rooms at a constant, steady flow. It was so inviting that she decided to open the little windows, and the door as well. She placed the finished loaves of bread by the window to cool, and went looking about her cupboards, taking inventory on her food stores. As she turned about and glanced out the window, she felt the presence of someone standing in the big room. She turned to look, expecting to see one of the children, but it was not Seamus or Molly. She gasped, and put her hand to her mouth. There, standing in her house, was an Indian. She had not heard him enter. They stared at each other for a long moment. Magdalena wanted to look toward the room where the children were sleeping, but did not dare take her eyes off the Indian. He motioned with the sign language that Indians commonly use, and it was easy enough to figure out what he was saying. He pointed to the loaves of bread, and put his hand to his mouth, then said something in his native language to her. It sounded strangely familiar. Slowly, Magdalena walked to the window where the bread was cooling. She picked up one of the large loaves and took it to the kitchen table. Then she slowly picked up the knife to slice it. The bread was still warm, and the dough pressed down and flattened as she sliced off an ample piece. The Indian watched her in silence. He stared at the knife in her hand. Magdalena stabbed the generous portion of bread with her knife. She held the knife way out in front of her toward the interloper, as to offer him the bread that was attached to the end of it. He took the bread from the knife and held it to his nose, and then tore a large piece of it off with his teeth.

"You have to leave," said Magdalena.

The Indian just stared at her as he chewed the bread.

"Leave!" she repeated, pointing the knife to the door. She knew that the Indian must have understood her own form of sign language, but still he did not move.

Then, from somewhere in the deep recesses of her childhood memories, an unfamiliar word found her tongue, and in her mother's Mescalero language, she said it again. "Leave!"

This time the stranger reacted. He looked at her inquisitively, and said something to her in his own tongue which was familiar, but not quite the same as her mother's Mescalero dialect. He repeated himself, and Magdalena understood enough to know that he was asking her how she knew that word. In her mother's language she struggled to tell him that her mother was Mescalero. All at once, the silent stranger began to spew words at her. She tried to catch them, but they came too quickly. She could catch one of every four or five. He wanted her to go outside, or look outside, something outside of the cabin. She looked at the open door and saw four more Indian men on horses. She wondered where they had come from; they were not there a moment ago, and she had not heard them arrive. She stabbed the remainder of the loaf of bread and again offered it to the Indian for his comrades. As the Apache reached for the bread, a tiny voice came from the door of the bedroom where the children had been sleeping.

"Mama?"

There stood Molly and Seamus holding hands in the doorway. Laz was standing in front of Molly with his lips curled back, announcing his disapproval with a low guttural growl. The dog knew the entire time that the Indian was there, but he never left

Molly's side, and kept his presence clandestine until it needed to be revealed.

The Indian spoke again. Something about a man. Magdalena's heart started to race. He was wondering where her husband was. She just shook her head as if to say that she didn't understand, but the Indian translated her sign language that she did not have a husband. He said one last word to Magdalena and walked out the door. She watched him walk to where the others were waiting on their horses. They divided the bread, and the interloper mounted his horse and they rode off. She had no way of knowing, but from that day on she would be known to the Apaches in that area as the Woman With no Tribe. She did not sleep well that night, and made sure that all of the windows and the door were tightly latched. The following day, Magdalena was still quite nervous. She repeatedly looked toward the east, and to the west for the trail of dust that announced visitors. A short while past noon, she checked again, and this time she saw what she was looking for. From the east there was a tiny trail of dust coming toward the Triple Bar M, and from the west, there was a large trail of dust. For days the only visitors had been five Indian men, and now it looked as though many visitors were coming. Magdalena prayed that they were not Indians. Moreover, she prayed that her father had finally arrived.

Chapter XXXVIII

The Reunion

They all arrived at once. From the east came Magdalena's father, along with several men and wagons. With him was Magdalena's mother, which was a wonderful surprise. From the west came Cotton and Charlie, along with the cowboys who had passed through earlier.

There was much commotion as the men halted their wagons and unhitched their hungry and spent livestock. The cattle and horses scattered toward the river and the premature foliage. Magdalena scooped up Molly, and she and Seamus ran to greet their parents.

"Oh, Papa! I was so worried! I was beginning to think something happened."

"Well, the only thing that happened was bad weather. We could not leave, and then when we thought we could, I decided to wait a while longer so that the livestock would have fodder along the trail. I did not want to take chances with your new herd. Magdalena," Don Sandoval paused. "Magdalena?" He pointed at Magdalena's swollen belly.

"It is Michael's baby, Papa. I was pregnant when he died. He did not even know."

"When is your child due?" asked Dona Sandoval.

"I am thinking the end of March or beginning of April, Mama."

"Well, we should still be here. I will help you deliver, and then I think you best come home with your Papa and me to raise these children proper."

"I will not leave, Mama. This is my home. This is my homestead. This is my mercantile. I will not leave it to someone else's care, and I will not leave Michael. I will never leave Michael; I intend to keep the promise that I made to him. Besides, Mama, I love it here."

"I told you, wife," said Don Sandoval. "It is of no use to try and change her mind, you might as well get used to the idea."

"I saw the beeves, Papa, thank you!" said Magdalena, changing the subject.

"We started out with thirty, but one of the cows gave birth on the way, and that held us up a couple more days," said Don Sandoval. "I wanted to give the poor calf and the mama a little time to rest. I thought about shooting it and having a veal dinner, but then I had second thoughts."

Don Sandoval chuckled at his poor attempt at a joke.

"You better not, Papa! I bought twenty head from a trail boss who came through here also, mostly heifers. He is there with Cotton now. When these new beeves are stronger, we will brand them with the Triple Bar M.

Cotton and Charlie have just arrived from Tucson. I sent them for grain and a few other things. I will have them feed the livestock some of the oats that they brought back. We ourselves have had a most lacking diet for the past few weeks. I do hope that you have brought some of your blackberry preserves Mama."

"You know that I did, Magdalena," she replied. "Along with some of my jarred peaches, and pickled cucumbers, and a few other things from the garden."

"How wonderful!" said Magdalena. "We will have one, big, wonderful supper this evening! I will invite the cowboys to join us. They rode back from Tucson with Cotton and Charlie. It is safer to travel in numbers."

"Come up to the house and rest, Mama, while these men take care of the livestock."

At that moment, Magdalena saw him. She felt a wave of anger come over her. A warm tingling consumed her body, starting in her face, and filling her entire being, right down to her little toes.

"Papa, you promised me! You promised that you would not bring Liam!"

"I had to Magdalena. That is his brother up there in that grave. He wanted to come, and I could not deny him. Besides, I needed him to help with the wagons. His mother and sister wanted to come as well, but I convinced them to stay and take care of the mercantile. I told them that they could come out on the next trip."

"Come, Mama, we have much to catch up on," Magdalena said taking her mother's arm and pulling her along toward the cabin.

"I will have the men bring up the beds I brought you," called Don Sandoval to his daughter as she and his wife, and the children walked toward the cabin. Magdalena glanced back at her father, but did not verbally acknowledge him.

"You brought beds for us?" asked Magdalena, looking at her mother.

"Of course we did. Your father wants you to be comfortable here."

They reached the cabin, and Dona Sandoval paused at the door. She looked around at the cabin and thought about the beautiful little casita that her husband had built for Magdalena and Michael. This cabin was nothing in comparison. Boards for floors, and the walls were logs. Magdalena had done her best to furnish it with the Navajo rugs and oil painting that once had adorned her casita, but it was not the same.

"How do you live like this Magdalena?" her mother asked.

"Live like what?" her daughter answered.

"Out here in this barren land with no neighbors, in this, this miner's shack!"

"Mama, I love my cabin. It is very cozy. And I do have neighbors. They are just a little further away than the neighbors in Santa Fe. It is what I have always heard you tell Papa that you wanted, yourself. To be out of the city and not so close to all those people."

"But Magdalena, this is so remote, so primitive."

"This is my home Mama. And it is not barren at all. It is bucolic. You will see when you open your eyes. It is beautiful here. I am glad that people do not know about this place, or it would soon be like Santa Fe, or Tucson, all dirty, and smelly, and spoiled."

Some of the men walked in with the beds and Don Sandoval instructed them where to set them up. More men came through the door with sacks of apples, potatoes, yams, beans, carrots, flour, coffee, and other staples that Magdalena had sent Cotton and Charlie for in Tucson. They opened the cellar door and began stacking up the food sacks. Then came crates of preserves, jarred fruit, pickles, dried fruit and jerky, and Magdalena's favorite, fresh green chilies.

"Mama! We could live on all this food for years! I will start making super now. We have many mouths to feed, and much to celebrate."

Magdalena asked Charlie to build two big fires outside; the kind they made on the wagon train. She asked him to bring two tri-pods and big pots from the barn. When the fires were hot and the coals were ready she put water and salt in the pots and brought them to a boil. One pot was for beans, the other for potatoes. She lit the oven in the cabin and put in several yams. She and her mother roasted green chilies and set them out to cool. Later they would skin them and fill them with bacon and cheese. Don Sandoval brought in a large ham. When the yams were finished, Magdalena would put the ham in the oven. There was no time for making pies, but the fresh ripe apples would be good enough, along with some jarred peaches.

"Mama, I have not eaten this well since I left Santa Fe," said Magdalena. Seamus, will you please put Molly down for her nap? Then you can go help the men with their doings."

"Yes, ma'am," replied Seamus as he went straight to the task.

"He is such a good boy," said Dona Sandoval. "Your father and I have come to love him very much, and we have missed him these past few months while he has been with you."

"Does that mean that you intend to take him home with you, Mama?"

"The house is so lonely without him, Magdalena. Your father and I would like to see that he has a proper education. It will not be long before he is a young man and can help with the business."

"Of course, it would be best for him. I am so pleased that you took him under your wing. He was great company to me on the trail. The poor thing, his mother was so unkind to him. I can see that he has thrived since being with you and Papa. It looks much stronger, and had grown much taller."

"It is truly a tragedy the way that his own mother treated him," replied Dona Sandoval. "But not an unfamiliar one. Life can be so hard and cruel at times. We all discover that at one time or another."

"Let us not talk of sorrowful things now, Mama. It is a celebration, all of us being together now. I am so happy that you have decided to stay on for a few weeks."

"Your father will take some of the men to the lumber mill for lumber to build your store. I think maybe I will suggest that he add on to your cabin. It is much too small for my liking."

"Mama," Magdalena laughed. "I like it just fine, and it is only Molly and me. We do not need another room."

The food was almost ready, and the long table was brought out of the cabin and put in the yard for a place to set all of the culinary dishes that the woman had prepared. Chairs were randomly placed as people brought them from the cabin, and all of the men used their own mess kits. Magdalena brought out tin plates, instead of her good earthenware dishes, for those who had none of their own. Finally, the large ham was placed in the center of the table, and Don Sandoval began to carve it.

"Everybody, please help yourself!" said Magdalena. As she turned, she came face to face with Liam.

"I am sorry if me coming upsets ya', Magdalena. Your father told me that you did not want me here."

"Liam, I," Magdalena stammered while she searched for the right words.

"No, it's OK," said Liam. "I really do understand. I just had to come, and I hope that you can understand that."

"I do Liam, I do." She gave her brother in law a hug to tell him that everything was fine.

"How is Fannie?" she asked.

"We'll be havin' a baby!" answered Liam. "She's seven months along now."

"That is wonderful!" said Magdalena. "The cousins will be practically the same age then!"

"Aye!"

"You must be starving, Liam. Go help yourself to some food now."

The news came as bittersweet to Magdalena. It was not fair. She would have to raise her babies without her husband. Fannie had her young, healthy husband to raise a family with. Magdalena tried to dismiss the thought and replace it with a happier one. Looking around, she noticed that everyone was eating. She then went inside to wake her still sleeping baby, and found her already awake in her cot, singing to Laz. Magdalena changed her baby's diaper, and told her that she was going to have a grand meal with her Grandpa, and Grandma. Then she took her hand, and Laz followed them out to the picnic. The skittish dog came out of his shell enough that day to make his rounds. People were offering him scraps and telling him what a good dog he was, while the other dogs kept creeping around the perimeter of the festivities.

"When did you acquire this passel of dogs, Magdalena?" her father asked.

"Oh, they came with the property. They are a bit wild, but feel free to throw them some scraps. They are used to me feeding them."

Magdalena's mother was about to protest when she suddenly froze. Five Indians on horseback were riding toward them.

"Indians! Indians!" she cried out in terror.

Some of the men ran for their guns.

"No! Stop! It is alright!" said Magdalena running between the pointed guns and the Indians. "They are friendly," she said.

Still mounted on his horse, the Indian who had visited her a few days earlier handed her a parfleche. She opened it, and removed a fine pair of high top deerskin moccasins. Then she removed another pair of smaller ones, that were shorter, not boots but shoes. Lastly was a tiny pair, soft with rabbit fur on the inside. Magdalena realized that the moccasins were for her children, even the one not yet born.

"Thank you," she told her Indian friend, holding the tiny moccasins to her chest. Then she told him again in Mescalero, thank you.

Her mother was shocked. It had been a dozen years or more since she had spoken to Magdalena in her own mother's native tongue. How did she remember after all these years?

"Magdalena!" said her mother as she hesitantly approached. "You do not speak Apache."

"Oh, but I do Mama. Thank you for teaching me, it has come in handy. I only wish that I could remember more."

Magdalena turned toward the Indian and said the word for "eat" using the sign language that he had used with her the day that he showed up at the cabin hungry. She pointed to all of the mounted men, and again motioned to eat, and then pointed to the feast on the table. They readily accepted.

Dona Sandoval was about to chastise her daughter, but Magdalena interrupted.

"This is like Thanksgiving!" she proclaimed. Then, she turned to speak to her mother.

"Of all the people present here today, Mama, I would think that you would be the most open-minded. I have to say that I am more than a little bit surprised. I need these Indians to like me. I need them to be on my side, be my friends. Can you not understand that? They have done nothing to me, and I have nothing against them."

"Are you forgetting about the Browns, Magdalena?"

"No Mama, I do not forget about the Browns. I saw them, dead, massacred, and mutilated! Remember? I was there! I saw their traumatized little girls, too. But these people could not possibly be the same Indians who killed the Browns. I will not condemn these men for what others have done. I could use your help with communicating with them, Mama. And in the next few weeks, I would like you to speak to me in Apache as much as possible. I need to relearn the language so that I may communicate with my neighbors."

"You must give them a gift in return," said Dona Sandoval. It would be best to give them all something. If you can, give them something better than the moccasins."

"Please watch Molly for me Mama, and feed her while I go to the barn."

Magdalena came back to the feast with five colorful Mexican blankets. She gave each man a blanket, and could tell by their faces that they were pleased. The man who had visited her cabin pointed to the carving knife that lay on the platter next to the ham. To the shock of the onlookers, Magdalena handed it to him without hesitation.

"They say that you must be very wealthy," said Magdalena's mother. "They wonder why your husband has turned you out."

"Mama, will you tell them that my husband is dead?"

"I cannot, Magdalena."

"Do it Maria," her husband commanded. "It will be fine."

"But they will know that Magdalena is a woman alone here!" she protested.

"Do it Maria," he ordered her again. "They know that there are men here with her. Surely they have seen Cotton and Charlie."

Dona Sandoval did as her husband instructed. She engaged herself in a conversation with the disbelieving Indians. She explained to them that she was Magdalena's mother, and that her own mother had been Mescalero. In reply, they told her that no harm would ever come to Magdalena by any person of their tribe. They were happy to have her as a neighbor. Magdalena saw a hint of a smile on her mother's face. Dona Sandoval was pleased with the conversation, pleased with herself. She knew now that she could feel better about Magdalena's situation in the Sonora Desert. She knew as allies, these Indians would protect her, and not harm her. Her daughter was very wise to foresee that, and that pleased her.

Turning to Magdalena, she told her daughter "They have given you a name. It is 'Woman With No Tribe'."

Magdalena smiled. "You must teach me how to say it Mama."

She looked at her Indian friend and said the word for good. Then her daughter Molly repeated it, and the Indian men laughed.

Magdalena put the little moccasins on Molly and said the word good again, and again, Molly repeated it. Then she handed Seamus his gift. His eyes became very big, and he wasted no time putting on the deerskin boots.

"These are the best shoes that I've ever had, Maggie. They are so comfortable. I feel like Davy Crocket! Or Kit Carson!"

Magdalena smiled and thought to herself, "This really is like Thanksgiving. And I have so much to be thankful for. Thank you God for this glorious day".

Before the Indians left, Magdalena wrapped up some meat, and put it in the parfleche. She added a jar of peaches which seemed to be their favorite dish on the smorgasbord, and handed it back to her Indian friend. Without any more words, he mounted his horse, and the five men rode away sitting on their new blankets.

The following day, the wagons were unloaded and Liam, along with the other men, left for Santa Fe with the empty earthly vessels. Don Sandoval, Cotton, and Charlie, were preparing to leave on horseback for Turkey Creek. They would buy more lumber to build the store. As Cotton saddled up his horse, Magdalena rested her chin upon her arm which was laid across the fence.

"I am sorry that we have kept you so busy, Cotton. You have missed the last two Sundays at Fort Huachuca. Annabelle must think that you have forgotten about her."

"It's the other way, Magdalena. The unmarried soldiers are keeping her busy at the fort, and she has asked me not to call on her anymore."

"Oh, I see. I am sorry, Cotton. You must be very lonely out here. You do not have to stay on you know."

"What do you mean Magdalena?"

"You are free to go back to Santa Fe. You need not feel obligated to me, Charlie and you. I do not wish to stand in the way of your dreams or future."

"Well, Magdalena, truth be told, I have sorta come to like it out here. Charlie has too, but I will relay your message to him. When things quiet down a bit, I would like to make another trip to Tucson though. There sure are some pretty senoritas there. The problem is, they never go anywhere without their parents. They are always surrounded by family."

Magdalena laughed. Cotton mounted his horse, and the men said their goodbyes to the ladies and children.

Dona Sandoval was leery of being left on the homestead with no men, but felt much better knowing that the Indians would not molest them. She and Magdalena spent that day on the porch, catching up on the news from Santa Fe, and speaking Apache.

Chapter XXXIX
The Notched-Nose Squaw

Magdalena and her mother sat on the porch with their sewing while the children played. They carried on a conversation, almost entirely in the Mescalero tongue. Magdalena was picking it up quickly, the words were coming back to her. As the two women sat talking, some sort of movement caught Magdalena's eye. It came from down by the river. She looked closely, as she had come to know that when this happened it normally meant that something, or somebody was there. She saw nothing, but a moment later Laz started barking and pacing back and forth with his head down, his ears pinned back, and the hair on his back sticking up.

"Children, go in the house," said Magdalena. "Now!"

Normally, Laz would follow Molly, but this time he stayed close to the river, his keen eye trained on something that Magdalena's own eye could not see.

"Mama, please stay in the cabin with the children. I see the other dogs watching. I will be all right." Magdalena reached for the scatter gun that was hanging over the door.

"No, Magdalena," pleaded her mother. "Stay inside with us and let the dogs handle this."

"I need to know what it is, Mama, I will live with worry until I find out. Latch the door behind me, Mama."

She walked outside, and slowly paced her way closer to the river. Laz stayed directly in front of her, always keeping two rods in advance. Then she saw what she had not been able to make out before. An Indian woman, small in stature, stepped out from behind a copse of trees and into full view. Magdalena greeted her in Mescalero. She asked if she was alone. The small woman replied by telling her that indeed, she was alone. Lowering her weapon just slightly, Magdalena slowly moved toward the woman. Laz kept close and on guard.

"What do you want?" asked Magdalena in the Apache language.

The woman answered. "There is a legend of a woman with no tribe. I came to see for myself. I too, am a woman with no tribe, but two nights ago I was a prominent woman in a tribe with a husband and three children."

Magdalena understood the words, but could not comprehend what the woman was telling her. She walked closer, this time letting the gun relax at her side. As she drew closer, she recoiled slightly at the shock of the woman's face. The end of her nose had been cut off. The wound was fresh, and the sight of it revolting to Magdalena.

"Come with me to my lodge," she told the woman. "I will clean your wound, and give you medicine, and something to eat."

The Indian woman willingly agreed to go with Magdalena. They sat at the table in the kitchen as Magdalena cleaned up the wound. She poured some brandy for the woman, and some time after the Indian drank it, Magdalena poured some on the open cut. The Indian woman winced slightly, but took her medicine bravely. She pointed to the cup, and Magdalena poured her a little more.

"Be careful with that," said Dona Sandoval. "These people do not handle alcohol well. It is like poison to them."

After imbibing upon the second cup, the Indian woman started rattling off words almost too quickly for Magdalena to decipher. Her mother was comprehending most of it though, and translating for Magdalena.

"She says that her husband caught her talking to his brother, and mistakenly thought that there was some sorted affair between them. He punished her by notching her nose, and banishing her from the tribe. Her husband is a sub-chief, and he felt that she had disgraced him. In their culture, he really had no other choice, in order to save his own face, pardon the play on words."

"Why, that is the most barbaric thing that I have ever heard!"

"Magdalena, it is not for us to understand their culture. I have heard of far more barbaric practices in other cultures. Be grateful that you have been born into a more civilized humanity."

"Indeed," she replied.

The Apache woman watched and listened as the two women spoke in English, although she did not know a word of it. She was, however, delighted by the fact that the women both spoke her language, albeit slightly different. Magdalena poured tea for the three of them and milk for the children. Seamus and Molly sat at the table in silence taking in the situation. The Indian woman pointed to the milk and asked what the children were drinking, so Magdalena offered her some. She found it very delightful, and finished what was in her cup. She then returned to the tea which was sweetened with a teaspoon of toasted sugar, finding it to be equally as delightful. The visitor joined the little family in a meal of ham, yams, and beans, and found it all very pleasing to her pallet. After their dinner, Seamus offered to wash the dishes so the women could continue with their visit. They moved to the porch and sat in the rocking chairs. The Apache woman rocked back and forth. She smiled, and Magdalena could not help but think what a shame that her beautiful face had been disfigured. She imagined what she must have looked like with her nose still in tact. She studied her dancing eyes, and perfect white teeth. This poor woman had just been mutilated and excommunicated from her children and tribe, and yet there she sat rocking, and smiling as though she had not a worry in the world. As the sun began to set, the woman rose from the rocking chair and said that she must be leaving. She had much work to do, in order to furnish herself with a lodge of her own. Magdalena instructed her to wait. She went inside and returned with a calico dress from her own closet, and a blanket. She made offerings of them to the Indian woman who was very grateful to have them. Magdalena told the woman to return, and she would alter the dress so that it would fit better. But the woman seemed happy with it the way that it was. As they were saying their farewells, Magdalena suddenly doubled over. She moaned and held her abdomen, and it was obvious that she was in pain. Dona Maria ran to her aid, and helped her into her bed. With every contraction came a shooting pain down Magdalena's back. Between the contractions, Magdalena kept counting to herself the months and weeks that had passed.

"I must have lost track of time being out here Mama. I really thought this baby was not due for another month or so."

"Well, you may have miscounted the weeks, or it may be that the baby just wants to come early. It happens sometimes."

The labor was difficult, and Magdalena was in much pain. The baby was just not coming, but the Apache woman knew what to do. She went outside to where Cotton had left some snake skins stretched out to dry, and pulled a rattle off one of the smaller ones. She crushed two buttons of it into a fine powder and mixed it with water, then instructed Magdalena to drink it. Dona Sandoval protested, but Magdalena took the potion and drank a few sips. She winced at the taste of it, but drank a small portion more. It was less than ten minutes before the baby came. The Apache woman took over the delivery. It seemed to Dona Sandoval that she must have delivered many babies. The woman knew just what to do, and in a matter of moments, the baby boy was swaddled and resting in Magdalena's arms. Magdalena asked for Seamus and Molly. She wanted the children to see Baby Michael.

"He's so tiny," said Seamus. "Why isn't he crying? I thought all babies cried a lot."

"Not all babies, Seamus," answered Magdalena. "He is a very good baby, and he is tired now. All babies do sleep a lot. Babies grow when they sleep, so we will let baby Michael sleep now, and he will grow up to be big and strong like his Papa."

The Apache woman told Dona Sandoval that she had returned a gift to Magdalena by delivering her baby, and now they were even. Then she disappeared into the copse of trees by the river, just as mysteriously as she had arrived.

Magdalena and her baby went to sleep, but when Magdalena awoke, her infant was not breathing. She cried out, and sobbed so hard that she thought she would not catch her breath.

"This is all my fault! I should never have named my homestead the Triple Bar M. I knew that another Malone was coming into the world when I applied for that brand, but I only accounted for Michael, Molly, and myself. Three bars! It should have been four!"

"You are talking nonsense, Magdalena," said her mother. "I know of your pain, but these things happen. You probably did not get the right nourishment to sustain the child growing inside of you. It has nothing to do with the name of your homestead."

Magdalena's mother tried to comfort her daughter while hiding her own grief. She knew only too well the pain of losing a child, and hated that she could not protect her daughter from that horrible, unforgiving feeling of helplessness and hollowness inside. After some time had passed, and Magdalena had calmed herself, her mother left her to hold the dead infant for a while longer while she and Seamus made a tiny grave for him next to his father's. They took the biggest rock that the two of them could carry together, and placed it at the head of the grave. When the men returned, Dona Maria would have her husband paint the baby's name on it.

Before she placed the swaddled baby into the tiny grave, Magdalena's mother drew the blanket away from his face and studied it one last time. She then replaced the shroud and interned the child to his resting place, all the while Magdalena sobbing and protesting. Tears rolled down the face of Dona Maria. She mourned the loss of her seemingly perfect little grandson. She mourned the loss of all of her own babies as this makeshift funeral conjured up the memories of each and every one of her losses. But most of all, she mourned her daughter's broken heart. Magdalena sat on the bench next to the graves of her husband and baby, while her mother and Seamus and even little Molly, stacked smaller rocks on top of the tiny tomb. They kept stacking rock upon rock, until Magdalena felt that they were being excessive. Dona Maria knew that the only thing that could possibly hurt worse than the death of the baby, would be to have his tiny body violated and consumed by wolves or coyotes. And so they kept stacking, rock upon rock.

Chapter XL

Returns and Departures

Magdalena was strangely quiet after the death of her baby. Her mother could not entice her to speak more than the necessary amount of words that were needed to convey a message. The children felt uneasy with her odd behavior. They, being so young, had recovered far more quickly from the tragedy than Magdalena herself had. She did, however, rise every morning and feed the chickens, collect the eggs, and milk the cow. She continued with cooking, washing, and sewing, and all of the normal day-to-day chores that she routinely preformed. Physically, she was healthy and healing. Mentally, she was in a state of emotional purgatory.

A week had passed when Magdalena noticed the familiar trail of dust that alerted her that people were coming. She sat on the porch sewing while her mother prepared supper. The children played a game in the yard, and Laz kept a vigilant watch over them. When Dona Sandoval stepped out onto the porch, Magdalena spoke to her.

"People are coming. They will be here in half an hour."

"How do you know this, Magdalena?"

"I see them," she replied. "I hope it is Papa."

"I hope so too, my precious daughter."

Just as Magdalena had predicted, it was nearly half an hour exactly when Don Sandoval and Cotton rode up ahead of the heavy wagons to greet the women. At first, the men did not notice anything unusual, but Magdalena's cold greeting was cause enough for her father to wonder. Then he noticed the change in her physical condition. She was no longer with child, yet nothing was mentioned about a birth. It did not take long for him to figure out that something horrible had happened in his absence. He dismounted his horse and handed the reins to Cotton, who had also detected the somber mood. Cotton took the horses to the barn and fed them some grain before turning them out. Dona Sandoval escorted her husband out to the porch, and explained what had happened. With tears in her eyes, she told him, "We could not even give the infant a decent burial. He was not even baptized! There is no church here, no minister, no religion!"

"Now, wife," started Don Sandoval. "God is all around us. Just open your eyes! That baby boy received the best sort of funeral that could have been offered. All of that other circumstance is just fluff. It does not mean a thing."

"A squaw came when Magdalena was in labor. She crushed up a snake rattle and gave it to her. I think it must have killed that baby. She killed that baby boy, I just know she did."

"No, Mama, she did not." Magdalena was at the door of the cabin listening. She stepped outside.

"The baby was not coming, I was in pain. She may have saved my life."

"But I have never heard of such a thing. My mother never told me of such a potion, and she knew of all the natural remedies that her people used."

"Just because she never told you of it, does not mean that she did not know of it. That squaw saved my life, I am certain of it. What cause would she have to kill my baby? Seamus, go get Cotton and Charlie, it is time to eat."

"They are helping the men from the lumber mill unload the wagons. Those men have to get back to the mill right away," said her father.

"Very well, then, I will pack them some food to take."

Magdalena returned into the cabin and made a lunch for the men from the lumber mill. Afterward, she and her family sat down to eat. Seamus took the lunch to the men, and when they had finished unloading the lumber, Cotton and Charlie joined the family at the table.

The group had a conversation while taking their meal, and it was then, that Magdalena had spoken the most words that Dona Sandoval had heard since the death of baby Michael. Dona Sandoval felt a tinge of relief. Perhaps now that her father was here, Magdalena would return to her normal self.

"Magdalena," said her father. "I have brought you a safe for the money you make at the mercantile, but I think that you should store it in your cellar." Her father was clearly trying to converse as though nothing had happened in his absence.

"I think that is a very good idea, Papa. Thank you."

"And I also bought a stove for the bunkhouse. Cotton would like to start preparing some of his own meals, and not rely on you so much."

"That is ridiculous!" replied Magdalena. "Cotton, is this true? I mean, I can see you needing a stove to heat your cabin, but you are always welcomed to take your meals with us. You know this. Charlie, what about you? Will you be having your meals with us, or are you with Cotton?"

There was a long pause. "Well, Miss Magdalena, you see, I have uh, I have decided to go back to Santa Fe with your parents. I am going to be the ranch foreman now, since Cotton is staying on here with you. I sure hope that will not put you in a bad way."

"Oh, I see," said Magdalena. "No, of course not. I understand, and we, I will miss you. Anyway, I have been thinking that I need to be more involved with the beeves. I need to learn how to do these things that you and Cotton do, and help more with the branding and doctoring. Oh, and Papa, I want to get some hogs, and sheep. Michael always wanted sheep. Maybe not right away, but when the store is finished and things are running smoothly. I also want to plant a garden. Did you bring any seed for the mercantile Papa? I will take some seed from the inventory, and start my garden. I want to plant melons and carrots, corn and potatoes. Oh, and yams, and pumpkins. Yes, pumpkins will be good. What we cannot eat the beeves will. Pumpkins are very nutritious. It will help them to stay fat, and healthy, through the winter. Will you help me put up a fence to keep the animals out of my garden Papa? Laz and the dogs will keep the smaller varmints out."

"Of course I will help you. I think we can get much done quickly with the help that we have. First the store, and then the garden. We will plow for you, also. Spring is here, and you should get started soon, my industrious daughter."

"Wonderful! I think I shall plant some peach trees and apple trees as well. I know where there are wild plums growing. They are small, but very sweet. I was told that the Spaniards planted them years ago when they came through this way. Perhaps it was your Grandfather who planted them, Papa! Last winter was just horrible. We lived on game meet and bread for two months. Next winter, I will be better prepared. And in a few years, I will have a small producing orchard! I cannot wait to get it started!"

Dona Sandoval turned her eyes upward and said a silent prayer of thanks to God for bringing her daughter back to her usual self.

The days passed quickly with all of the work that had to be done. Dona Sandoval took charge over the children, while Magdalena helped to set up the mercantile. Twice, wagon trains went through the Triple Bar M on their way to California. Magdalena always made sure to introduce herself to the trail bosses. She wanted to get the word out that she was opening a supply post and would be fully ready to receive customers soon. She also made certain that they knew they could pass through, but not camp on her homestead. It was understood and appreciated.

When the structure was completed, Magdalena went about setting things in order. She would stock her mercantile with practical items. There would be no need for fancy dresses and hats, or dishes or curtains, or catalogs, like the store in Santa Fe. She stocked shelves along the walls with one pound sacks of sugar, yeast, salt, soda, and coffee. Twenty pound sacks were stacked up on the floor containing corn meal and flower. There were blankets, and yard goods of linen and calico. There were dry goods, and practical clothing like slickers and dungarees, boots and gloves. She also had a good supply of cotton for baby diapers, knowing how hard it was to keep a clean supply on hand while traveling with a wagon train. Behind the store's counter there were guns and ammunition. There were traps for wolves and bears, tobacco, brandy, laudanum, and peppermint oil. In one corner there were bridles, bits, spurs, horse blankets, and even three very practical work saddles, as well as several pack saddles. She stocked tin plates and utensils, pails, and pots. She had so many chickens now, before long she would find herself with too many eggs. They also could be sold in the store, and the roosters, too, along with some jarred fruit.

When the store was stocked and organized, Magdalena put her hands on her waist and looked about. She was very happy with her mercantile. The men had almost completed the two square acre fence for her garden, and the plowing would begin soon. Magdalena had selected an area not too far from the river, since she would be dry-land farming. If she needed to carry water, she did not want it to be too far. Still, she did not want to be too close to the river knowing that the javalinas enjoyed spending much of their time there. They could ruin her garden very quickly.

The men plowed the fenced-in grounds into rows, and Magdalena selected the seed that she would plant. She would wait for a rain before planting, so the seeds would germinate. The hard work was finished, and the next few days were spent resting, and visiting, and preparing for the long trip back to Santa Fe. That day came too quickly. In the morning, Magdalena boiled all of the extra eggs that her productive hens had given her. She wrapped them up and gave them to her mother for the trip home. She gave them a bottle of milk, two pounds of butter, and several dozen biscuits.

"My darling daughter," said her mother. "Charlie is a very fine hunter. Please do not worry about us going hungry on the Gila. I will write to you from Fort Craig, and I will write to you when we arrive home. I hope that you will write to us often as well. Your father says that he will come to see you at least two, maybe three times a year. I do not know who will come with him on the next visit. Perhaps I will come, or perhaps Michael's mother will come. Someone needs to stay behind and watch the mercantile. I will pray for your safety every day."

Dona Sandoval fought to hold back the tears. Magdalena stood strong. She hated to see her parents leave. She would miss them, and Charlie, and Seamus. How Seamus entertained and amused her, and Molly too.

The next goodbye was from her father. "Do not worry, Magdalena. I know that you are a strong young woman. I have total confidence in you. Cotton will be a great asset to you here. You are truly a pioneer at heart, my daughter. You have the Sandoval spirit. I will be back in a few months with supplies for the mercantile. I will look forward to seeing you every day. Be strong, my daughter, as I know that you are!"

Next Charlie stepped up. "I feel like a deserter," he said.

"Oh, Charlie, do not be so silly. You have been such an important part of the establishment of this homestead. I truly appreciate your help, and could not have gotten along without you these past months. Now that things are all laid out, you can go and help Papa with his ranch. I will see you again soon. You shall see, and everything will be just fine. Thank you Charlie, I will forever be in debt to you, and hopefully someday, I will be able to amply repay you for all of your support."

Still holding strong, Seamus approached to say his goodbyes also.

"I will miss you, Maggie. I will miss Molly, too. I wish that I could stay here with you. I love you, Maggie!"

This goodbye was almost more than Magdalena could bear. She choked back the tears, and swallowed hard, looking out into the horizon. For a long while, she held her little brother and said nothing. Then, finally, she spoke.

"My little brother, Seamus. I love you so much, more than you will ever know. But you must go home with our parents now, and go to school. You will need to learn many things so that you can help our father with the business, and you owe that to him for what he has done for you. Now you go get up there on that fine Palomino of yours, you hear? You write to me often. I will want to see how much you remember of the words that I have taught you to read and write. I will keep track of your progress through the letters that you send to me. Remember, Papa will be making many trips out west to visit me. I am sure that you will be seeing me again soon. I love you, Seamus. You are a ray of light on the darkest day. I love you my little brother."

The boy did as he was told. Magdalena's heart was very heavy to see her family leave, yet she was determined to settle right where she was, and make the best of her life. Michael was with her, she was with him. She knew that day that she waved goodbye to her family, that she would be with Michael for the rest of her days.

Magdalena brought her apron up to her eyes and wiped the tears away. She waved one last time and watched the wagons until they became that familiar trail of dust in the horizon. For the longest time, she and Molly stood on the porch, watching that trail of dust.

"Come now, Molly, let us go inside. It is just you and me now, just the two of us. This is our home, yours and mine. This is our homestead, the Triple Bar M."

ABOUT THE AUTHOR

Statia Button Dougherty

Statia Button Dougherty grew up in Southern California and lives today in Eastern Arizona with her husband and four dogs. Statia has always nurtured an affinity for the old west. She enjoys taking road trips and exploring and photographing ghost towns and mining camps. In preparation for this book, she and her husband embarked on a journey from San Diego California, to Santa Fe New Mexico along what use to be the Gila Trail.

A Promise Kept

Lightning Source UK Ltd.
Milton Keynes UK
UKHW021147090120
356646UK00012B/1185/P